THE
CUT OF
PRIDE

A NOVEL

THE
CUT OF
PRIDE

A NOVEL

JAMES A. MISKO

For information regarding special discounts for bulk purchases, please contact Northwest Ventures Press, book sales at 907-562-2520.

Cover and interior design by Frame25 Productions

Manufactured in the United States of America

10 9 8 7 6 5 4 3 2 1

Library of Congress Cataloging-in-Publication Data

ISBN: 978-0-9640826-3-2
eBook ISBN 987-1-59433-281-4

Misko, James A. 1932 –Fiction
For What He Could Become.
The Most Expensive Mistress in Jefferson County

Non-fiction
Creative Financing of Real Estate, Prentice-Hall 1981
How to Finance Any Real Estate Any Place Any Time, 1994
How to Finance Any Real Estate Any Place Any Time—Strategies that work, Square One Publishers, 2004 www.squareonepublishers.com

Only God knows what a man lives with in his heart that he won't tell his family, his friends, or himself, but that haunts his very soul. Anyone who knows him can guess it, for it's the thing men are born with that keeps them from crying alone in the world.

CHAPTER 1

When the sheriff turned his key in the lock I woke up and looked at the opening door.

"You can go," he said.

It took me a minute to loosen the kinks from sleeping on the jail cot, something I was certainly not used to. I had slept on various kinds of bedding since leaving the security of a paycheck with room and board at the motel in Seaside, but nothing as uncomfortable as this place.

At the front desk the deputy handed me my pack. It was dirty, the pockets open and my ID tag broken. It had been searched and that was okay. There wasn't anything in there that would scare anybody. Clothes, some dried fruit, jerky, and a couple of apples I had picked off trees as I left the valley.

"Don't change directions when you leave town," the sheriff said.

I nodded and threw a pack strap over my shoulder. It looked like a good clear day on the Oregon coast. That was a rarity.

"What's the shortest way out of this burg?" I said.

He jerked his thumb at the mountains rising on the eastern edge of town.

"Up over those, huh?"

"Yep," he said. "Highway goes through. You ought to be able to find your way."

"Where's the highway go?"

"Willamette valley, Eugene, Salem, Roseburg—wherever. Just get outta here."

Outside I checked my wallet. Five hundred dollars left. I must have high graded the wine and steaks with that pretty assistant manager at my last stop. I thought I left Seaside with $800. Technically I wasn't a vagrant, but I could see the sheriff's point. Sitting on a curb, pack on my back, long hair, beard, I could have been wanted for something somewhere. He just needed time to check me out and I had no fear he would find anything. After all—it was 1955 and some of the Korean War vets were raising hell but I wasn't among them.

I checked my notebook. It was where I recorded thoughts and ideas and impressions of places and people. That was what writers were supposed to do. I'd learned it in college from a poetry professor who thought someday I might write decent fiction. I didn't know how many things I needed to record before I could start writing from the notebook. Most of my early stories and articles came fresh from an experience that I hadn't had time to record.

Normally I worked my way, stopping here and there to gather writing material, make a few bucks, meet new people. I was heading back to graduate school to get some more writing classes. The work in Seaside ran out when the summer season ended.

I was friendly with mountains. I liked everything about them except the poison oak at the lower elevations in Oregon and California. If the highway went through the mountains to the valley there would be game trails, foot trails and logging roads that would lead the same way. I decided to hoof it over the mountains. I could head northwest from Bandon, come close to Coquille, and connect with the highway there. I had a month before college opened.

Down the street half a block was a mom and pop store. I picked up a half pound of raisins, three apples, some beef jerky, and a sack of M&Ms and then left the main street and walked into the coastal range that smelled of early fall, leaves on the hardwoods just beginning to blush, the hint of moisture in the air from the early morning fog and patches of clouds. I thought I smelled mushrooms but didn't take the time to look for them.

Imprinted in the mud overhung by fern fronds was a fresh elk hoof print. The tracks drifted uphill at a good angle and showed signs of four animals; their hoof prints left a clean impression in the damp soil.

The uphill slogging was heavy work. Sweat beaded on my brow and trickled down beside my eyes. Hiking up mountains was not something I had done all summer at the motel. Several times I stopped, peeling off first my jacket, then my sweatshirt, ending up in my tank top with OREGON blazed across the front.

By late afternoon I was almost to the crest when the trail spilled into a natural amphitheatre carpeted with ferns, a small round basin maybe twenty yards across, in the middle of which was a small spring oozing the most delicious water I had tasted in six months. I bedded down there. I gathered dead branches from beneath the drip line of the firs, shaved some starter chips and coaxed a decent fire that released smoke tendrils straight up into the gathering darkness. While the tea water heated I broke and piled dead wood to feed the fire through the night. Compared to the city jail this was a five star motel.

Just after dawn, which was coming later each day as fall crept in, I breakfasted on spring water, jerky and an apple, then shouldered my pack and followed a game trail to the top. It led through heavy vegetation and old growth firs that had probably been there when Lewis and Clark wintered over on the coast. It was getting lighter and I could see patches of blue sky through the thinning tree branches straight ahead. I was cresting the pass and in ten steps the landscape changed.

Like opening a curtain on a window I could see in all directions the silent charred destruction of an old forest fire. I paused to look at the mute testimony to a searing fire that had at one time wiped the side hills clean of life. There was no wind. I could hear nothing.

I started through the burn. The tops of young fir trees seeded by squirrels and birds were now ten feet tall. It was like walking on foam going through the green grass and springy undergrowth that takes over after a fire. It had been logged and charred stumps of cedar and oak and fir stood like blackened soldiers guarding the landscape. Two thirds of the way through the burn the trail passed beside a fir stump that loggers call a barber chair. I tugged off my pack and sat on it.

It was peaceful. If there was a way to make a living trouncing through the mountains I would opt for that. Lonely though. You'd have to come to town every so often to get stuff and talk to some people. The summer I had spent on the forest service lookout had been like that. Days with just me and my dog then a one day trip to town, shop, get back, and suck in the solitude.

I drank water and let my eyes get used to the distance.

Far below me was a sturdy barn tucked into the crotch of two ridges, painted brick red. Below and to the right squatted a one story farmhouse with a sag in the roof sided with plain lumber and a front porch held up by four posts. Off to the left there was a pile of peeler-core firewood. It was in a heap beside a dirt road. The road had been cut into the side of the hill and crawled up to a three story skeleton of a house gray and austere. The house was set like a monument on a level piece of ground overlooking the entire Coquille River valley. A brick chimney rose up three stories and stuck out of a rusty tin roof that was steep enough to drain off rain and snow. Plywood covered the windows. The two doors that I could see were open. Below and to the right was a cobbled up shed and the shiny top of an Airstream trailer reflecting the sunlight.

A movement caught my eye. It was a dog walking from a shed behind the woodpile down the dirt driveway toward the farmhouse. The dog limped, taking cautious steps until he slowed to a stop at the edge of the driveway and sat down. Then he tilted back his head and let the front legs slide forward until his body rested on his stomach. He surveyed the driveway before settling his head on his paws. Twice he raised his head and looked from side to side.

Behind the dog and the house was a pile of tin cans that reflected the sun from their naked surface like mirrors. There was an outhouse, and to the left behind it, a stack of wire pens that looked like discarded rabbit hutches. A large area had been leveled out and graded to drain downhill toward the river. It was fenced and held ten long metal-roofed sheds positioned parallel and looking like some sort of military barracks.

My eyes watered from the glare off the roofs and I lay back and rested. I breathed in the cool coastal air and wondered how far I had come since morning. Sometimes I could get thirty to fifty miles in a day if I pushed it. Hadn't done that all summer; probably hadn't come more than six miles. The dog barked and I sat up.

A pickup truck drove up the driveway, stopped and backed up to the low shed across from the house. The driver emerged and dropped the tailgate. He unloaded three calves into a corral. A woman came out of the house and shouted, "How many?" Every word amplified as it drifted up the hillside clear in the damp morning air.

"Three," the driver said. He lifted up the tailgate on his pickup and reached over to pat the dog.

The woman turned and went back into the house to emerge in seconds and gave the man something. He nodded his head, folded it and put it in his pocket. Then he doffed his hat, climbed in his truck, closed the door and spun his tires in the soft mud.

The woman returned to the house. The dog went through the process of sitting, stretching out his legs and resting his head on his paws. Quietness enveloped the place, and swallowed everything that had happened.

The calves started milling around in the small corral and bawling. I could tell from the sounds they were new-born.

Little threads of steam rose from my thighs and arms as the sun dried my clothes. The river out beyond the house was flowing high and muddy with debris from the recent flood caught in the low tree branches along the banks. Tops of fence posts outlined the near fields where they stuck above the water.

I stretched out my leg and grunted into a kneeling position. I felt a kink in my back tighten up and then relax. I used to be good at sleeping on the ground. Maybe I'd lost the knack. I got up, hitched up my pack, and followed a cow trail down toward the house.

The dog barked.

As I passed by the house I could see people looking at me through the window. The woman who had dealt with the man for the calves walked out through the rough lumber door. A gust of heat from the house followed her out and touched my face with the odor of frying meat and potatoes and fir pitch burning and the close smell of people, old clothes and tobacco.

"What do you want?" she said. Her head was cocked to one side and her straight hay-colored hair, which looked home cut, hung from the part. Dressed in gray sweats and black rubber boots, she looked as stern as a battleship.

"Wondered where I was."

She crossed her arms in front of her chest. "You a convict or something?"

"No," I said. "Get many of those around?"

"Enough to make it worth questioning."

I slipped one arm out of my pack. My knees were wobbly from walking the downhill trail. "I'm on my way to Eugene. Came over the mountains instead of taking the road."

"Looking for work?"

I shook my head. "No. I'm headed back to the University."

She lowered her head and smiled. "I need a hand. Why don't you stop here for awhile?"

"If you'll just tell me where I am, I'll find my way to the highway sooner or later."

"Well—you're on River Branch Road out of Coquille, Oregon in the United States of America. Now put your stuff in that trailer and come on down for dinner. We can always set another place. It's what we do around here. Feed things."

"I've just left a whole summer of working. Not wanting to do that right now."

She looked straight at me and ignored my statement. "I don't want you if you can't take responsibility and if you can't learn you're no good to me. I got another guy working for me and he can't learn. My old man's not much better and I'm in a hell of a fix. I've got two cripple boys in there and nobody to take care of them. I can't be both places at once. I need someone like you to help with the mink."

"Mrs..."

"Helner. Rose Helner."

"I just need to keep moving toward Eugene. I've got fall classes to enroll in and things I need to do before that happens."

"What can you do?"

She had a way of not taking into account anything I said. It was interesting to me as a writer and learner of people's traits but it was difficult to deal with standing there.

"Do? Well most anything," I said.

"Huh," she snorted. "Last fella said that I fired him in a week. Said he could do anything and I caught him fixing the wiring on one of the mink sheds all wrong and he admitted it. Said maybe he just thought he could do anything."

"Well—I wouldn't try something I know I couldn't do, but there isn't much man invented that a man can't figure out if he uses his head," I said.

"That's right. Can't isn't in my dictionary—is it in yours?"

I twisted my head and smiled. "No. Impossible is though."

"Impossible is in everybody's book." She looked me over with intent gray eyes and a smile formed on her face. "You look sturdy enough to do the work. Ever worked on a mink ranch?"

"No. And I don't intend to." I slipped an arm through my pack strap.

"Start this afternoon. First month is $200 with room and board."

I chuckled. "Do you ever take no for an answer?"

"Haven't lately."

"Well—sorry to disappoint you but I need to be moving on. I take it that road at the end of the driveway heads somewhere."

"Turn left and it goes to Coquille. Turn right and it goes to Seven Devils Road."

"Thanks. Been nice talking to you."

"Wish you'd stay. I sure need help and you look like you could do a good job of it. Just try it for a week and see if you don't like it. School will still be there this winter. If you'd stay it would give me time to find another man and you could leave then."

"Thanks, but no thanks. Goodbye, Mrs. Helner."

I TURNED LEFT AT the road and had walked about a quarter mile when I heard a horn beeping behind me. I pulled off the road to let them by. The car stopped beside me. Rose Helner leaned out of the window, her hair fluffing in the wind.

"What's your name?" she said.

"Jeff. Jeff Baker." I kept walking.

She idled the Buick along side me. "Jeff. Come to work for me. I need a man and you remind me so much of what my son's would have been. I know we'll get along fine."

I shook my head. "Mrs. Helner, I'm headed for the University."

"Just give it a couple of months. I need help now."

"I'd like to accommodate you but I can't keep putting things in the way of my life."

"You're young. You've got your whole life ahead of you. Just give me a month or two." She stopped the car and I turned to face her. "What so important about that school that it can't wait two months?"

"Look. I'm twenty-four. I've got enough money for school. I'm going to be a writer and I'm going to school now. Thank you for your confidence but the answer is no."

"I like a person with goals. Got those myself." She sat in the idle car and I walked on.

HALF A MILE DOWN the road I caught a ride with a logging truck into Coquille. He dropped me off at a Laundromat near the sawmill that had a public telephone. I called Dave in Eugene to tell him I was on my way.

"Better bring plenty of money," Dave said.

"And that means what?"

"Tuition has just gone up to $1,200."

I dug out my wallet and counted my money. "I've only got $500."

"You'll need to find some work then. How long you going to be getting here?"

"Depends on if I keep walking, hitchhike or buy a bus ticket."

"I'd hustle up here if I were you and see what you can find for extra work."

"I'll think on that. See you soon, my dime is running out."

With tuition at $1,200 I was behind at the starting gate. I was going to be in debt all year even if they would let me start without paying full tuition. At the A&W Root Beer drive-in I bought a burger, shake, and fries and sat on one of their outside benches that had lovers initials carved in the seat and table.

I could probably find work; I always had, but clearing $700 during the semester was going to be hard on part time work. The Korean War Vets were hustling and getting the good jobs. They were getting the girls too. Apparently young women could listen to war stories for hours in the backseat of a car.

A heavy gray cloud bank drifted over the sun. That was enough sun for an Oregon day and it looked like rain coming in from the coast where it always came from. The rain was either with or followed by the wind, daring you to stay dry and warm. I put the rain cover on my pack, dug out my poncho and hat and started out.

ALL I COULD HEAR was the rain driving down on the roof and my poncho as I stood outside the window. Mrs. Helner recognized me and opened the door.

"Come on to the porch out of that rain," she said. "I hoped you'd come back."

"How long do you need me?" I said.

"As long as you'll stay."

"Four months okay with you? Can you find someone by then?"

"Always have."

"And the pay again?"

"$200."

JAMES A. MISKO

"Plus board and room?"

"Plus board and room."

"After that?"

"It's up to you."

"What's the highest you'll pay?"

She cocked her head. A smile formed on her face tracing lines that I hadn't seen there before. "I don't know. No one's ever gone that far." She sucked in her cheeks.

I smiled. "I will." I stuck my hand out from under the poncho and she shook it.

"You're all wet," she said.

"That I am."

She kept her smile and her gray eyes softened. "Stow your gear in the trailer house there and come have a bite to eat."

The door was unlocked. I went inside and sat on the bed. The place smelled musty and damp. On the window ledge were old cigarette butts, shrunken and brown stained with age. I cleaned the ledge, and put the books I carried, East of Eden, The Old Man and the Sea and my notebook there and hung up my change of clothes. The books leaned against the side of the window and announced that this was my place. Gave me a sense of belonging.

Well—now I'd done it. Shot fall semester at school. This had better work out.

The trailer had a wood burning stove for warmth, a sink, cupboards, a bed, a small mirror and an Esquire calendar. It was dirty and unkempt like the rest of the place. I turned on the cold water, dashed it on my face, combed my hair and walked over to the house.

The knob was fastened to the door with a piece of wire. I pushed it open and looked into a tableful of upturned faces. I saw half a dozen red-haired kids, a man of about forty years, a heavy-set woman next to him, the woman who hired me, a round-shouldered man of about fifty with gray hair curling around his temples, and a young man in a wheel chair with a wide-eyed expression that looked more past me than at me and who responded to my greeting with a half smile and exaggerated motions.

"What'd you say your name was?" the woman said.

"Jeff Baker," I replied. The heat was oppressive.

"This is Ralph and Olive Johnson and their kids. This is Paul and West and that guy in there," indicating a white emaciated figure, "is Ronny." He appeared to be about thirty. He had a white patch pasted over his left eye and lay sprawled on the davenport in the next room.

"Glad to meet you," I said, trying to pass the few words around to them all. A vapor rose from a tin can on the back of the stove that smelled like tar and kerosene and pine pitch and burning nettles.

"Sit down there," she said, indicating a chair just vacated by the man she had called West. I sat down and watched the old man walk away from the house. The rain had stopped and he had put on a sweatshirt to go over his overalls, both of which looked to have been worn for a year or more without change.

"That's my old man," she said.

I smiled and felt uneasy being the only non-eating person at the table.

"We're like pigs here, mister. Just fill your own plate and get to eating."

The woman called Olive handed me a plate and I took my first conscious breath since coming into the house. The heat sucked my energy. I longed to be eating from my pack out in the open air but I took the plate and scooped a little of the food on to it.

The milk was raw and unpasteurized and warm and it felt slick as I drank it, the lumps of cream sliding off the back of my tongue.

Paul, the son sitting at the table in a wheelchair, was about twenty-five. His eyes looked blind. He seldom blinked and retained that wide-eyed frantic expression all the time. When he let his head come forward and looked down it was with that sullen passiveness that blind people sometimes affect that looks like meditation. He ate with his hands and drank milk from a quart jar which he drained in one long drink, broken only by sounds from his lips and throat which ended with deep gasps for breath.

My skin crawled from the scorching heat and the smell of house dust, fat meat frying and the sweet odor of warm milk. My stomach rolled.

Paul wiped his lips after a gulp of milk. "Where'd you come from?"

His question caught me with a full mouth. The bacon was undercooked and greasy but I swallowed it. "The coast."

"What were you doin' there?" Paul said. The other people seemed occupied with their food.

"I worked the summer at a motel in Seaside."

"Haven't been there," he said, turning his head towards me. "Is it nice?"

"It's a coast town. Caters to tourists in the summer."

"Mom said you came over the hill?"

"That's right."

The sounds of chewing and flatware clinking on plates filled the room.

"How come you didn't take the road?"

"You've got a lot of questions, Paul. Do I need a lawyer?"

He scoffed. His wheelchair rolled back a few inches. "No—I'm just curious."

"I like trails and mountains. I worked all summer in town and it was a good break to be alone for awhile. Nice country between the coast and here."

"You don't have a car?"

"Nope. Had a nice '36 Ford but my brother burned the motor out of it."

"Dad's got a Plymouth you can buy." He paused, put his hands to his face. "Course it don't run. Hasn't got an engine."

Everyone laughed.

Supper was over none too soon. My mental facilities regained control out in the cool, damp air coming in from the coast.

Back at the trailer I pulled out my notebook and sat with pen in hand looking out the dirty window onto the driveway. The dog was looking up at the window. I smiled at him and he wagged his tail. I opened the door. He came over and stuck his nose into my hands. He was probably half Collie and half Australian Shepherd. We cemented our relationship right then and there. Then I did two things. I took a rag from the closet and washed the window inside and out. Afterward I took my notebook, sat on the step with the trailer door open and pet the dog with one hand while I wrote with the other.

Walked over Coast Range for two days after night in jail at Bandon. Stumbled onto a mink ranch out in the boonies. The owner, Rose Helner, gave me a job. I took it because I'm awful short of money. I didn't ration my summer's earnings well. Now here it is fall and shelter, food, and money make a good combination. Plus—I've got a place to myself where I can write.

This place and the people are unusual. There are two young men—they call them boys—who are handicapped. Paul, the younger one, gets around in a wheelchair. The other one, Ronny, can barely move and stays on the couch or in bed.

Too dark to see what I'm writing now. More later. Oh yeah— making $200 a month + room and board. Not as good as the motel work but I should be able to save it all and get back to school for the second semester in January. Nothing to spend it on out here.

CHAPTER 2

The next day after dinner Mrs. Helner followed me out of the house over the heavy ruts in the driveway to the mink yard. We went through a homemade gate of 2x4s and wire, green with moss and slippery from the soaked up rain. The mink yard had been chewed out of the side of the hill, leveled and fenced, the ground rutted, just gravel and mud and the rotting hay, moss, and lumber carpet over-laid with musk.

We walked through the aisles with mink pens on each side. The mud was an inch deep. "Don't usually have this mud but the floods brought it in and we haven't had time to fix it yet. West just went after some gravel to put in here."

"Now who's West again?" I asked.

She smiled and motioned with her cigarette. "He's my hubby."

"Oh." I felt sort of foolish for having to ask so soon but she passed it off with a quick laugh and we turned up one of the aisles. The little animals came running to the end of the pens stood on their hind legs, looked at us with beady eyes and sniffed us as we passed.

It was all very curious and pleasant except for the slight mink odor, which I didn't mind. We stopped beside the last row of mink and she drew out another cigarette, offering me one with a flick of the package in my direction. I shook my head no.

"You and your husband build all this yourselves?"

"This is the first year the old man has helped me any," she said after blowing smoke out. "He's been mostly working in sawmills and lumber camps all his life."

"You didn't build it all alone?"

"Me and Jack built this place up," she said. "Good man, Jack. Wish I knew where he was now.

Ralph stopped at the end of the row of mink cages. "What should I do now?"

She glanced at me but looked at him as she started speaking. "You could clean up the slaughter room floor. Get ready for more calves."

It was getting hot and I wasn't listening much but looked back up on the hill where I had been so footloose a few days before and wondered if I shouldn't be there now. My stomach was full and it felt good. "That Ralph," she was saying now, "He's a poor worker. I told him to grind the feed and he was over there forty minutes with the grinder running in reverse throwing meat all over the slaughter house." She laughed and bored into my eyes as if she expected me to agree or disagree with her and she was ready to take on either. I didn't know how to look at her.

West drove the truck up the driveway and turned it around swinging the back end close to the mink yard. .

She looked at her watch. "That took him long enough," she said.

I glanced at her out of the side of my eyes. We started down toward the truck and she said, "You don't ever want to trust the old man—he's always got some skullduggery afoot. He tried to

JAMES A. MISKO 17

kill me and the kids one time but Jack picked up a chair and would have brained him but I stopped him." As we came within hearing distance of West she stopped talking.

West climbed up on the bed of the truck as we passed. I paid more attention to him this time. He didn't look like a killer but I didn't know what a killer looked like either.

"Did you pay for it?" she said.

"No, you didn't give me any money," he replied, his voice soft and slow.

"Well, for Christ's sake," she said and walked on to the house leaving me standing there.

West shrugged his shoulders and pulled the tailgate out letting some of the gravel fall. He kicked out some more and I found a shovel and he used that and not until he was done did he say another word.

"What did she tell you to do?" he said.

"Nothing. I guess I could go take a nap."

He smiled a funny half smile and his eyes were moist and danced under the bushy eyebrows. I smiled back. He seemed pleasant. Not the killer she made him out to be.

I shrugged. "I might as well help you."

He looked at me and didn't change his expression but turned and grabbed the tailgate. I picked up the other end and we stabbed it in the holes in the bed.

"We'll spread this gravel in the aisles so when we feed we don't have to walk in the mud all the time."

"You don't like walking in mud?"

He smiled and licked his lower lip with a tobacco stained tongue.

WE BOTH SHOVELED UNTIL the wheelbarrow was full and I wheeled it down the aisle while he scooped the gravel out and threw it down in the wet places. We worked through the whole truckload in no time and sat down on a couple of log ends to rest. The dog came over, body wiggling, tail wagging, ears laid back and nuzzled West's hand. He massaged the dog's neck.

His hands were big and rough, the nails yellow and cracked. Every hair on him was white, even on his hands and throat— and thick. He reached under his faded sweatshirt with one hand and brought out a package of cigarettes, lit one and ran one hand over his throat like he was stroking a cat. The smoke curled up around his ears, his eyes squinting against the sun. He was round-shouldered and slightly stooped with age, but his frame looked stout, and even when he walked with a little wobble in his legs, he looked strong.

I pointed up at the old gray house on the hill. "How long has that been there?"

He looked at the house for a moment and then turned away. "Since '45," he said.

"How many rooms?"

"Too damn many."

I wondered if I was prying into a sensitive area.

"You build it?" I asked.

"One guy helped me."

The five redheaded Johnson kids dashed past the truck and into the berry patch and jumped over the fence into the mink yard.

"Looking for duck eggs," West offered.

"You eat them?" I asked.

"Feed 'em to the mink."

We were sitting in the sun that was playing peek-a-boo and had just punched a hole through the layer of clouds when Mrs. Helner came out of the house and headed towards us. She handed West a check.

"Pay for that gravel and pick up some chicken feed in town and don't take all day doing it, either."

He hesitated a moment. "We need some hay for the cows too," he said.

"Well—get it then, but your cows are supposed to pay for their own hay and this is the last time I'm buying your hay!"

He folded the check in half, then in half again making sure the edges were even, then slid it in the breast pocket of his overalls buttoned his pocket and climbed into the truck cab. The engine started and he roared down the steep driveway.

When he turned left on the dirt road to town I could hear the shifting of gears. He was driving it like a race car, the frustration bleeding out of him at each gear change. Could he really get mad enough to kill somebody?

Her old man, West, doesn't act like a killer but what do I know. So far she has told me Johnson is not good help, West is a potential killer and some guy named Jack helped her build this mink farm. Not bad for the second day.

I've always found new work interesting. On the other hand, I've not stuck to something long enough to let it get to me. Summer jobs and part time work during school have kept my bank account from being overdrawn. The old man and I seem to have hit it off. Haven't run into Johnson on the job yet. She is a piece of work—no doubt about that. Talks, smiles, wheedles, smokes, pushes. So far so good.

CHAPTER 3

"Come up here with me, Jeff."

"Okay Mrs. Helner."

She turned and smiled at me. "Call me Rose."

I followed her up to a shed where she put one foot on a bucket and pointed at a jumble of wiring attached to the wall.

"Know anything about electricity?"

"A little," I said.

"I want to tear down this shed and build a new one. I need these wires disconnected. I'll go turn off the juice and you disconnect them." She was wearing large rubber boots and the tops flopped in and out with each step which made it seem like she was waddling away towards the slaughterhouse. Soon her head emerged and she shouted, "Okay!"

I removed the wires from the insulators, taped the ends and coiled them around a stick, which I hung on the wall.

"Ok!" I yelled.

She switched the juice back on and waddled over. She handed me a pry-bar and taking a crowbar for herself, started smashing down the shed, the slick mossy crude cedar shakes, the sheeting, rafters, and 4x4 posts. She rested often, to breathe and smoke, while I banged away at the remnants of the shed.

"How'd you get started in this business? Doesn't seem to be the normal type of business that I've ever heard about," I said.

"They started as a hobby," she blew out a smoke ring. "But I've built them into a good business and the ole man would like to get his hands on this place. That's why he tried to kill me and the kids once." She drew on her cigarette, cocked her head and squinted.

I kept swinging the iron bar.

What have I gotten myself into? She really seems to think West is out to kill her and yet they work together all day. Now stir me into the mix, the two handicapped sons, and the full throated Johnson family. It's strange.

"What would you think of a man who's never apologized in the thirty-five years we've been married?"

"Did he apologize for anything before you got married?" I asked.

She straightened up. "He never did anything to apologize for before we got married." She looked at me funny and I saw it before it passed through her face and was gone.

"Do you infect easy?" she said.

"No."

"Ralph does. First week he was here he got infection in his hand and couldn't work for three days. Last week he got infection in his knee and he thinks he can't work yet. When they hired out to me, Olive said Ralph was slow and I'd have to teach him about the mink but I didn't think he would be this slow. He's been here three months and still doesn't know anything."

I didn't want to talk about the Johnsons. I changed the subject. "Whose beginning of a house is that up there?"

She laughed and turned her cigarette over in her fingers. "The old man started that in '45 with some money he saved from the logging camps. He got it that far and then asked me to put the roof on it and I did. Sixteen hundred dollars! Then he tried to mortgage the mink but he couldn't do it so that's as far as it got. When I save enough money to put radiant heat in it for the boys—we'll finish it."

"The boys," I said. "Will they understand and enjoy it?"

"Oh I think so. Paul talks about it from time to time. Course—neither of them can see it. They've only heard about it."

I swallowed and wondered if I was stepping into a mine field. "How did they come about their condition?"

She shifted on the pile of lumber she was sitting on and lit her third cigarette of the job. "The old man was putting up hay and Paul was up in the hay mow with him. Somehow he fell out and landed on his head on the concrete floor of the milking parlor."

"Holy cow."

" I carried him in and he was unconscious but the Doc said he'd be okay and just let him sleep." She squinted.

"That's why I don't trust doctors anymore. A person can do more for themselves if they use common sense than a doctor can do. Anyway—it hurt his brain and that virtually blinded him and put a kink in his mobility. He can see a little out of one eye and gets by with his wheelchair and his wheelbarrow push cart. He was such a beautiful baby." She smiled and turned to me. "He'll be twenty-nine in December."

She sucked in on the cigarette until her cheeks were hollow, held it, and looked at me with an intensity she hadn't shown before. She blew out the smoke and said, "You're good-looking like my sons would have been. They should be out here working with me, building this place up instead of dying a little every day in that hell hole."

I made a good swing at the shingles and a whole row came flying off.

"Ronny's got meningitis," she continued. "Got it when he was two years old. I've had them all over the country—even the Mayo Clinic, but there isn't a doctor that can help them so I keep them here and try to make life happy for them."

I shook my head. "That's a tough shake you got."

I had most of the shingles off and I hit the post at the far end with such a blow that it broke off at the ground. She laughed and grabbed one end of the shed. I took the other and we pulled.

The first pull didn't do it, but we pulled and grunted and it gave a little more. Then she smiled and nodded and we came forward together. It tumbled down in a heap of rotten wood. The moldy wood smell was strong and little bugs scurried out of the cracks. We laughed and pointed fingers at each other over the way the cobwebs and splinters and dust had made white rings around our eyes and covered us with a gray powder.

We sat down while she smoked another cigarette. She looked up the hill toward the corral and stood up. "Ladd—no." She turned to me. "That damn dog is digging in the corral again. Must have buried a bone in there or something. West hates it when he digs a hole in the corral. Thinks his precious cattle are going to break a leg in it. Ladd—git!"

I breathed in the musky smell from the mink yard alternated with layers of cool air drifting down the hillside. The land was framed with fir trees and the river curled across the end of it making a setting that except for man, was idyllic, warm, and friendly. I leaned back, my muscles took their ease and I watched the day grow old.

CHAPTER 4

It was a hell of a way to take a shower but I didn't feel right about using their bathroom with eleven of them already using it. Anyway, it was all right with the hose looped over the rafter in the slaughter house with the nozzle turned to a fine spray and the cold water running fast down my bare body into the gutter.

The three calves we had killed that day lay on the floor with expressionless clouded eyes. It didn't bother me to look at them now. But when West took a steel pipe off a stand, swung it like a baseball bat, and struck them behind the ears, my knees buckled. The calves collapsed in a heap on the concrete floor. They were day old bull calves nobody wanted. Milk farmers kept only the female calves to build their herd and either sold or killed the bull calves. I had held my breath during the ten seconds he took to kill them. When I let the air escape it occurred to me that I too, was a young bull calf.

I closed the trailer door and walked down to breakfast. There was no warmth coming from the woodstove in the kitchen and nobody talked. Rose looked tired. She moved slowly with half-closed eyes looking through dirty spectacles. West shuffled through the door with an armload of wood for the heater. Ronny wasn't up yet and Paul was screaming for his razor.

I was ill-at-ease waiting. Then the Johnsons, seven strong, walked in the front door without a word and sat down. Olive, who was the cook, offered a half smile and said, "We overslept," to anyone listening, tied a dishtowel around her bulging middle and hurried to get the dishes and silverware on the table while the bacon cooked.

It was a healthy old-fashioned breakfast, a cowboy breakfast of pancakes, bacon, eggs, toast, coffee, and fresh milk still warm from the cow's udder. I was very full when I walked out into the morning air and wondered if I could work or would have to take a nap to let the food settle. It was sure a break from my past fare of dried beef, apples, raisins and creek water.

Rose followed me out the door and West went down to the barn, his gray-striped overalls flapping against his old-man legs at each of his hard-put-down steps. I heard her light her first cigarette and blow the smoke into the foggy air. She led me into the slaughterhouse where the gray wet cement made it seem much colder. The three dead calves lay in a row—eyes glazed, tongues protruding from their mouths, hair matted. Three dead young calves morphing from romping hopeful infancy to ground-up meat in the belly of a mink and ultimately fertilizer on the ground. Nature is harsh on the young.

"You know anything about knives and skinning?" she asked while her fingers danced over the edge of a knife she had drawn from the rack.

"A little," I said.

Rose bent over and turned the water on into a bucket, then grabbed a steel and whipped the blade across twice, then the tip of the knife two times, turned off the water and pulled up one of the calf's front legs. She inserted the blade into the hide below the hoof and ran it down to the brisket to meet the cut from the throat that had bled the animal. She peeled back the hide from the brisket on both sides of the leg without cutting it. She skinned well.

A little grunt floated up from her throat as she moved to the other front leg and repeated the process. Then she cut down the middle, through the navel to the bung and grabbing a hind leg cut from hoof to bung and the same on the other leg and then cut around the bung and stood up, her face swollen and red and wrinkled.

"That's how we do it," she said.

"Looks easy when you do it."

"You'll get on to it. I can out-skin most people but I learned from a butcher and I pay attention to people who know more about something than I do. The old man doesn't."

I grimaced. A shudder crept over me. Would I not be worth a damn either?

"Let's see you skin the other one," She said and handed me the knife. "This was my knife and when you get to skinning you always want to keep your own knife 'cause everybody sharpens their knife different. This one can be yours."

I took the knife and grabbed a dead calf. It was cold and the hair was stiff with blood and water. The keen edge slipped down the leg to the brisket and I fleshed a bit of hide to hold onto. Fleshed the other side and cut a hole.

"Three holes make it a glue hide," she said. "We don't want those—they're half price. Those damn Jews!"

The knife was so sharp I hardly noticed that I'd cut the hide. I finished the other front leg and cut down the middle but the blade went deep, opened the stomach and the guts and paunch spilled out on the floor.

"Don't cut that!" she said.

Good advice, but too late. The knife slipped through the paunch with the calf's last meal spilling out looking like cottage cheese and smelling like soured milk and eggs.

"You cut too deep—keep the point just under the hide." She gave a deep heavy laugh and launched a bucket of water across the cement, washing the contents into the gutter.

I moved the knife around the bung and made two extra cuts that affected the price of the hide—and she told me so—and then maneuvered down the back legs and straightened up, my face red and my back stiff from five minutes bent at the waist.

She chuckled. "You'll get used to that when we have sixty or seventy calves to skin. West will finish these."

"What do you mean finish these?"

"They need to have the hides pulled off." She pointed to a winch anchored to the wall with a line running up through a pulley. "We used to have to skin them out but now we use the winch to pull off the hides after we do what you and I just did." Her whole face smiled forcing me to smile with her.

"What do you do with these naked calf bodies?" I said.

"Next we gut 'em and grind 'em and then feed 'em."

She pointed to a small refrigerator-sized object against the wall. "We grind them up in that grinder with some meal and feed it to the mink." The look on her face told me she thought that was a pretty clever idea. Her smile and dancing eyes confused me for a moment. I couldn't quite get around grinding up a whole calf, bones and all and feeding it.

"Bones, guts and all?"

"The next step is to gut them, but we leave in the heart, lungs, liver and kidneys. They make good feed too" She watered the area down again and started out. "Come on," she said and led out toward the mink yard.

West was stooped over with a carpenter's apron on, his mouth stuffed full of nails. He straightened up as we stopped.

She looked at the stakes he had driven in the damp soil and the yellow string that ran from one end to the other.

"What the hell did you do that for?" she demanded.

His eyes glittered above the silver whiskers and he was slow in answering. "To get the sides straight."

She coughed. "Jack and I got the sides straight on the other sheds without wasting all this time putting up stakes."

He sort of smiled and pointed at the other pens.

"What are you snickering about!" she said.

He extended his arm along the line of the water pans that stuck out from the pens and it was plain that they wavered and that the side was not straight.

She glared at him. "And you know why those are crooked— because you didn't stretch the wire when you put it on like I told you to!" She walked away and started up an aisle talking to the mink. "Hi there girl... well poor baby . . . what's the matter? . . no water? . . .well—we'll fix that for you . . . poor mamma."

I stood transfixed. In my life I had not heard a wife berate her husband with the venom that Rose spewed on a daily basis. Had I walked into a hornets nest just to earn some money for school? It was not hard to conceive that I could be next and that the decision I had made to stay here for four months was ill conceived.

West shrugged his shoulders and walked back to the stakes and yellow string. A truck started up the steep driveway the engine emitting a high whine. It was in low gear and loaded to the top boards. It took a long time to pull the hill and then it roared into the turnaround and stopped with its nose pointed down hill.

"Better go help Charlie," West said to me. I walked over through the mink yard and around the truck to where a muscular young man was tipping the calf guts out of our barrel into a box. He looked up at me.

"Hi." He smiled through nice-looking teeth.

"Hi," I said. "Need some help?"

"All the time." He moved fast. "You working here now?"

"Yeah."

"Like it?"

"Don't know . . . haven't been here but a day."

"You'll learn fast . . ." the young man said. He motioned to the box full of calf guts and feet. He grabbed one end and I the other, we walked to his truck and on three, heaved it up over the side. I jumped up on the rail and looked in to see two dead cows, a horse, bones and meat scraps, three chickens, some beef guts, a whole calf, and our stuff. It smelled pretty rank.

"You pick that stuff up around here?" I said.

"Yeah."

"What do you do with it?"

He grabbed the hose and washed off his boots and hands. "Take it to Eugene to the rendering plant. They cook it into bone meal. Thanks for your help."

"Sure."

He was gone with a whine of the starter and squealing brakes as he slid the hill. I walked back to the shed project and the two of them were there together.

"How the hell are you going to build it that way?" Rose said.

West lifted both arms in frustration. "Just the way it ought to be built."

"Why don't you do it like we built this one?" she pointed to the other shed.

"That's no good. It won't last as long as this way."

"Oh, bullshit!" She stood with one foot on the rail, her hip canted out. She stood that way with a hand on her hip, cigarette smoke curling up and coiling around her neck and face up through her hair. Then she walked off to the house.

West shrugged his shoulders, a half smile on his face and bent down to the stake with the string tied to it.

"Will you check the string on those stakes, Jeff?"

I went up the line. It was okay. He hollered to bring back the posthole digger.

"I'll build this shed so it will last and we won't have to be tearing it down in three years again. What does a woman know about building?"

I dug the post holes and we set the 4x4s in and with West working the level, I tamped them tight into the spongy earth and we put up the posts and nailed braces across to keep them straight and then added the side braces that would hold the pens and put the rafters together and placed them every three feet. It was still wobbly.

"I think this will hold when we get the pens in and the sheathing on the roof, don't you?" he said.

"I think so." I looked at the framed building and tried to imagine how it would be but I couldn't quite put it together in my head.

I scampered up on the rafters and took the sheathing he handed up to me and nailed it on. We skimped on that because we were using all the materials we had torn out of the old shed and it wasn't much good. In fact the whole shed was mostly out of the old lumber because she couldn't afford to buy new and didn't want to waste the old so we pulled nails and sawed off rotted ends. I put the last bit of sheathing on and climbed down. He looked up at the job.

"I can build if I've got wood to build with—not this crud."

He turned his head and looked in my eyes to see if I believed it.

"You built that house, didn't you?" I said pointing to the big, gray hulk of a house on the hill.

He turned to look at it and I could see his eyes going over the structure from the roof to the windows and doors. He nodded his head and his lower lip curled up.

I swallowed. It sounded like a waterfall in the silence and he looked at me.

"You're a pretty good man," I managed to say.

He flashed his eyes on me in a smile. "Some guys say they're as good at sixty as they were at twenty. That's a lot of bull. They just think they are." He took out his pack of cigarettes, shook one out and put it between his lips and reached beneath his faded blue sweatshirt and took out a lighter, lit it and returned the lighter to his pocket. "A fifteen year old kid could stomp the hell out of me."

I took in his shoulders and forearms, swollen and knotted with muscle, "I'd put in with you in a fight," I said.

He snorted.

I grabbed one of the posts now supporting our rafters and sheathing and tried to wiggle it. It wobbled a bit and the nails creaked but it looked fairly stout.

"They'll be all right, Jeff—the sign of the moon is good."

"The sign of the moon?"

He smiled again. "You put in posts when the moon is growing in the first and second quarter and they'll stick so tight you'd think they were in concrete."

I must have looked like I didn't believe it.

"That's right," he added. "And in the last quarters for some reason the posts just never get tight. Some people plant their spuds and corn by the sign of the moon." The ashes got very long on his cigarette and they hung down but they didn't fall on his big lumberman's hands.

"Really," I said, unbelieving.

He nodded.

His squinted eyes were looking at the high country toward the coast where I had come from when I first saw the place. He nodded toward the green hill that was still damp from morning fog but now glistened all over where the sun touched the dew on the leaves of the rhododendrons.

"I wouldn't be too proud to take a shot at a deer walking across up there," he said.

"Do they often do that?"

He pulled the cigarette out of his mouth. "I saw two this morning when I went up to milk." He looked at me again. It seemed that he needed to verify every statement he made, to search my eyes to see if he could tell if I believed him.

Ralph walked up. It was the first time I had really paid any attention to him. He was slight-built and red-haired and I looked at him wondering where he fit in. West glanced at him and then looked down at his boots and didn't speak.

Ralph stood there looking at West and me. He had broken in on something. He stood with one hand massaging his chin while his other hand jingled change in his pocket. Finally he said, "Anything to do?"

West looked at me and I at him knowing from where we stood there was plenty to do.

"Why don't you water?"

"Yeah—I guess I could do that," he said, and wandered off.

We heard a holler from the house. West looked at me and then turned to listen again.

"West!" came the cry again. "Ronny needs you!" Rose screamed.

"Finish the cross braces," he said. "It'll be dinner time pretty soon."

"OK."

He walked toward the house with that funny gait of his, stopped and looked up the aisle where Ralph was watering and then kept on going to the house.

I SAWED A BRACE AND nailed it in position and looked up to see Rose standing there. She glanced down the aisle toward the house, then back to me, walked inside the shed dodging the boards and stooped to pick up a nail. She stood beside me and fixed me with a sharp-eyed look.

"Don't believe anything the old man tells you. Me and Jack built this shed over here. It was perfect until hubby started to put the wire on it. He wouldn't listen to my directions so it came out crooked like everything else he does." Her eyes narrowed.

"Does he understand the mink?" I asked.

"Thinks he does. I've supported the family, paid the doctor bills, bought the car and everything...he hasn't done a damn thing but drink the beer I buy for Ronny.

"I used to have a good man here...that was Jack. Sure he was an alcoholic, but he hadn't taken a drink for three months when the old man ran him off." She squinted her eyes. "He'll never do that to any hired man of mine again. I've got me a little pistol that I pack and a permit to carry it and he'll get hurt the next time he tries that."

I shifted my feet and stretched my back and shoulders. "What happened to Jack?"

Her eyes half closed, lips pulled so tight they were just lines across her tired face. "He disappeared." She breathed out her cigarette smoke and looked away up the river. "Disappeared and never heard from again."

I nodded, wondering. She glanced down the aisle.

Ralph was close.

"Who told him to clean out the pans?" she said.

I shrugged my shoulders. "West told him to water."

"I'll be damned...he can't even do that right. See what I'm up against?" She stomped off to the house.

Ralph walked up, his face blank.

"You like the work?" he said.

"Not bad...seems to go all right. You?"

"Yeah...time goes fast anyways...interesting work." He shifted his weight to the right foot, the hose dripping down into the ditch.

"She doesn't pay much though. I was making $1.55 an hour digging ditches back where I came from and she said she'd raise my pay here but hasn't yet." He raised his eyes and his lips formed a bare smile. "What she giving you?"

"Same as you—two hundred."

"Yeah." He was figuring in his head. "Seems like a guy ought to be able to get ahead these days. Just seems like a day then a week then a month goes by and you don't get anywhere. You're fed and you sleep and you work but in the end, I mean—when the time is up, you haven't done anything but stay alive."

I nodded. "Know what you mean."

His eyes lost their questions. He stared down at the water running from the end of the hose then looked off to the house on the hill. "We live up there," he tilted his head indicating the house. "But it isn't much more than camping. I wouldn't call that board and room would you?"

"I guess it depends on how high on the hog you want to live."

"Well—yeah." He worked up a smile. "Well...I guess I better finish this watering." He ambled off, the water trailing a black streak in the drying clay.

Rose stood at the gate motioning me to come to dinner so I called Ralph and together we headed for the slaughterhouse to wash up. I washed first and stepped outside the cement house for a dash of sunshine. Suddenly, Olive, her arms folded across her huge bosom, and a sly look in her eye, came over to stand beside me. She half smiled like she was going to apologize for something and whispered, "Do you like this job?"

"Not as bad as some I've had," I said.

She looked toward the house and then whispered again, "We've never got our raise she promised us and we're going to get out of here. She charges us a quarter a meal a piece for the kids.

"Really?"

She nodded. "Soon as we get our paycheck we're leaving here."

"Where you going?"

"Ralph has been offered a job on a mink ranch in Astoria at two fifty a month." She was still whispering.

I looked down at the house and saw Rose looking out of one of the small glass panes. Olive saw her too. She stopped whispering, spun on her heel and walked away.

I'm here a couple of days and all of a sudden I'm father confessor.

I went down to dinner wondering if it would be digestible.

CHAPTER 5

Paul had a firm grip on his wheelchair and rolled it forward. With his head bobbing, he smashed into the sofa, turned a little to the left and headed straight for the stove. His shoe hit it and he turned to the right, heading for Ronny on the sofa again, Rose yelled; "You're gonna hit Ronny's feet!"

He twisted his head towards her and screamed, "I know it!"

He turned the wheels harder and upset the water on the table when he hit it. Rose grabbed his chair and wheeled it into his place at the table, sticking a piece of firewood behind the wheel.

"Dammit! Why do you always put that wood behind the wheel?" he yelled.

"So you can't roll back!"

"Well, I can hold it here!" He struggled to reach the chunk of wood. His fingers clutched it and he tried to lift it, but the small back wheel jammed tight with his weight holding it against the wood. His muscles wouldn't work together and he fumbled and got a sliver.

"Dammit to hell!" Finally he closed his fingers around it, lifted it and flung it across the room.

No one said anything and we ate in silence around the big table where you could reach anything you wanted except the milk and I had to say, "Please pass the milk."

I left the table early and walked away from the heavy smell of pork roast and the constant prevailing odor of that black liquid bubbling on the back of the stove that sent its vile stench through my clothes, my lungs and everything in the house.

I walked up the grass covered hill past the spring where a frog jumped in the pond, the water rings spreading to the bank, and continued up the high hill enjoying the new sunshine. The smell was lean and new—the kind of smell that dried the mold from your throat and pushed the heaviness from your limbs.

Near a rhododendron bush I saw a fresh deer track. A doe, from the size of it. I sat down. It reminded me of when I sat on the stump looking down at the place before I knew it and before I worked it and suddenly I wondered if I could see the coast from the crest of the hill. I almost got up but instead I sat there just looking at the place again. I was surprised that I didn't want to leave. I could have walked away but I didn't really want to and I wondered at this feeling in me that didn't want to move on.

At the bottom of the hill I saw West step out from the porch and stop to put his hat on and look around. I waved.

He saw me and I stood up and walked down the grass, past the pond making the frog jump again with a "waauk", down to where West stood inside the slaughter house, smoking and pulling the hairs on his throat.

"Just working a little of that dinner off," I said.

He turned to me and smiled. "I want to fix up my motor to this winch."

"Need any help?"

He shook his head.

"We've only got three calves so let me show you how to skin them." He pulled a dead calf up by the ear. "You take the hook on the floor chain and push it through an ear. Dammit! She didn't leave any hole for the hook. Hand me that knife. Don't cut the hole too big or the hook will tear through the ear."

He threaded the hook through the ear, reached for the handle and wound up the winch by hand. The carcass started to rise by its back legs, the ear chained to a steel ring in the concrete floor. The low-geared winch pulled the hide off the carcass until the naked body was left swinging by the winch chain, its skin on the floor.

West grabbed it, cut a slice in the membrane between the tendon and ankle on the back legs and hung it on two hooks suspended from a rafter in the middle of the floor. Then he unhooked the winch chain from the calf's neck and the animal hung head down over the gutter.

He cut down through the bung, through the pelvis and through the brisket, reached his hand in and pulled the guts and lungs out and with a stroke of his knife cut them loose from the back. He cut one of the tendons and as the carcass swung by one leg, he scooped it in his arms, lifted it off the hook and hung it on a heavy nail driven in the back wall. Now it was my turn. I had the ear hooked on the second calf and up it went. He handed me the knife. I did poorly but did get the insides out and hung it up beside his.

"You'll get on to it," he said.

Rose was standing there when we looked up. "Jeff, come with me and I'll show you how to water." She turned and walked away.

I followed her out to the yard and up to the hose pipe. She turned. "The watering hasn't been done right for six months and ever since I've had sick mink. You've got to keep the water pans clean. If the mink get sick it costs money to get them well and I can't stand carelessness. Can't afford it."

I winced.

She picked up the hose, squirted the pan and brushed it hard to clean out the green moss. The little mink came out of their boxes, ran to the pans and pushed their paws into the water. Some dug at the water with both front paws like they were playing in it and some dashed back and forth climbing up the sides of the pen or jumped up and down beside the pan.

"Here," she said. "You try it."

I took the hose and brush. The mink showed intense interest in my scrubbing their pans and stuck their front paws on the wire, small dark eyes covering every move of the brush, biting at it if they could get to it. It was simple work.

She turned to me. "Do you believe in the stars?"

I chuckled. "My Mother does...I don't know...the moon has a lot of pull on the ocean, maybe the stars have pull on us."

"When's your birthday?"

"September 15."

"I thought so—under Virgo." She stopped to light a smoke. "The old man doesn't believe in horoscopes, but I do. Everybody that was any good with the mink that I've had here was born under Virgo. The old man and Ralph were born in February and that's Aquarius."

I cleaned and watered more pans.

"You're catching on fast to the skinning and this mink work. Did you skin before somewhere?"

"Well—just some deer and rabbits."

"Jack's birthday was the same month as ours and he was good with mink."

This Jack," I said, "who was he?"

She shifted her weight to one foot, put on that glinty-eyed look and inhaled again.

"He was a drifter. A guy who worked wherever he stopped. West says he drank too much but he used to come in the house and play bridge with us and buy the whiskey and West sat there and drank as much of it as he did. Finally Jack said to hell with him. He wasn't going to buy West's liquor for him and so they started getting at each other."

"You mean really getting at each other—hard?"

"No—West was jealous 'cause Jack worked so hard. Last year when hubby busted his leg I looked after him like a baby besides taking care of everything out here. Sometimes Jack and I worked sixteen to twenty hours a day while he lay in there bitching about his leg and the food and everything.

"Jack knew how to do anything. He used to be an electrician in San Francisco and was a smart man but he got to drinking too much and he ended up here. I thought I could make him quit drinking." She smiled between puffs. "I did for a while. But he started again and was gone for a week. The sheriff called me to come and get him out of jail so I did and when he came back he promised not to drink anymore and he didn't for three months until the old man chased him off."

I glanced down at West who was intent on building the new pens.

"I'd sure like to know where he went," she said. She walked off toward the house and shouted over her shoulder. "You know how to do it now, so finish the rest of the rows and then help West with the building." She threw her cigarette butt in West's direction as he came from the slaughterhouse.

I heard West call Ralph to grind the feed. Then slipped onto the seat of the little battery-powered cart and drove it into the shed.

Something made me look up on the hill and, standing like a battleship against the blue sky, was the house, gray and cold, the doors swinging back and forth with the slight afternoon breeze.

Inside the Johnsons lived in a portion that was boarded off with strips of tar paper and lath and heated with a little iron stove fueled with broken shingles and odd bits of wood.

I finished the watering and turned off the pump. I felt good and even though the clouds came over and covered the sun, I was warm. When the rain started to fall and West put on his rain clothes, I sat dry under the shed and fastened mink pens together until supper.

Later I sat in the living room reading the paper. Paul swung his wheel- chair in front of the radio and with his head down and eyes closed, he dialed the tuner until he found a ham operator on the short wave.

"That's Bill in Eugene . . . I think," he said. Every time the voice crackled he would raise his head and chuckle. Then he dialed to another ham and repeated the procedure until he had checked off four of them. He alternated listening to each of them until the last one shut off for the night.

"Jeff?" he said without looking at me.

"Yeah,"

In a voice which was slow and affected a drawl he asked, "Would you play the piano for us?"

"Don't know how."

He laughed. "Sure you do. Everybody knows how on ours," he said. He turned his wheelchair toward the piano, lifted the bench seat lid and pulled out a piano roll and fastened it into place with exaggerated movements and when he finished said, "There!"

I climbed on the seat and pumped. The music was clear and full of bass and warm sounds.

"Sing with it," Paul said.

I pretended to gargle, did a few runs up and down the scale and then turned loose my rusty tenor voice and sang the words inscribed on the scroll.

"Mine eyes have seen the glory of the coming of the Lord; they have trampled out the vintage where the grapes of wrath are stored..."

Paul and Ronny laughed when I sang ahead of the music or when I tried to harmonize with the melody and slipped.

"Come on," I pleaded. "Give me some help here." I looked at Paul, thinking he could probably see me well enough to know I was serious.

"Can't read a word of music," Paul said.

Ronny gurgled a laugh in his throat and threw his head back.

A second later Paul closed his eyes, opened his lips and his throat swelled. From out of his chest came a baritone voice that filled the room with sweetness and a fullness and a magnificence that transformed the player piano into a full orchestra with stage, lights, curtain and audience. I pumped the pedals, not believing what I was hearing. That this damaged human being who lived shut away in this falling-down house could produce a sound like that.

When the disc was over I sat stunned.

"Paul, that was wonderful," I said.

Rose looked very pleased. I looked at her and West. West was reading a magazine. Ronny had his head against the back of the couch. Paul's face had returned to normal, uninterested with eyes down toward the floor. He wheeled over and removed the roll. I stood up and he put it under the seat and closed the lid. It was very quiet with only the popping of the fire in the cast iron heating stove to touch our awareness. What had begun had now ended.

It was very homey there with just the five of us. We poured hot chocolate and got out a jar of raisin cookies that Olive had made that morning. When I finally went to bed I felt full and looked forward to rest on a soft bed. But as I walked from the house to the trailer I knew it was something more and I liked it—more than I should, more than I wanted.

The sheep dog was outside my door and walked up to me when I stopped. I sat down on the little iron step West had welded to the trailer and the dog sat beside me while I stroked his damp hair.

"Well, Mr. Dog . . . what gives for you tonight?"

He nosed my hand.

"And your name is Ladd, is it? All right, Ladd. We'll be friends. I'll tell you everything and you keep it all a secret and we'll be friends . . . huh?"

It was good to pet a dog, to know that a dog never did me any ill. I guess that's why people like dogs. They always forgive human temperaments and never hold a grudge. I wouldn't doubt but what maybe dogs are smarter than some people. They can always leave if they want to. (The green grass on the hill in the moonlight looked cool). Course they usually stay because things are easier than flitting around on their own. (The sea, and the sand look nice walking alone in the dark with your memories when you know tomorrow will hold a new challenge).

I hit the bed but hadn't been asleep long when I heard Ladd bark. Then I heard Rose holler, "Jeff . . . Jeff!"

I pulled on my boots and pants and jumped out into the moonlit night shirtless. "Yeah!" I shouted.

"Mink out!" She yelled.

Rose was alongside the fence with a flashlight and West was just coming from the house pulling on a sweatshirt. I jumped the fence and ran up to where she was.

"He's under those boards. Get some gloves," she said.

I grabbed some heavy welding gloves and she lifted each board carefully. It was a huge dark male who kept heading for the furthest corner under the boards. When Rose lifted the last board he bolted straight for me. I threw up my gauntlets. I felt his wet fur slide by my arm as I barely closed my hand on his tail. West was standing beside me and he jumped as the mink swung back and forth. He reached up and took hold of the mink's head with his gloved hands.

"He's got a broken leg," West said.

"Let's see," Rose edged over.

They looked him over while he squirmed in West's firm hold.

"We'll have to pelt him then," she said.

The old man pulled the mink tight against his body with both hands and then put his left hand around its neck and slid his right hand up under the mink's chin, pushing the chin up until the top of its head was flat against West's chest. Then in a lightning move, he shoved the head down hard and I heard a crunch as the neck bones slid over each other and broke. The mink went limp and a green smelly fluid leaked out his back end.

We went back to bed, but it was hard to sleep.

CHAPTER 6

Getting used to that inside the trailer feeling made me restless. When the sun came up I dressed and walked outside. Ladd raised his head, stood and stretched, arching up like a Halloween cat, and walked over, wagging his tail, heavy with dew.

"Morning, Mr. Dog . . . did you sleep better than I did?"

I yawned and looked to the east. A bank of heavy clouds hung over the valley toward town but the sun struck through the fog over the river and hit our side of the valley with warm streaks. Ladd and I walked up the hill, loosening up for the day. We followed a cow trail, then branched off when the scrub alder gave way to grass and burned stumps.

Ladd picked up his head and stood motionless. I followed where he was looking then he was gone. A streak of black and white, low and close to the ground after the yearling doe. She jumped and bounced, her white tail like a ping pong ball against the black clouds to the west. I sat down on a stump to wait for Ladd to come back and watched the sun lose the battle with the clouds. Before it really started raining I was down the hill and taking the first bite out of those buttermilk pancakes that Olive could fry pretty well except for the burned edges and an occasional one that was served doubled-up because she didn't flip it right and the two wet sides welded together.

The Johnson kids came dragging in to breakfast after I left. They almost missed the school bus. Olive shouted for Toddy to put his jacket on before he caught his death of cold.

There weren't any calves to skin so West, Ralph and I worked on the shed. It was standing stouter every day and West said that before the month was out we wouldn't be able to wiggle it.

"I told you the sign of the moon was good," West said.

I tried to shake it.

"Well, we've got it better braced since last time," I countered.

"Try that one," he said and pointed to the shed Jack and Rose had built.

I grabbed the corner post and shook it. All the mink ran out from their nest boxes and up and down the wire. The metal roofing squeaked and one nail popped out and slid down the roof.

West smiled and returned his eye to the bubble in the level he was working. "Up . . . up some more . . . a little more . . . that's it." Ralph nailed the board.

I was driving nails out of the old wood and making it ready for use on the shed when the rain moved across the hill top and started a light trickle, the drops hitting the few remaining leaves sounding like a far away drum corps marching closer, then the sound doubled in volume and doubled again until no conversation was possible. We ducked under the shed and watched the heavy drops splash onto the soaked ground.

First a little stream wiggled its way down between the stones and clods and then more and more until the whole ditch was filled with water carrying mink manure, pieces of duck eggs, straw and hay down to clog up the drain. The ditch started to overflow and run over the path. I ran out from the shelter and lifted the filter screen off the drain. The water rushed down the open pipe while I pounded and pulled the matted stuff out of the filter. When I replaced it bits of grass started piling up again so I pulled it and stuck the pitchfork there to catch the big stuff and ran for the slaughterhouse, the soaked heavy clothes clinging to my body.

Rose was standing under the eaves laughing and puffing on a cigarette.

"Just let it flood," she said.

"Cotton picking water will float that house right off, cook and all," I said.

"We wouldn't lose anything either way," she said.

"How good can you cook?" I asked.

"Anybody could cook better than Olive. And when it comes to cleaning house Paul does better on his room than she does with the two rooms I asked her to keep clean."

"Well, tell Paul I'll give him a buck to clean the trailer house for me."

"Can't you keep that clean? Jack always had it sparkling clean. He even wanted to fix the outside up but the old man wouldn't let him fool around with his trailer." She took a drag on her cigarette and let the smoke drift out between her open lips. "He never wanted anybody to do anything on his stuff but just him doing it the way he wanted."

"Isn't a man entitled to that?" I said.

Her face tightened. "Maybe."

I wrung the water out of my sweatshirt and steam came off my body like I was afire. She looked at my chest. "You've got a good build. My boys would have looked like you if they hadn't been injured." It was silent for maybe twenty seconds, then she looked away. "You know, it's funny what happens in a person's life. You start out thinking the world is your oyster.

You get through school. Get married. Have kids. The Old Man is making a living and the timber business looks like it can last a hundred years and then, wham." She turned back to me.

"Life isn't fair but we all have to get through it," I said.

Her smile crept back. "I wish you could have known Jack. You would have liked him." She looked over at the shed where West and Ralph stood under the roof looking our way. I waved.

"Jack liked his whiskey and hot women, but I guess that's every man's privilege."

She cocked her head. "Ought to be every woman's privilege, too, then."

"I think women who take care of house and family don't have time for whiskey and hot men." I looked for a change in her eyes. A wry smile danced across her eyes and the tip of her tongue slipped between her lips. She took a step away then turned back.

"You know, Jeff. . . Jack did everything for those kids. Built them shelves and bought them that recorder. Bought me this watch when he was stone drunk. He bought the old man whiskey until he got sore cause the old man never bought any. One day he told him to go to hell and that made West mad." She looked at me like she had a secret to tell. She had been building up to something but I had no clue as to what. I waited and wrung my sweat shirt.

"That's when West started that rumor about Jack and me," she snarled. "I said where would we have a place to go—out in the mink yard? One night I got so mad I told him we had a secret place and we wasn't going to tell him where it was. Boy, I was burned up." She looked at me hard, her stone grey eyes challenging me to think, to decide, to weight in on one side or the other.

"You know, Rose," I shook my head. "This pounding on West and building Jack into some kind of great guy isn't helping my work. Let's keep our eye on the goal here, which I believe is to make money with the mink. I'll do my work but I'm working every day with West. I can't stand to hear him undermined all the time."

She turned away—unsatisfied.

I stood there, the cold pushing goose bumps up my body. I pulled on the damp sweat shirt and it began to steam. A car started up the driveway and she poked her head out under the overhang to look. Suddenly the rain let up. Only a drop now and then splashed into the pools that had gathered in every depression. She walked off to get money to pay for the calves in the car and I ambled over to where West and Ralph had come out from under the shed. West looked into my eyes when I walked up; those soft blue eyes questioning without a word. I couldn't look at him.

We worked for another hour until it was dinnertime. Ralph and Olive got in their car with the radio and heater and white sidewalls and went to town. Ralph had his red hair plastered down slick as they slid down the steep driveway.

Olive had prepared the dinner and left it there for us.

I washed the green slime off my hands from the old boards. Paul pulled his chair up to the table. Ronny sat very still on the sofa. Rose asked him if he wanted a milkshake and he didn't answer.

"Ronny. . .you gotta eat something." she said.

He screwed up his face and hollered in a broken slurred voice, "I don't want anything, gawddamnit!"

She slammed a glass down on the counter and served up the meat loaf and potatoes and carrots. I prayed short and silent, giving thanks for the meal, and filled my plate. Ronny writhed on the sofa and Paul looked absently out the window, his head bobbing out of time with his jaws chewing. The food was cut in big chunks on his plate, and he held a greasy chunk of meat loaf in his hand.

Suddenly Ronny wailed. I looked up at West. He was concentrating on pouring gravy on his potatoes and a slice of bread. Ronny groaned again and knocked his drinking glass to the floor. Rose went over and sat beside him on the sofa. She picked up the glass.

"If you'd eat something, this wouldn't happen!" she said.

He tried to answer but nothing came out. His head dropped down to his knees and his feet jerked in spasms.

"Dammit-to-hell. . .hell. . .," he spurted out.

"Quit your damn swearing" she said.

His lips drooled a little, *"Shut up!"*

West's jaw revolved around the food in his mouth which turned like a water wheel, his gaze out the window, a wistful look in his eye, everything slow and deliberate, staring at the green hills fresh with the rain. I couldn't eat; everything doubled in size in my mouth. My tongue choked me and closed off my throat.

Ronny quieted down and sat still as death with sweat trickling down his forehead into his reddish beard. His breathing was labored but regular. Rose lit a cigarette and eased it between his lips. Then she massaged his shoulder and with a mother's hand, pushed his hair back off his forehead several times until it stayed in a rough curl. He didn't object. She sat quite a while just looking at him. Finally she came to the table and sat down but didn't eat anything.

I tried to eat again. West and Paul had their plates empty before I started. The old man pushed away his plate, lit a cigarette and sat with elbows on the table smoking.

"What'd they go into town for?" West said.

Rose answered without shifting from her position looking out the window. "Haircut. And so Olive could make the car payment."

West flicked the ashes onto his empty plate and returned the cigarette to his lips. He took a long pull on it and inhaled, embedding the smoke in his lungs. A hollow tick-tock, regulated and mechanized, filled the living room and kitchen, blanketing all of our thoughts. It was like sitting alone in a cave with giant pillows covering my ears and feeling sure everything had stopped living.

Paul coughed. "Dammit. . .I'm getting Olive's cold." He coughed again.

"Well, the way those kids run around and the things Olive wears," Rose said. "They'll have colds all winter long. They can afford a new car but the kids run around in the mud without boots or rain clothes. And then they put their sick kids in the living room with Ronny, when they know he's got no immunity, and leave them there all day where he can get it." She turned her head and hacked.

"I was never sick until they came," Paul said.

I looked at West.

He smiled but they didn't see. "You know. . .there wasn't so much sickness before tin cans," he said.

"Oh," I said.

"Say they've got some stuff to line the inside of the cans with, but...." He shook his head.

"Well, no wonder they're always sick," Rose said. "Olive knows nothing about nutrition. No green vegetables every day and look what they ate before they came down here to eat. A pound of wieners for the eight of them." She shook her head. "When I found that out I invited them down here for dinner and they've been down ever since. They wanted free board for all of them when they first came."

"Really?" I said.

West looked at me, that startup smile curling his lips. "I took them around looking for a house when they first came. Took two days off and hunted them a house. We found some they didn't like—better than this house," he said, his face holding the grin. "And then I found one that Ralph said he guessed was all right if he didn't need the first month's rent right away." He looked, trying to pull an expression from me. "Why didn't he tell me he couldn't pay for a house in the first place instead of after I'd spent two days looking for a place?" He expected me to think about that.

"Their rent was only $20 a month where they came from and they were $70 behind. The owner's keeping their stuff until they pay for it." He flicked the ashes off and looked back at the hill, his steel blue eyes steady. "Here comes Ladd. He must have been running deer again."

I looked out the window. Ladd was coming down the hill, wet from top to bottom and muddy all over.

"I'm going to get rid of that dog," Rose said. "Maybe I'll get a shepherd."

West stood up and shrugged his shoulders. He pulled his sweatshirt over his gray head, turned the old hat over in his hand and walked out, pulling the door shut behind him. I followed him out. I heard him cough hard and spit and I knew he was getting the flu, too. I hoped I wouldn't get it. He stopped at the outdoor privy and I walked on to the slaughter house and waited.

He came out shortly and stopped in front of me. "Those eight people are filling my toilet overfull. You'd think a man would dig his own toilet for eight people. We gotta even buy their toilet paper for them." He looked at me for confirmation and then said, "Gotta fix that motor on the winch tomorrow," as an afterthought of the thought of having to dig another toilet.

We walked out to the new shed. A mole was pushing the ground up beside a post and we watched him. When he stopped, West scooped up the fresh mound with a shovel and the mole came with it. He brought the shovel down like a pole driver and cut the mole in half.

Suddenly West looked up. Ladd was digging in the corral, in the corner where the cows usually stood with their butts to the wind and rain making continual slurry of new and old manure, dirt, rain water and apple tree leaves that drifted down the hill. West had the shovel in both hands and walked fast toward Ladd. Ladd glanced up for just a second but kept on digging. The shovel hit him broadside full in the chest. He yelped and half jumping, half reeling turned sideways in the air and ran across the corral, managing to slip between the two bottom rails.

I jumped up, fists clenched. Rants formed in my mind. My lips parted but nothing came out. Every muscle and sinew tuned to throw myself into the battle. Then my brain stopped and nothing rational that I could say or do formed. Anger flooded over my senses.

West threw dirt into the hole, patted it down with the flat of the shovel and walked back to where I stood with my mouth open. The whites of his eyes were large, the pupils dilated. I stood with my arms hanging at my side, fists clenched. Vulnerable. Exposed. I tensed thinking I might feel the flat of the shovel any moment.

We stood a few feet apart. He blinked several times. The whites of his eyes diminished as the lids closed around them. The pupils retreated. His eyes defused and in a minute had returned to the grey passive glaze that I saw every day.

West set the shovel against the shed. "Don't like him digging."

"You don't have to brain him with a shovel."

He stood as still as a post and looked me in the eyes. "I guess he's my dog."

"Your dog or not, I don't like you hitting him with a shovel."

We stood there silent facing one another. I felt a shudder pass from my shoulders to my hips but I don't think it showed. I inhaled through my nose—a big breath—big enough to settle things.

West walked over to the wall, took his apron down from the peg, pulled it over his head and tied the strings behind his back.

I blinked several times. I felt like a witness to an accident who couldn't describe with any accuracy what had occurred.

I put on my apron and climbed up on the sheeting. West handed me the aluminum roofing to nail on.

He shook his head. "I think this will be strong enough, don't you?"

"I think so."

CHAPTER 7

He handed me another sheet and we finished the whole shed before Ralph and Olive got back. By the time Ralph got his boots on and his apron tied, we were ready to water the mink and he had to grind the feed.

West started to split wood from the wood pile, holding the wood with his left hand and splitting it clean with one swing of the axe. He bent over like everything hurt, picked up the wood and I could tell just from watching him slow down that he had the flu.

I ran down and turned on the pump and walked back up the water line to check for leaks. The rain had done a good job of watering the mink and I skipped along pretty fast until I got to the sapphires with their inside pans. I hadn't seen the sapphires much because of the work on the new shed so I stopped to watch them play in the water. One huge male with a heavy grayish-blue coat that fluffed out like a wolf at his ears and eyes stretched full out to look at me, his beady eyes alive and darting, his nose moving from square to square on the inside of the wire mesh. I thought he was the most beautiful animal I had ever seen.

I traced my finger across the wire and he followed it with his black nose and then suddenly, faster than I could think, his nose slammed against the wire, his teeth slipped through it and he held my thumb in his jaws. I jerked back. The flesh tore. I snapped his nose with my other hand. Blood started running down my knuckle. I grabbed the hose and shot water up his nose, then hit him with it but he still held on and now the thumb began to throb and ache as he worked to pull it through the wire.

I squirted him again. He coughed and sneezed but held on. With my free hand I reached in my pocket for a match, struck it against the pen and shoved the blazing end up his nose. He jerked loose and licked the blood from his mouth, drank a little water and went into his nest box. My thumb had three holes in it. Blood was pouring from each one of them.

When I finished watering I turned off the water and headed toward the house examining my black and blue thumb. Rose let out a howl and could hardly tell me where the band-aids were for her chuckling. She finally got me some black goop to put on it.

"Now you're a mink rancher," she said.

"It really takes that, huh?"

"Look here." And she showed me several scars similar to the one I expected to have.

I slopped the black goop on and taped on a Band-Aid. It felt a little better.

"Which one did it?" She asked.

"That big sapphire at the end of the row. He just bit and hung on good."

"Jack got bit by him too."

Olive didn't say anything but she looked bad. She coughed a couple times right over the drying dishes. The window over the sink fogged over a bit when she coughed.

"I'd be out there helping you but Ronny's sick and I gotta stay here with him," Rose said. "If the old man ever gets that shed done so we can put mink in it before breeding season, it'll be a wonder."

Olive coughed again. I felt unclean. The house was unclean. West came in with the paper tucked under his arm, put on his glasses, sat down beside Ronny and read. I took off my coat and sat down listening to Paul trying for a Texas station on his radio. "Almost gotcha. . ." he'd say and then, "Dammit. . . where are you?" The government records had come in the mail for the boys and Ronny wanted to hear them but Paul wanted to try for that station. And Olive wanted some wood for the stove and she said, "We're out of wood, Mr. Helner."

West put down the paper and looked at her. He folded his glasses into their case, stood up, and walked to the nail where his hat hung, put it on, and walked out to the woodpile. I grabbed my coat and followed.

"I'll take some, West."

He looked at me then turned and coughed. I loaded up and walked to the house. I came back out for another load and he carried in the rest. I let the wood tumble on the pile beside the stove next to the wall and rubbed the pitch from my hands. I kicked the door closed behind the old man. He dumped the wood and turned to me, "Thanks," he said. I nodded.

Rose turned and looked at him in amazement and Paul stopped to listen. For a second were we all three aware of that one word. I looked out the window at the house on the hill. It stood like a ship, gray and dull in the fading evening. The wind banged a shutter. Then the second was over and it was like it had never really been there.

The kids returned home from school and Ralph came in from feeding the mink with his nose and ears red. We all sat down to the big table, the adults on chairs and the kids on apple boxes and Toddy and Billy on one chair together. They all coughed on the table and when the food got to me I didn't want any, especially the bread after they all had fingered it.

They passed it to me and I passed it on. I took some meat from under the pile and passed the bread and the carrots and the potatoes. When Olive reached my glass and filled it with milk I saw the thumb print on the rim and turned the glass to drink from the other side. I felt like not breathing but I took in a small amount of air through my nose. West turned his head and coughed.

"We're almost out of wood," West said.

"I know it. I'll have to call tomorrow," Rose said.

"Should have called a week ago," he said.

She scowled at him and raised her voice. "They'll bring it to me 'cause I got good credit and they know the boys are sick!"

West looked down at his plate. Ralph coughed. He had the bug. They all had it. Ronny and Paul had to blow their noses all the time. I was glad when dinner was over and I could retreat to the trailer. I was going to write a letter to the girl I had dated when we both worked at the motel in Seaside but then I decided not to. How did I explain the situation I was in now with incriminations as my daily fare? I didn't even write in my journal but I had no worries that I wouldn't remember what was happening around me.

I slept better. The morning was cold and wet and the fog hung in tight. I couldn't make out the last row of sheds and I just barely saw West walking through the cloud to the barn. I dressed and stepped out putting on my raincoat. Ladd came out from under the trailer favoring his right side. A car drove up with a calf in the trunk. I put the calf in the corral, went to the house and got the money under the clock where Rose had showed me she kept it, and paid the man. He had some trouble turning the car around in the mud, but he made it and I went down to breakfast.

Only Olive was there and she was half asleep. I went back out and chopped some wood and brought it in and stoked up the heater with big chunks of alder. The wind blew in through the cracks between the window casings, fluttering the newspapers that were rolled up and nailed in the cracks. I left my coat on.

Rose came out but didn't say anything. She went back into her room and then came out again.

"Was that a good calf?" she asked.

"White face. Sturdy little fella."

"Bull?"

"Yeah."

"Take it up to the pelting shed and put him in there. I'll be out in a minute to feed it. I'll feed him for beef next fall."

The calf didn't mind being carried to the shed with his legs dangling and he kept slipping his rough tongue in and out between his lips. Rose came out smoking a cigarette, the smoke mixing with the fog so you couldn't tell one from the other. She carried a nipple pail and handed it to me over the fence and then came in and fastened the gate behind her.

The calf took the nipple and sucked with as much enthusiasm and noise as if it were its mother's udder, nudging it every so often to increase the flow. Rose turned to me.

"Now that I've got a chance to talk to you without *him* around I want to tell you to keep your ears peeled."

"Why?"

"I've had it from three different people that I should fix it for the boys." She patted her chest. "I carry me a little pistol and he better not try it again."

"Try what again?"

"He's going to try to kill me. He's been talking about it to them!" She raised her voice. "I think he killed Jack."

I was deliberately slow. My head was having a difficult time switching from feeding a day old calf to the murder plot. "You think he killed Jack and means to try and kill you?"

She went on like we were on a picnic or jaunty outing. "His birthday was yesterday and I forgot it. He was in a killing mood last night and was packing his suitcase so I gave him a fifth of whiskey I had for Ronny and told him it was for his birthday." She sucked in on her smoke.

"He always needs something for his birthday, but he never buys anything. Not for me or the kids." She glanced towards the barn.

I looked down at the calf which had finished his feeding but still fought with the nipple. A swift version of the shovel beating passed behind my eyes.

Could West be capable of murder? Where in the hell was I in this complex mess?

"You're probably making too much of this," I managed to say.

"He's fixing to leave again." She looked straight at me. "He left me in 1945. Just packed up and left me with everything to take care of, no money or anything."

"What'd he do?"

"Just bummed around until his money was gone and then came back wanting me to take him back. I did it, but never again. My lawyer said I was a fool to let him come back the first time. And when he goes again, and it looks like he's going to, he won't get a second chance."

"A second chance is one thing. Murder is another. Have you told anybody you think he killed Jack?"

"No. Can't prove anything. But you know how you get those feelings that won't go away? And I'm too busy to go snooping around trying to prove my husband killed someone."

"You'd think," I said, "that both of you working together every day would mend those old wounds."

"Or make them worse," she offered.

"That's possible."

For a moment, just the calf's noises could be heard. The heavy fog shut out all other sights and sounds and we stood there like conspirators having met in a dark alley.

A thought came to me. "Do you think if you finished off that house up there and moved in and really got going again, it would change things?"

She looked up at the house. "I doubt it. That dream is as old and weathered now as that building. As I told you yesterday, when you are young and have two handsome sons, the sun never sets on a bad day. Then..." her voice trailed off as a car drove up the driveway. The car was towing a trailer with a calf cross-tied in it bawling its head off.

She walked out the gate. "Remember . . . keep your ears peeled."

Can he be that bad? Except for smacking Ladd in the ribs I haven't been worried about him. But I'm more alert now than I was—especially with her telling me all this stuff. It's all hard to believe—but possible. Anything is possible.

"Better come to breakfast, Jeff," she said, her voice coming from out of the fog, and I started after her.

She stopped at the end of the row. "Jeff, did you put the male and female from the end cages somewhere?"

"I haven't moved any mink," I said.

"Look—they're gone."

The cage doors were open. I looked around. They had to be right there somewhere.

"Check the area. I need to pay for that calf," she said.

I ran the perimeter but saw nothing. Then I went aisle by aisle until she called me to breakfast again.

"Any luck?" she said.

I shook my head.

WE ATE BREAKFAST WITHOUT Ralph or the kids.

"Couple of mink out," I said as I took a seat.

West looked up from his food. "We'll find them after we eat. They can't get out of the fence.

Paul was shaving and wouldn't come out until he was through and Ronny didn't want to get up yet, so I ate with Olive and Rose and West, who were all sick with the flu. Ralph and the kids were sick too and stayed in the big house. They didn't want to eat. Ralph didn't want to work.

I felt like the last man standing. The newest person on the farm was suddenly the only one who could make a decent accounting for the day. I ran some options through my head then guessed at the priorities. Finding some firewood; mink feeding; calf killing; skinning and grinding all came first. After that we built sheds, mended fences, salted hides, helped the gut hauler and anything else that needed doing. But first—I had to find those missing mink.

CHAPTER 8

There was one job that was more consistent than handling the calves that got dropped off at the ranch: mink feeding. Twice a day we patrolled the aisles chucking the uneaten food on the ground where the ducks would find it. After that we brushed the top of the wire cage where the food was dropped, then reached into the bucket of ground-up meat, meal and water, and dropped a handful on top of the wire cage. The mink were usually right there waiting as soon as you started scrapping the old stuff off. Fingers were at high risk while that was going on. We wire brushed the dried food off and often put drops of medicine in their water dishes to counteract any potential infection that might get started.

I was halfway down the second aisle when Rose came around the corner and worked her way toward me.

"Jeff," she said. "I don't want you to think that I don't appreciate your work here. I do."

I had my hand in the feed bucket and was rolling a piece of bone between my fingers trying to decide if it was too large or too small to cause a problem with the mink. They wouldn't mess with a big bone but often got small bones stuck in their teeth. When that happened you held the mink against your chest with one hand and pulled the bone out of his mouth with the other. It was not the beginning of a great day.

I realized she was going to go on so I pulled my hand out of the feed and wiped it on a towel hanging at my waist.

"I've got a lot of responsibility here. I'm the breadwinner—the decision maker. When West was logging I had to take care of the boys and run the place. It wasn't as big then but I started it.

"I studied catalogs at night after the boys were in bed. Studied the mink market. I learned about how to make pens, different kinds of feed, diseases. Even took a correspondence course on how to figure the finances of a mink ranch. One month I ran up a $100 phone bill calling all over the states to talk to people who knew more than I did about this business.

"When the logging got slim and West couldn't make us a living at it I spent most of our savings and went to the national fur farmers convention. Came back with a dozen females and one male mink. That's what started us."

She waved her arm around the mink yard. "This is the result. I can't take care of the house, the boys, and this place without hired help. I appreciate what you do. I've done it all myself and I know it is hard work. It's hard and it's dirty. West works at it too. But other than carrying Ronnie from bed to couch and back again he doesn't do anything else around the house. He acts like it's a logging camp. That there's a bull cook to wake him up, cook his meals, wash his clothes, give him a piece of pie at the end of the meal and see that there is wood for the stove.

"That's why I let him have his precious cows and that worthless dog Ladd, so he can have something to call his own. He's lost without logging and the guys and their talk. Sitting around chewing snus, spitting and telling jokes."

Ralph passed by the far end of the aisle and Rose hesitated. He glanced up our way and kept going with his bucket and wire brush.

She took out her cigarettes, shook one out and lit it. "I knew the timber business would play out. Hell—they were logging everything they could get their hands on. Anybody would know they couldn't do that forever. Then the fire hit and burned up the mill and they shut down."

Her eyes softened and she exhaled her smoke. "I wanted a business that the whole family could work at and where we could keep the boys at home. I think I found that."

Just like that, she stopped. I had let my mind wander a bit and was yanked back to what she said at the end. Something that would keep the whole family together. I wasn't being challenged and no question had been asked. I nodded my head.

"Well?" she said.

"I appreciate what you're saying but working here is like being tied to a buzz saw. You talk about West being a killer, Johnson no good, nothing is done right. I'm always on pins and needles wondering if I even know how you want something done.

"One day you're mad at West and today you're making excuses for him and letting him keep a cow and a dog so he owns something.

"I'm not used to working under this kind of pressure. Frankly I've been thinking it's time for me to leave."

Here eyes grew steely. "You promised me at least four months."

"I know, but this see-saw you've got me on is ruining my perspective on life in general and on mink farms specifically.

"Will you make your promise good and stay four months?"

I thought about it a minute. Thought about school, being short of money, being locked out here on this foggy dead-end road and finally nodded. "Ok, but start looking for another worker now."

"I need your help and your cooperation, Jeff. Promise me you'll stay."

"Yes, I will. But only until you find another worker."

She dropped her cigarette butt in the aisle, twisted her boot on it, looked up into my eyes and smiled. "Let's feed these hungry mama's. Then we'll do a good search for those missing mink."

"Right," I said. The bucket of feed was wet, cold, and clammy but I pulled out another handful and plopped it on the wire. "There you go, mama."

I wasn't sure where to put this information; where to file it. I finally decided to just hold it until I got to the trailer tonight where I might be able to sort it out and compare it to what I'd heard from others. I couldn't verify anything around this place.

Sure getting conflicting stories around this place. Seems like two sides drawn up to do battle and each side is recruiting me. I'm going to be more regular recording events in my journal because it is getting difficult to recall who said what. We've lost a couple of mink today. Rose thinks they can't get out but I've covered the grounds several times and seen no sign of them.

This is not a life. It is barely an existence. The emotional trauma is constant unless I'm with West and I don't ask him some question about something Rose has told me. Johnsons are just as bad. They sneak around not making any noises but whisper their plans on leaving and asking my opinion on the job, the food, the pay—everything.

Sure miss seeing some girls after a summer of beauties. Well, it's only for four months. The money adds up fast with no expenses. I can stick it out that long.

CHAPTER 9

I went out after breakfast to clean up the kill floor. West took his good axe, his felling axe, honed it until he was satisfied with the edge, and then went to look for wood to split for the fire.

The job of killing, gutting, and skinning the calf fell to me. The calf sensed something wrong. He ran around in the pen, avoiding me and the iron pipe that we used for killing. I swung at its head when it turned at the corner and I knew as soon as I swung that it was going to miss the kill spot. It bounced off its skull, stunning it. The calf wobbled, went stiff legged, its eyes wide and bloodshot as I swung the pipe across the back of his skull for the kill.

He went limp. I dragged him out of the corral onto the cement floor, drew my knife and stuck the blade beneath the lower jaw, then ripped open the throat down to the chest cavity. I punctured the heart and the blood ran dark red over my hand down to the gutter.

I honed the blade. Stroked it keen with the steel and drew a bucket of water from the hose. I skinned out one leg and was starting on the head with only one hole when Rose came in.

I straightened up. "Hey, where you going all dressed up?"

She looked very nice. "To get a German Police dog. Also some mink feed. Anything you want me to bring you?"

"No."

"I'm gonna see about that pen wire too," she said.

"My gosh, you got sixteen rolls in the pelting shed..."

"Well, Jeff... that won't even start to make enough pens for two thousand mink."

"Two thousand?" I said. I hadn't counted but I guessed there might be two hundred mink out there going through their short lives in a wire pen. "Wow."

"With you here, I've got some time to work on new colors. The fur business is gonna boom soon and I want to be first with desirable colors and pelts. You see—there used to be just wild furs—one color—and then we found out we could breed for different colors and that opened up a whole new market. Fashion. Women love to wear mink coats and we are going to provide them." She started out then turned. "Really look hard for those two mink this afternoon. Can't imagine where they're hiding out."

"You've got my word on it," I said. Then as my mind got around the concept I blurted, "Two thousand mink! You know how many calves we'll be killing to feed that many mink?"

She smiled and left. I heard the truck start. She didn't warm it up before she engaged the clutch and let it chug down the driveway in low gear.

I finished the calf, washed up and stepped out into the drizzle. I took a deep breath to rid my lungs of the dry sweetness of warm blood and newborn calf smell. West stood outside the slaughterhouse, leaning on the felling axe. It would make a good killing instrument.

He turned his head to me. "When you gonna get these two thousand mink?"

He had overheard our conversation. My heart skipped a beat. "Not me," I said, "her."

He cracked a faint smile and bent over the piece of wood he had just split. As he straightened up his voice took on a harsh tone. "Where's she gonna put them?"

"Here," I said. I squared my shoulders and took a deep breath.

He spit tobacco. "Humph. Not enough water for two thousand mink."

I shrugged. "Why don't you buy some mink of your own, West, and raise them the way you want to?"

He looked straight at me and I could see his eyes dilate.

"Buy?" he said. "A lot of my money has helped buy these mink." He motioned with his hand toward the sheds. He looked back at me with a sideways glance and reached for a cigarette. He put it to his lips and patted his overalls looking for his lighter. He found it in his pants pocket.

After he expelled the first draw his voice softened. "I work seven days a week here."

"Does she pay you any wages?"

He stroked his throat. "I won't take any."

"I bought this place," he whispered. "Every nickel I earned went into this place. All the fixtures and everything—"

I didn't know how to look at him. I didn't want to turn away from this man who asked of me understanding and yet I didn't know how to face him. I felt ill at ease when he looked straight into my eyes, still stroking the white hairs at his throat. So I looked back at him without answering, stayed looking at him even though it got uncomfortable until a mutual appreciation welded us there.

He got up and split the rest of the old log he'd found and I helped him carry it in the house. With everyone gone, we sat down to a cup of coffee and a piece of cake. Paul was in the living room listening to his radio. After West finished his coffee, he got up and went into Ronny's room and carried him out to sit on the sofa. Ronny's daily routine was to sit on the sofa until he wanted to go to the toilet and then West carried him to it, set him down on it, and waited and then carried him back to the sofa.

After our snack a car with four calves in the trunk came in. I got the money from under the clock on the piano and walked out.

"Where's the boss?" the man said.

"Gone to town for a dog," I said.

"How many do they need?"

I shrugged my shoulders. "She wants one to guard the place."

He chuckled. "Where's the old man?"

"Inside."

"He know about the dog?"

"Guess so."

"He oughta kick her butt clear out of this state and run this place right," he said.

"Here's your money," I said.

"Thanks." He folded it two times and put it in his overalls pocket. "How long you been here?"

"Almost a week."

A smile started on his face. "How do you like it?"

"All right." I tried to keep my face open and unreadable.

He got in his car and slammed the door and started it up. "Well, if Jack knew you were here, he'd probably take back his threat—you're a pretty good sized boy. Well, we'll see you." He released the brake and the car slid down the driveway and out on the gravel road with just a little spinning on the wet stones.

West walked out the door and came over.

"Four?" he asked.

"Four," I said.

He moved in to the winch and pulled a small crescent wrench out of his overall pocket and started unscrewing the bolt from the winch cogwheel. "We'll put on the motor today."

"Hey, West. What's your take on this Jack character?"

He turned to me and stopped what he was doing. He lit up with a short smile and then it turned down. "Don't know why she always brags about that drunken sonofabitch. I never saw him skin a calf by himself or grind feed or build a mink pen."

"What did he do?" I asked.

"Just water and feed the mink." He smiled. "They want him on a bad check charge now." He had a way of looking at me, straight into my eyes after he made a statement that made me feel that I should make up my mind on each thing he said so it could reflect in my eyes when he looked.

"Well, from what she says, he must have been a half god or some such form of creation."

He laughed with a slow chuckle.

I went on. "Told me that between the two of them they put out fifty-eight calves in two hours and had them hanging on the nails."

He turned to me. "Do you believe it?"

"I don't know. That's pretty fast. But from what she says about him, he could do it by himself."

"She was always out here helping him, shoving calves to him from the corral or skinning for him. He'd get drunk and go up town saying things about me and Rose and the kids and ole Doc would hear them and tell me. Jack would come back after three or four days and say Doc had been saying them things."

"Who was Doc?"

"He was a guy that worked here but she didn't like him 'cause he told her she was lying half the time." He smiled.

"Was she?" I asked.

He nodded his head. "Jack threatened to kill anybody who took his job so he could get back on. Even said he'd kill me. He could have got into some bad trouble after he left here. Never heard about him since."

"So that's what that guy meant about him taking back his threat."

He nodded.

I picked up the kill stick and knocked the calves in the head and stuck them and skinned them while West rigged the electric motor up to the winch.

The motor worked pretty well but the belt kept slipping and by noon it was working only when I leaned on the motor to keep the belts tight and by then Rose was back with the truck and the feed and the new dog, a German Sheppard that she named King. He was all brown and tan except for a black nose and a black tip on his tail.

Ladd nosed him over but wouldn't have too much to do with his playfulness. He just retired under the trailer and growled when the puppy came near. West looked at the dog once and took a load of wood into the house and we sat down to hot dogs and carrot sticks.

After dinner West and I started the process of grinding the calf carcasses to put in the freezer for later use. I put the grinder together and he lined the boxes with wax paper. He flicked on the grinder switch and I lowered the carcass head first into the twisting auger. The head bounced on the auger twice and then caught and the powerful motor pushed the auger through to the plates. The calf went through the machine in seconds, only slowing down a little when both shoulders were being ground at once.

He turned it off and I smoothed out the ground meat in the box with my hand and lifted it to the battery cart, replaced the box underneath the grinder, and pulled another carcass from the nails and stuck it in as the auger picked up speed.

Just as I lowered the second calf in there was a whunk of metal against metal and before West could shut off the grinder the vibration almost shook it off the concrete foundation it was bolted to. I pulled the headless calf out.

We took the grinder apart. The first blade and the small plate were okay, but the second blade had one of its three knives broken and it had chewed up the back plate and had so tightened the plate to the casing that it gouged a ditch in the auger when the blade stopped but the auger kept going.

Rose was right there. She had heard it in the house.

"What the hell did you do now?" she said.

West didn't answer and neither did I.

She vented at West. "You trying to wreck everything I own?"

"I told you to get that fixed a month ago," he said.

"Gawddamnit, I haven't got time to do everything around here. Take care of the boys and the mink and the machinery too. You've got to do something to earn your keep."

I looked at West. His jaw muscles tightened and pulsed which made it look like something was living under his skin.

"I suppose it didn't hurt it any when that drunk dropped the steel in it?" he said.

"Oh my Gawd!" she bellowed. "He knew how to fix it, but you have to take it down town and spend money to get it fixed. You and your chasing off my men."

She stared at me. "What did he do?"

"I was grinding a calf..."

"What was *he* doing?"

I shook my head and pointed to the meat box. "Standing there I guess."

"Oh bullshit. That grinder didn't break on its own. He did something to it—what was it?"

"Look," I said. "Neither of us did anything to break it. It broke doing its job."

"Look me in the eye when you say that."

"We're doing our best out here. Things break. West didn't do anything to break it and neither did I."

She walked off. West watched her go and I thought he would throw the blade at her back but he just stared at her as she walked away.

When she was gone West pulled back his right arm and with a move that used his entire body's strength, threw the broken blade across the concrete floor. It skipped twice off the floor and thunked into the wall. I picked it up and put it in a bucket along with the pieces I lifted out of the grinder.

"Bring the auger," he said.

I pulled it out and put it in the truck with the bucket of pieces West had carried over.

"We'll take these fresh calves over to the locker since we can't grind them and feed some of our frozen stuff tonight."

I backed the truck up to the kill floor and threw on the carcasses hanging on the nails and threw some empty sacks over them and then I got five boxes of ground-up, frozen calf meat out of our freezer and laid them where the air could circulate around them and grabbed my gloves.

By then West was ready to go and he eased into the seat, dug out a cigarette from under the sweat shirt and struck a match on his overalls button. He drew in long on the cigarette and blew out a gray haze.

"Thanks for sticking up for me."

A thin smile formed on my lips. I nodded. "You were in the right."

"Don't seem to make any difference around here. Anything I do she downgrades it."

"Pretty much."

He looked out the windshield and expelled a lung full of smoke before he pulled the brake off and coasted down the hill to start it.

We bounced over the holes in the gravel road up to the gas station and stopped for some gas and a candy bar.

When West paid for them the owner asked, "The river coming up?"

"A little," West said.

The man shook his head. "Suppose the road will be closed off again?"

"I've only seen it open one winter in the 25 years I've been here," West said. "Hear they plan on building a new road higher across the hills to the coast."

"Yeah," the man said. "The bastards want to go through my station here." He cocked his hat on his head and looked out of the corner of his eyes at West and me.

"Why—they won't pay half what its worth."

"Never do," West said.

I un-wrapped my candy bar and took a bite. The conversation sort of dragged to a stop.

"Well, we'll be going," West said.

I turned and walked out in front of him and we took off on the old road to the highway. West drove fast. The truck made a lot of noise so we didn't say much but my mind was turning over the comments that Rose and West had made to me about Jack.

I shouted over the burned-out muffler noise. "Was Jack really drunk a lot of the time?"

He glanced at me and took the corner fast, looking in his rear-view mirror for any cops. "I filled two gunny sacks with whiskey bottles from the inside of the trailer house. All the cup-boards were full and I found two boxes of them in the slaugh-ter- house where he had them stashed away."

I laughed.

"I don't begrudge a man a drink of whiskey, but I can't see him drunk all the time." He looked out the side view mirror. "I suppose your Dad takes a little whiskey now and then, don't he?"

"Used to," I said.

"Huh?"

"Used to," I shouted over the roar of the truck.

He nodded his head. We hit town and parked in front of a machine shop. West and I pulled the box of pieces and the auger out, lugged them into the shop and dropped them on the floor.

A big man turned down the lathe before he took off his goggles and the machine whined to a stop.

"What do you need?"

"Some welding and brazing," the old man said. He looked small beside the welder.

The welder picked up the pieces and fitted them together, looked at the auger and thought and looked some more.

"When do you need it?" he said.

"When can you get it done?"

The welder smiled. "A week,"

West turned to me, and then looked back up at the welder. "How about tomorrow?" He had his hands hooked in his overall straps and stood on one leg with the other stuck out to the side.

"Okay."

West nodded and we turned to go out.

"Who shall I charge it to?" the giant asked from back inside the dark shop.

"Charge it to the dust and let the rain settle it," West said.

"Like hell..." he bellowed from inside the cave.

"I'll pay you tomorrow."

"Okay." His voice mixed with the starting whine of the lathe.

We drove to the fish plant where Rose rented a walk-in freezer. West backed the truck right into the spot where it was easiest to throw the calves into the cold hole on top of the frozen carcasses. I threw them in while West urinated behind the door. Afterward we sat in the front seat of the truck while he smoked.

Across the street a pretty Negro lady pulled up the blind on the tavern window and unlocked the door, stuck her head out and looked up and down the street, then walked out to the paper box in her nightgown that was a beautiful white with lace around the neck. When she walked it split open. Her legs were nicely shaped. West and I both watched until she closed the door behind her and then we looked at each other. A faint smile creased his lips.

"Rose used to have legs like that. When we got married and I took the garter off her leg it was evident to everybody else too."

"That the first time you saw her legs?"

He snorted. We sat there for a minute in silence.

"I suppose we best be getting back or she'll be on the war path," I said. He didn't move. One hand held the cigarette and the other pulled at the white hairs at his throat.

"Yeah...and when we get there, she'll be telling everybody I broke the grinder and she got it fixed," he said.

"Didn't you know?" I said. "She built the best mink shed and paid for the team to clear the land and she and Jack made that place what it is today

"Jeff, I get so discouraged. I work like a dog around that place and what do I get for it?" He looked at me. "I asked her for money for a new pair of overalls and a new sweat shirt and she said no." He rolled down the window and spit. "So I sold that old grinder for twenty dollars and bought them. I work all day and then she says I don't do nothin'. First thing she tells a hired man is that I'm no good." He turned to me. "Ain't that what she told you?"

I nodded. He turned back to look out the window.

"Mink ranchers come here and she called me to catch some mink so's they could look at them and she wouldn't introduce me."

I shook my head. I didn't want to speak for fear of stopping him. When he spoke it made my heart sore and I wanted to talk with him but I had to search for the right words.

As an after-thought he said, "She's gonna get paid back for her spitefulness with those boys. Paul don't like her much any more and Ronny's been turning against her for quite awhile. He bawls her out every so often for something now."

"Yeah, I noticed that the other night."

He just stayed looking out the window and I felt maybe he wasn't talking to me, but to himself, so I didn't look at him. We both stared across the street.

"You think things might have turned out differently if those accidents hadn't happened to the boys?"

He turned to face me. "Who told you about that?"

"Rose did."

He took a deep breath and flicked the ashes off his cigarette. "The boys are what they are. We can't go back and change any of that. Things were pretty good when I was working the lumber camps. We had a house, car, some savings. The boys were growing up good. Rose worked from time to time but mostly she had her eyes set on raising mink. She was always good with animals and kids. I thought we'd have some more kids but after Ronny got meningitis and we spent almost everything we had trying to get him well, we just never got that done.

"Seemed we got to spending all our daylight hours solving little problems and taking care of Ronny. Then Paul had his accident—" West swallowed and looked out the window.

He tried again. "That's what's made her mad. When we come back from the hospital I could see her change." He looked me in the eyes. "There was no good going to come from that and it got worse every year. I don't know what to do. I've got no place to go and no money to do it with. Hell—I'm as much a cripple as those boys."

I slumped in the seat. Here I was at the beginning of a productive life and West was looking back at a shattered life. Living it day by day in a struggle of desperation. Knowing each day would repeat the day before and at the end of it the best he could hope for was some family peace, a decent supper, and a smoke. Maybe he had friends, but I hadn't seen or heard of any.

Neither of us spoke until the cigarette had burned down to his lips. He lowered the window and threw it out. Pretty soon he started the truck and we rolled down the ramp and out on the street crowded with homeward-bound cars. He didn't drive so fast now and even when we were out on the highway with no cars around he didn't go over forty. We didn't talk. Each of us in a private funk. When we passed the little service station it started to rain again. It really rained hard going over the bridge. The water was coming up higher but it would take a lot more rain to cover the road.

When we pulled up the driveway we saw Rose on the right, standing beside the old wheelbarrow. Down at her feet was her new whiteface Hereford calf that she had been feeding for beef, very stiff with rain drops hitting the open eyes and parting the hair on its bloated side.

I rolled down the window. "What'd he die of?" I asked.

"Scours," she said and walked off.

The gray day suddenly became very dark and Ladd barked a couple of times. I got the shovel and buried the calf up behind the old house because the gut man wouldn't ever come up our driveway when it was that slick. Ladd followed my every move. I bent over and pet him and he closed his eyes and leaned against my leg.

Suddenly I straightened up. I didn't know why, but I had a funny feeling. I listened. Then I heard a baying that came from up the hill. Ladd sat, mouth closed, ears and eyes alert, looking at the hillside and barely breathing.. West and Rose came out on the porch. It came again and again and then drifted away with the rising wind. The coolness made me shiver. For the first time I noticed shadows that moved on the side of the hill and then the rain came down hard again.

West came out with his jacket on and looked at me. "Gonna put the calves inside. I think that's coyotes headed this way."

"Need help?"

"You can hold the gate open."

I lifted the gate and drug it across the opening. "You've lost calves to coyotes?"

"They've killed some of everything on this place."

"Maybe they got those mink we're missing."

He wiped his running nose on his sleeve. "I doubt it."

Ladd followed me back to the trailer and stood at the bottom of the stairs when I went in. "You know where you sleep," I said. He lowered his eyes that had followed me with a pleading look and crawled under the trailer. Before I closed the door I heard the baying again. It was a haunting sound.

CHAPTER 10

A Ford pickup pulled up the driveway with smoke coming out under the running boards and a fan belt squeak so loud it drew me out of the salting shed. It stopped and a small cloud of exhaust engulfed the car, passed over it, and dissipated against the slaughter-house. Two men got out. The driver, the smaller of the two, took off his hat and rubbed a handkerchief around the inside of it then settled it on his head, turned and looked at me.

"The missus around?"

I shook my head. "Gone to town. Can I help you?"

The larger one put his hands on his hips, stuck his head out and glared at the driver. "I told you we should have called first."

"Can we see the hides?" the driver asked.

"Who are you?" I said.

"Hide buyers."

"Let me ask Paul."

I found Paul in the living room listening to the government books on records that had been delivered by mail this week.

"Paul—there are two guys here say they're hide buyers. They want to see the hides. Do you think it's okay?"

His head snapped upright. "I'll come out."

"You don't—"

"I'll come out. I get ten percent of the hide money."

"Okay. Need any help?"

"Yeah—I took off my shoe that was hurting me. Can you put it on?"

I found it half under the couch. Ronny was asleep.

Paul said, "Those Jews—we gotta be careful with them. Every hide is a throw-away when they look at them. Let me think a minute."

"Maybe we ought to tell them to come back when Rose or West is here," I said.

"Naw. We can handle 'em. Help me get out the door to my wheelbarrow."

I pushed his wheelchair through the living room and kitchen and out the door to the porch where he kept his wheelbarrow parked.

It amazed me that Paul, who lived in his wheelchair inside the house, had enough leg strength to push the wheelbarrow up the hill to the slaughter house. It was a heavy contraption that West had fashioned from a wheelbarrow and two car wheels. Paul would lift the rear by the two handles, shove it forward and take a couple of awkward steps behind it, then set it down and catch his breath. But today, with the hide buyers already in the salting shed, he made the entire distance in two drives. Two level boards placed between the handles provided him a stable place to sit between drives. When he got to the hide shed he positioned the wheelbarrow near the entrance.

The two men stood on the concrete floor looking at Paul and me.

Paul, his head tilted down and shaking in his typical mode, turned his face up to the men and smiled like had just found his long lost brother. "Hi, gentlemen. I'm Paul, their son."

The two men looked at one another, then the driver leaned forward and stuck out his hand. "My name's Sydney."

Paul lifted his right hand. It waved around but Sidney followed it, caught it, and then shook it. "Glad to meet you, Paul."

The larger man stood looking at Paul, his hands still on his hips in the reverse mode with thumbs pointing forward, elbows back.

"Where did you guys come from today?" Paul said.

The driver looked at the other buyer. "Eugene," the big man said.

"Good weather there?"

"Usual for this time of year. How many hides you got?"

"I like Eugene. It's a nice clean town and the girls are wonderful there."

The big guy turned his head away.

"You guys live in Eugene?"

"Yeah—near there—in Springfield."

"You ever been to the saw mill there on the main road?"

"Drive by it all the time.

"My Dad used to work there. Back in the late forties. He worked the mill pond."

"Look—we've got several places to go today and we need to see about your hides. Can you make a deal on them or do we need to see your folks?"

Paul waved his right hand and his head moved up and down and in circles like a showman. "I am authorized to make hide deals. I'm a part owner of the hides. Have you seen them yet?"

The big guy moved forward. "We'd like to do that right now."

Paul twisted his head when the big man spoke. "Have we met?" he said.

"This is my brother, Mort," Sydney said.

"He's with you?"

"Yes. We go together to buy the hides. Could we see them now?"

Paul turned to me in an authoritative manner with a mild frown on his face. "Jeff, will you please show these gentlemen the hides and be sure to count them."

We kept a paper tally sheet on the outside wall of the hide shed so that we knew how many hides had been put in there, salted, trimmed and ready for sale.

"Here's our tally sheet," I said.

Mort didn't even look at it. "We don't go by that." He climbed in the hide room and pulled the top hide up, turned it over, ran his hand over the hair side and pinched the neck skin. Then he pulled the next three up and did the same. "How many you think you've got?"

Paul looked toward me, the frown still on his face as he worked at putting a pinch of snus in his lip. "How many, Jeff?"

"The tally sheet says 460 plus 300 in the freezer."

"That's 760 then," Paul said. "Let's see—at $4.00 apiece that's..."

Mort interrupted. "We haven't paid $4 since the war."

"Now, Mort," Sydney broke in. "Don't get argumentative. These people want to sell their hides. We buy hides. We need to come to an amicable agreement." He seemed to be thinking on it with the edge of a hide in his hands like looking at it longer would give him some special answer to the price. After a pause that allowed Paul to complete the act of getting the snus from the can to his lip and then cap the can and return it to his top overall pocket, Sydney said, "$2.50 is the best we can do in this market, with $1 off for any holes in the hide."

Paul snorted and looked away. I didn't know how much he could see with his damaged eyes but he had positioned the wheelbarrow so that Sidney and Mort were back lighted from the window and he looked away from them.

"Jeff—when did that other hide buyer say he would be out to look at these?"

I hadn't heard about any other hide buyer. I didn't want to lie, even to help him in his negotiations. "I don't recall," I said.

"Oh, that's right. You weren't in the house when he called." He lowered his head and sucked on the snus. "Four dollars a hide is a fair price," he said.

"I've looked at ten of them and two have holes in them," Mort said. "That's twenty percent. If you have 760 hides and twenty percent have holes in them we could go maybe to $2.75 each. More holes we'd have to cut the price."

Paul jerked his head up. "I doubt you'll find ten percent have holes. But I'd let them go for $3.50 each right now."

Mort moved toward the door. "Let's go, we're not getting anywhere here."

They both started for the car. Mort pulled the passenger door open as Sydney reached for the door handle and turned. "Paul. I like your bargaining stance. You've got a good head on your shoulders. But the market's not that good for calf skins right now and there is a flood of them on the market. Before we go, can we make a deal right now at $2.95 a hide?"

In a move that I'll remember the rest of my life, Paul stood up and crossed his arms across his chest. He spit the snus into the gutter, wiped his lips and smiled. "I'll let you have 'em for $3.00 a hide with no discount for any holes. That's my final offer."

Mort got in the car and slammed the door shut. Sydney opened his door and started to get in. He put his left leg back out and stood half in and half out of the car. "We gotta deal at three dollars a hide?"

Paul nodded.

"OK. We'll send the truck by to pick 'em up. He'll have a check for you then. Seven hundred and sixty hides in all."

Paul nodded.

I didn't think the pickup would start but it backfired once, and the starter seemed to get some juice from that, and it started with a burst of exhaust, and down the driveway it went.

Paul fell backward onto his wheelbarrow, his arms flailing and laughing so hard I didn't think he would be able to catch his breath. "Two thousand two hundred and eighty dollars," he said.

"Less what is owed to the Johnson kid for salting that day," I said.

"That don't amount to nothing." He squirmed on the wheelbarrow seat like a little kid. "Don't that beat all. Three bucks a hide."

"What did you expect?" I said.

"I wanted more than the two-fifty they paid last time. The car companies are using calf hides for trim in their cars and I thought the price might go up. Heard it on the radio market report."

"Well—I'll be damned."

"Those guys drive Cadillac's in town. When they come to buy hides they dress poor and drive that stinky old pickup."

"Could you see that Sydney's hands?"

"No."

"They were soft and well-manicured."

He nodded.

"You want any help getting back to the house?"

"Yeah. That would be nice."

I turned the wheelbarrow around and pointed it in the right direction. Paul leaned on the handles and started it down the slope dragging his left foot. He stopped twice going down. I helped him into the wheelchair and through the front door. We barely got through the door and he yelled out to Ronny.

"Ron—I got 'em. I got 'em."

Ronny twisted his face and gave his version of a laugh.

"We got two hundred and twenty-eight dollars for our share."

Ron squirmed on the couch and brought his left leg up off the floor. I got the feeling they had something in mind for the money.

WEST AND ROSE GOT back late in the day before the last feeding. At supper everyone acted normal so I didn't mention the hide buyers.

Just before coffee and desert, Paul lifted his head and turned to Rose. "When do I get my check?"

"What check?"

"My ten percent check."

Rose acted confused. She put coffee and a chocolate layer cake on the table. "I don't know of any ten percent check."

"Sure you do."

"For what?"

"The hides."

"The hides?"

Paul nodded. "Buyers came by today and I sold them."

"You sold them?"

"Yes."

Ronny was giggling on the couch, his left leg rising and falling.

"I never said you could sell the hides. We do that," she said.

West cut a piece of cake and gave it to Paul then cut another for himself.

"I sold 'em."

Rose looked at West. He shrugged and put a bite of cake in his mouth.

A smile started over Rose's face as she poured the coffee all around. "And how much did you get for them, Mr. Businessman?"

"Guess."

"Two-fifty?"

Ronny pounded the couch with his left hand, his face contorted in a facsimile of a smile. Paul could hear him and half-turned his head to acknowledge his brothers antics.

"More," Paul said.

"More?"

Paul nodded.

"Two-seventy five?"

This sent Ronny into convulsions. Paul was sucking in air and snorting as he shook his head. "More," he laughed.

For the first time since I had been there, Rose looked perplexed. "My god, Paul. Did you point a gun at him?"

Paul slapped the table with the flat of his hand, threw his head back and the whole table shook with the vibrations of his laughter. I thought Ronny would fall off the couch. West turned to look at him to see if he was going to have to leave the table and catch him.

"Three dollars," Paul finally blurted out.

"How much off for holes?"

Paul shook his head, his smile widening as it moved from side to side. "Nothing."

"No hole discount? What am I missing here?"

"I heard it on the radio on the market report. Calf hides were up so I thought I'd see how far. I started at four dollars."

"How many did we have?"

"Jeff said 760."

"My gosh, that's..."

"Two thousand two hundred and eighty dollars," Paul threw in. "And ten percent of that is my check for two hundred and twenty-eight dollars."

West stopped chewing and looked up. "That's more money than I've got."

It was silent for a minute. Even Ronny quieted down and sat very still.

Rose smiled. "Paul, honey, you don't have a bank account so I'll just hold it for you."

"You could cash it and give me the money."

"You'd just lose it. It's yours and Ronny's. It is to be used for something you need."

"I want to feel it and count it."

"Honey," she said as her voice softened and she put her hand over his arm. "You couldn't see to count it."

His head dropped into his traditional chin-on-his-chest position, accentuating the bones on the back of his neck.

Ronny was dead still. Partially wrapped in a blanket, he looked like a mummy escaped from his tomb.

"I just wanted to count it," Paul said.

"I know. I know."

The only sound in the room was the tick-tock from the clock on the mantel underneath which the calf money was kept.

Rose stood up to clear the dishes from the table. "OK. When I go to town Friday, I'll cash the check. How do you want it?"

Paul's head snapped up. "Twenties. There'll be more of them."

"Twenties it is then."

Paul's lips formed a grin that went clear back to his molars. He tossed his head back toward Ronny, who had come to life and was thrashing his left arm and leg through the air.

"Hot damn," Paul croaked out. He turned his wheelchair and pushed himself in toward the couch. When he got close to Ronny they bumped legs and both of them tossed their heads back, laughing.

"Paul. Watch your swearing," Rose said.

West had both elbows on the table, sipping his coffee and looking out the window at the unfinished house on the hill.

CHAPTER 11

Thanksgiving and Christmas came and went. We drank a little whiskey and played Canasta on New Years Eve and the four months I'd bargained for were turned into a month by month commitment. Rose had not found my replacement; The Johnson family was still there and the work was constant.

The money I saved encouraged me to hang around. As repugnant as the calf killing was it hadn't ruined my sleep and each new day was an experience. It was late in January when I made the decision to stick it out until at least summer.

It was rare to go to work without rain gear so I was wet outside from rain and inside from sweat. My hands were wrinkled like skin on an elephant.

THE FIRST SUNNY MORNING, Ladd and I sat on the front step of the trailer before breakfast just letting the light and warmth seep into us. The high spots on the clay driveway started to dry out where the tires hadn't rutted it.

I watched the road that led from the house on the hill to see if Olive was going to come down, but pretty soon smoke started curling out of the lower house chimney and I knew Rose was cooking. The smell of fresh bacon and eggs came on the soft breeze that drifted across the driveway past the open window in the kitchen. She hated cooking but when she did it she smiled and whistled and the food she turned out was good. Usually when a person can do something well he likes it, but boy, until she was committed to cooking—like when Olive didn't get there in time—it was hell to pay around the kitchen. But once she started cracking the eggs and mixing the pancake batter she turned into a regular Aunt Jemima, all warm and happy and smiley.

"Morning."

Rose looked up. "Morning."

West nodded and I could hear Paul's razor running and once in awhile, Dammit," (the razor stopped) "Ungh..." (Started again).

I stacked an armload of wood in the wood box and fed a couple sticks to the new fire.

Pretty soon Olive came down the hill looking half alive. She had run a comb through her hair a couple of times and there was sleep in the corner of her eyes. Fat—pale face—breasts that bounced on her chest when she walked. She mumbled something about over-sleeping as she came inside, grabbed her apron and set the table.

I walked down to the end of the driveway to get the paper. The tension in the kitchen with Rose in the full and Olive pussy-footing around to make up for her tardiness made any kind of conversation suspect. West started his first cigarette opened the paper and sat waiting for the household to wake up. I sat, my energy stunted with the heat and cigarette smoke, and let my mind go blank. It was almost like sleep without dreams.

One big cloud hung over the town to the East but was dis-appearing, and I thought it was the most wonderful day since I had come here. How the time had gone. Monday the breeding season would start and I would learn something new about the mink. We had just finished the shed and except for the prospect of not having enough pens when the baby kits came, and dealing with forty to fifty calves a day, we were pretty well caught up. West said the calves would come faster now as the milk cows had their birthing sessions.

Breakfast was good and filling. West went to clean his cow barn and I drew the skinning job. I didn't mind skinning when the calves were warm, but when they got stiff and cold and the water was freezing and the cement floor was hard and damp, it took more concentration and effort not to cut holes in the hides. But today the sun was shining and I dragged the dead calves out to the sunlight at the edge of the floor to skin them.

I honed my blade, drew the blade across the steel – twice on the edge and twice on the point – tested it cutting hair on my arm, stuck the tip through the hide on the front leg and cut. You don't pay much attention to time when you're skinning. The number of calves on the pile to be pulled out of their hide is what counts. Every calf on the pile means one less on the floor, then you straighten up and feel the kink in your back hurt bad at first, and then pound, pound, pound with your heart beat until it is gone, and then you bend over again and pass the kink in your back down to your hips.

West came in and honed his blade. He skinned five to my four and I watch while he skinned the last one. He doesn't make so many passes at the same place and he pulls long strokes that slide nicely along the hide without cutting a hole and leave the flesh on the calf where it should be. I rig up the winch to pull hides off and clean my knife so it won't rust with the acidic blood on it.

Not so bad. He used to skin three to my two.

He looked up and smiled and threw the calf on the pile. I put the steel hook in the ear, he flicked the switch and up went the calf and off came the hide. The carcass swung naked across the floor and back.

West gutted but he couldn't find the soft place in the pelvis. He tried three times. I handed him the cleaver and he split it off to the left and then took his knife and finished the gutting. I grabbed the carcass and hung it on a nail by the back leg tendon. On and on it went until all twenty-four were up on the wall.

Ladd and little King walk in. Ladd is visibly annoyed by the new addition and growls when the pup bumps into him. West cut a hunk of meat from the rump of one of the calves and gave it to Ladd. The pup sat looking into West's eyes. West cut another, smaller chunk, and the pup takes it between his puppy teeth and trots after Ladd, his tail erect.

West smiled. Standing there I thought how he would look if Rose ever shot him. Really shot him. I guessed he'd smile that funny sort of half-smile right down to the bottom of the grave. It was getting so I enjoyed meeting him every morning. I wanted to put my arm on his shoulder and walk with him after the cows, him and his old man's walk, pant legs flapping against his skinny legs.

Rose came out with her smoke between her wrinkled lips. She pointed her cigarette towards the new motor on the winch. "How does it work?"

"Whole lot easier than by hand," West said and glanced at me with that look that announced he wanted me to back him up.

"Fast," I said.

We all stood there in the sunlight, wanting not to leave it for the cold, dark, salt shed or the slop of the mink yard. There are times on the coast that you'd sell your soul for some sunshine and when it's there, easy for the taking, you want to shed your shirt and stand with your back to it until all the damp is cleaned away. We might have done it had West and I been alone but not with Rose there. She walked away.

"I'll salt," I offered.

West nodded. He took the cover off the gutter and started to clean it so the water would go down the pipe that slanted underground to the river.

I trimmed off the ears and tails and threw the hides in the salt shed, then climbed in the small opening into a room about the length and width of a single bed. The enclosure hosted odors of wet hides, blood and salt. I picked a hide up and lay it out, hair down, on the knee-high pile, stretched out the legs and cut the navel out. Then I scattered two coffee cans of salt over the moist surface. I picked up another hide, a black and white one, cut the navel and sliced some flesh off the side where it had stayed on. I salted.

I could salt about thirty an hour if I did it right, but like skinning, it took time to learn and it wasn't really the time that counted. It was the height of the stack of hides.

Some more calves came in and I peeked out of a crack in the siding. I could see a new Buick and I heard laughing and a young voice. I heard Rose telling about her new man and then saw a pretty young girl step around the car behind Rose coming toward the shed.

She brought her over on the pretext of showing her the hide pile, but I knew she brought her over to meet me. I smiled and said hello. Her face was pleasant and her figure was good, but she looked country-girl all the way. I was polite while I salted the last of the hides and followed them out to their car. The bright light made me flinch and shield my eyes. How they got three calves in the trunk of that Buick was beyond me. I hoisted the calves out for them. I saw her watch my arm as I picked up a calf and I knew my arm muscle lay flattened out alongside the calf's ribs. She was more appealing in the sunlight. The wind spun her hair around strong shoulders and caught the sun making it glisten.

The twinkle in Rose's eyes was something I hadn't seen there before—she liked playing cupid. The girl's mother asked if I wanted anything from town.

"No...not that I know of," I said.

"You coming back out shortly?" Rose asked her.

"Just as soon as I do the shopping," she said.

"Do you want to go in for an hour or so, Jeff?" Rose said, her eyes sparkling.

"Oh...I'm pretty dirty for traveling," I begged off.

"That's all right," the girl said.

What's the deal? We've got calves to finish, feeding to do....

I looked across the fence and saw West looking at me. He turned away and walked into a shed. The women were talking. I got into the car and they had the heater going full blast. I could smell the salt on my boots and dried blood on my Levis, but they didn't seem to mind. The girl and her mother were in the front seat. They talked and the mother laughed but I couldn't get what they were talking about.

We stopped outside the Safeway and I opened the door for the girl. They got out and I said, "Will you excuse me for a few minutes? I want to check on something. Be right back."

I turned and walked up the block and down to the courthouse and up the stairs in the hot sun. I had to find out.

THERE WAS A SIGN half-way down the marble floor of the courthouse that announced the Sheriff's office. Behind the counter stood a green-shirted sheriff with a little .32 stuffed in his back pocket chewing on a Mississippi Crook cigar. I could see his big chest move against the tailored shirt as he walked over to me.

"Hi," he said.

"Howdy." I said.

"Something I can do for you?"

"Yeah... are the files for concealed weapons open to the public?" I said, a little nervous.

He nodded and turned. "I can tell you about anyone if you want to know," he said.

"Mrs. Rose Helner," I said biting my lip.

"Is that the old gal out on the mink ranch?"

"Yeah."

"I think she has one, if I'm not mistaken. Think she got it last year. He opened a drawer and thumbed some files. Yeah, here it is. Expires June 2." He handed it to me and turned to answer the questions from a man about someone stealing his farm.

I looked at the permit. "Permission to carry concealed weapon. A .22 automatic. Reason—alone in big mink yard with hired man. Two character witnesses."

"Thanks," I said.

"Wait a minute. Is everything all right...she's not threatening you with it or anything?"

"No," I said. "Just checking to be sure."

"Well...okay."

"Thanks."

WHEN WE LEFT TOWN the girl got in the back seat with me and sat close. The ranch smell had almost disappeared outside in the sunshine and I felt more comfortable with her now. She reached across my legs and took my hand. I felt my face flush. I hadn't washed my hands that well and the salting smell to me was ever present.

"I'm sorry. I forgot your name," I said.

"Rassel." Her smile was contagious and I chuckled and smiled with her.

Her hand was small and warm. From my side view she had a nice profile. Good thick hair that hung past her shoulders. Full lips. Nice.

"I'm Jeff Baker. We'll have to do this more often," I said.

She nodded her head. "I'd love to."

"I don't have a car. Could we take a walk sometime?"

"I'd like that," she said and I squeezed her hand.

We stayed holding hands until her mother stopped the car in the driveway.

"Thanks for the lift to town and your charming company," I said.

"Any time we're going, you're welcome to go along."

"Thanks."

"Goodbye," Rassel said.

I saw West emerging from the slaughterhouse.

"What are you doing?" I said.

"Defrosting the freezer.

"Oh." I reached in my pocket and pulled out a plug of tobacco I had picked up in town and tossed it to him. He caught it and smiled. He ground out his cigarette under foot, then with his calloused and cracked lumberman's hands he opened the cellophane on the plug like you would open a Christmas present, and touched it to his nose.

He didn't look up. "Thanks, Jeff. That's just what I needed." He bit a chunk off with his front teeth.

"Didn't think my false teeth would bite it off like that, did you?"

"Didn't even know you had false teeth."

He chewed. "You know...a chew of tobacco tastes good."

I nodded. "What was the deal letting me go to town with so much work to do?"

He smiled, shrugged his shoulders and started off for the barn, then turned and grimaced at me, letting tobacco juice run down his chin. I picked up a calf foot and threw it at him. It went over his left shoulder. He reached up and snagged it like a tight end and started prancing like a football player, his feet coming up high and hustling as if he could still move fast, spitting tobacco juice to his left while he jigged to the right.

CHAPTER 12

It was late when we finished work and Ralph came down for supper and so did all the kids. They coughed and sneezed and I only ate what I saw didn't get the treatment. Between the roast and dessert Olive poured us coffee then set a chocolate cake on the table.

"What religion are you, Jeff?" Rose asked.

Her question interrupted my bite of cake. "Why?"

"I saw you praying over your food; I just wondered. And you don't very often take coffee, you don't smoke or drink."

"Nazarene," I said.

"I knew a Holy Roller once who didn't drink coffee," West said. "When we were harvesting, her boy...oh, he was about your age, 23, or 24, decided to have a cup 'cause it was so hot out and she told him to stir the devil out of it before he drank it."

I smiled. "Really?"

He closed his lips tight and nodded his head, his eyes twinkling light blue in the electric light.

Rose cut a piece of cake for each of the boys and a small one for herself. "I used to be a believer," she said. "But this business has driven it out of me. There are so many no good skunks—you can't believe anybody. Most of the people that go to church are hypocrites anyway, so I gave it up."

Olive and her family, unwilling or unable to enter the conversation, rose from their chairs in unison and walked out the door. West stared at the table top mouthing his cake. I wondered how it went with the tobacco plug.

"Well," I said. "I think church is a good place for a hypocrite to be, don't you?"

She glared at me.

Nobody else picked up the conversation. Not a word was said until West got a package of playing cards and started shuffling them. The cake was gone, more coffee was poured and it seemed like a family gathering, one that only started when it got dark, all of its members were fed, the day's work was done and it was warm and dry inside.

We stayed up and played cards until late and I finally said good-night and headed across the road to the trailer. I could see the clouds coming in over the coast and I felt sure that that day was our last day of sunshine for a long time. Ladd walked over with me and even he sensed it. At the door he stopped and whined.

"What? You want to sleep inside—is that it?" He wagged his tail. "OK" I held the door open, he jumped over the step and headed for the bed.

"No, you don't. That's my bed." I put a blanket on the floor. "Here." He watched with a great deal of interest while I got on the blanket and curled up like I was going to sleep there. When I got off the floor he turned, circled three times and lay down on the pad beneath my bed. I could touch him and I rubbed his neck for a long time thinking about Rassel. He was asleep before I was.

I felt lousy in the morning and Olive's pancakes didn't do much to pick me up. Maybe I was getting the bug. Everyone else was over the worst of it and they all kept on working. I was right about the clouds. It drizzled all morning while West and I killed and skinned calves. It was a little easier because we didn't kill them last night and they were warm and much easier to skin.

West killed twenty and bled them while I lined some boxes. He had picked up the fixed grinder yesterday when I was in town and he wanted to check it out and grind some to put in our freezer before we hauled a load of carcasses over to the walk-in.

I knocked thirty-two in the head and that made us fifty-two for the day. It was about noon before the rain stopped and we still had seven more to skin. The sun broke through for a few minutes and Paul came out the door in his wheelchair. He had his coat on and lifted himself by his hands into a leaning position behind his heavy wheelbarrow.

He worked the homemade cart up the hill, pushing it a foot or two and then using it for support and pulling one foot up and then leaning on that leg and the cart and dragging the bad foot up and then with jerks and wide eyes he would shove the cart forward a foot or two and follow that up again until he was at the slaughterhouse.

"Whew!" He sat down on the cart. His shoulders and chest rose and fell from the labored breathing. It took some time for him to settle. And when he did he had a glum look on his face that I had not seen before. Usually talkative, he sat deflated and mute.

We pulled the hide off the last calf and I gutted it and hung it on a nail. West walked out to Paul who had his can of snus open and was trying to find his mouth with a pinch between his fingers. When he got it in, he relaxed his eyebrows which always formed little pyramids on his forehead when he concentrated.

West stopped in front of him. "Give me a chew of your snus, Paul."

Paul turned his head toward him. "Why should I?"

West stood anchored, his eyes searching his son's impassive face. I thought he might be wondering what he had done in his life to deserve this. He tilted his head down as if seeing where his feet were planted would ease his dismay. He stood like that, weaving a little, then turned and walked to the house.

"You shouldn't say things like that to your father," I said.

"I don't have no father!" Paul shot back. "I ain't had no father since he left us in '45."

"He came back," I said. I had never heard him bash West before and it took the wind out of me.

"Hah. He came back when he ran out of money. It wasn't for us."

"I mean he didn't leave you for good. He left for a short time and then came back. Cut him a little slack."

"I don't know why he left. He just up and left."

"I understand, but that doesn't mean he doesn't love you."

"He never talked to me about loving us. Never."

I looked at his passive face chewing the snus, looking for a spitting place with his sightless eyes and I wanted to cry for him.

"Paul—just because he didn't say he loved you...and Ronny, doesn't mean he doesn't love you. Look how he works on this place...carries Ronny to the couch..."

"He left. Didn't say goodbye or nothing. One morning he wasn't at breakfast and that's how we found out." He spit. "Mom told us."

I looked around at the place. Battered old house with a sway in the roof, weathered gray like the fence and the pens and the barn and the slaughter house and the house on the hill and the clothes they wore.

"If you could see it, Paul, you'd know it isn't much to come back to. He had to love his family to return. And the house on the hill..."

"I don't want to talk about it," he said.

A truck loaded with calves appeared at the bottom of the driveway and started up the hill, interrupting our conversation and changing the subject.

"Better move it, Paul. That guy wants to back up right here," I said.

He didn't move. "He knows I'm here."

I left him.

West came back out with a chew under his lip and some money in his hand.

"Look out, Paul, that truck's backing up here!" West hollered.

Paul turned his head, "Aw, shut up!"

West looked at me. "I'll be damned. That makes a fella feel like working don't it?" He handed me the money and went into the freezer.

I gave the man two dollars for each calf, except one nice-looking white face that he kept to take to the auction. I herded them in to the slaughter room and grabbed the kill pipe. As I raised the pipe I felt it stop at the top of my swing. West had come around the corner and taken hold of it. I lowered my arm and he took it from my hand, his eyes burning and every wrinkle in his leather face etched with anger.

I backed out of the shed. He starting smashing calves right and left, swinging with all his power. I herded them to him, watching them drop on each other and bawl, hurt, kicking and then his pipe searched them out and silenced their cries. One stumbled but didn't fall and he jumped over the dead calves and swung a side blow that smashed into the shoulders of the calf and made him bawl more. He raised the pipe again and brought it down across its skull, making the left eye pop out, but the calf went down for good.

West stood panting and looked at the pile of dead calves around him. Tenderly he reached down and turned over the one with the bulging eye. He wiped the pipe with a rag, hung it up and took his knife and slit their throats, lining them up like fallen soldiers to bleed in the gutter. He straightened up; sweat dripping down his nose, his sweat shirt dark in patches. His face looked vacant. And then in a quiet voice he said:

"Need some six-penny nails."

I nodded, my response a hoarse whispered sound. "Some in the pelting shed," I said.

His eyes were still burning. West picked up a hammer in his right hand and walked past me out towards Paul. Paul turned his head but couldn't see him. He knew he was there. The sound and shuffle of his steps told him.

"Huh!" he said with disgust and turned back facing the house.

West raised the hammer. His grip on the handle tightened, flexing the tendons in his hand, making them stand out like ropes under a canvas. He kept walking. He had killed so many calves with the same blow. One sharp crack behind the ear. I watched. I could hear the pulse of blood in my ears. He slowed down and stopped, and silent and tired, stood looking down at his son.

In a soft voice just above a whisper, he said, "Go on in, Paul, it's going to rain."

I didn't realize I had held my breath until it began to leak out. Paul squinted up at the sky as if he could see it. Mentally he must have agreed because he struggled up, stood weaving a bit and started the cart down to the house. West disappeared into the pelting shed. I got a drink of water and stood by the hose pipe taking deep breaths until Olive called us to dinner.

CHAPTER 13

The clinking of flatware on plates was the only sound in the kitchen. The tension made my stomach tight. But I ate dinner anyway. I could see in his face that West was still thinking about what Paul said, and once in awhile he would shoot a glance at him, his eyes wrinkled around the edges with no shine in the pupils, and then resume looking down at his plate.

For the first time, I didn't eat any dessert and Rose said, "You sick, too?"

"No."

"Too full for dessert?"

"No. Just don't want any."

Rose put on her glasses and got her checkbook and pen and sat down at the table again.

Ralph coughed. He guessed he'd go into town this afternoon and see the doctor. Maybe he could do something for the way he felt. He guessed he could. His eyes darted around the table and then returned to his hands folding and unfolding on the table.

Rose looked at West. "Take some carcasses into the freezer and pick up two tons of fish from the Pearl Harbor on your way back," she said

West spun his head. "Us?" Lately, it meant him and me when he said "us".

"Hell yes, you. Who'd you think?" She wrote on the check.

He smoked with his elbows on the table. "What you going to do with them?"

She looked up at him. "Oh for gawd's sake…freeze them!"

"Got so many calves in there now they're gonna rot," he said without changing his position looking out the window.

"I can't help it…the fish are there and we need the fish. You've got to do something—I can't do it all around here."

I got up from the table and went out to the slaughter house. I counted over fifty fresh calves hanging on nails. In the freezer we had over 100 boxes of ground up feed and maybe sixty frozen carcasses. It was hard to tell with them piled up and frozen. There was room for a few more but it would have made our work harder trying to get the feed out.

We put the fifty fresh calf carcasses on the truck, threw in our aprons and gloves, and slid onto the seat.

We were tired and didn't talk much driving over to the lockers. We just listened to the groan of the truck and leaned with the curves. West backed it up into the unloading space in front of the freezer door. Their freezer unit had an outside entrance. Huge thick insulated doors that swung out on massive cast-iron hinges and locked with a simple padlock.

His hand hung on the key a second and then dropped to his lap and we both sat there looking across the street through a big glass window at a black man playing the pinball machine in the café.

West pulled out a cigarette and lit it. I took a deep breath before the smoke got over to me. He looked at me and sort of smiled—his way of smiling where you could tell that he was mildly tickled but not enough to smile big or laugh out loud. We looked at each other with a tired look, the kind where the eyes are droopy, the head hanging a little less than erect, and the shoulders sagging.

And now West and I sat there waiting to get up enough energy to go to work. We were thinking about different things I suppose, him with his left hand stroking the white hairs on his throat. The steady drum of rain on the truck cab dulled our thoughts. Streaks of rain zigzagged down the windshield, mesmerizing us and washing away conversation. I started to talk about something else but the gun deal came out first.

"Do you know she carries a gun?" I said.

His head turned toward me. "I don't think so."

"I checked the sheriff's office yesterday and she has a permit to carry a pistol, a .22 automatic."

He looked stunned and then a smile crept over his lips as he sat there. "She's crazy enough to shoot me if she got mad."

"You *and* me," I added.

He snorted. The cigarette smoke curled away from his mouth and out the open window. We sat there for a long time. "She's crazy..." he said.

"She's neurotic," I said. "She needs a head doctor."

"She wants me to go to one."

"What did you tell her?"

"I told her I'd go when she went with me."

We sat quiet for a minute or two then he started talking. "You know, Jeff...I work there seven days a week and never get pay for it. I used to buy horses and cows and pay for them with cash when we were first getting started in the mink business. She don't have no record of it so she says she paid for them all." He was telling a long story now. It was coming out like infection from a wound.

"All my gas and tires and trailer went and got that feed before the mink started paying for themselves. And what have I got?

"I bought the cement and gravel for the slaughter house floor...she couldn't pay for it. I built the drain, dug the ditch, laid the pipe, everything." He stopped to knock the ashes from the cigarette.

"I dozed the mink yard with a team of horses and my Fresno and pulled the pens over from the old place. I bought the lumber for those pelting sheds and me and Frank built them. I paid him for his time.

"And then when I broke my leg I hobbled around and stuck calves for them and gutted too; I couldn't bend down to skin, but I gutted them and even skinned mink with the cast on. And then she says she did it all and the mink are all hers."

"That's not what she says." There was more bite to my remark than I had planned.

He turned to stare at me.

"Says she waited on you hand and foot while you were laid up with the leg."

He turned back to look out the windshield, the wry smile just creeping across his lips.

"Well," he said. "There's gotta be some truth somewhere. I guess you're free to think whatever you want."

He took a long drag on the cigarette then threw it under his foot and crushed it. He stared out the dirty truck window. His eyes looked sad not understanding this thing. He was looking not at the bar across the street and not at the cloudy day or the work ahead, but back.

"All the money I've made has gone into the place."

We sat there waiting for nothing to happen. It might have been two minutes or five or fifteen, I couldn't tell you. At last we each moved out our side of the truck and put on our aprons and gloves, unlocked the freezer door and pitched rain-wet calves in on the carcasses frozen purple at zero degrees.

We didn't have to drive far to get the fish but we had to wait for a grocery store truck to get the good fish off before we loaded the scrap. I tried to doze but the clank, clank, clank of the winch hauling up the net from the hold kept me awake.

Finally West moved the truck into position to take on the fish. Thirteen boxes with 300 pounds of fish in each of them were heaved up out of the belly of the ship. They swung over high enough to clear the truck's sideboards and then the winch dumped them to slip and slide off the pile. I jammed them into the corners to keep the pile down. The truck really buckled with two tons on her. The overload springs were lying straight and when the old man took her down the ramp she didn't even bounce over the railroad tracks.

I could hardly see the road for the rain that smashed into the street like it was going to break through the asphalt. A river of dirty water ran in the gully by the curb.

"Had three yards of gravel on her once," he said. "And it acted the same way." He locked his elbows straight out to hold the wheel. His arms and chin were jiggling with the vibrations of the steering wheel.

All the way home the truck weaved and wheezed threatening to take our half of the road right out of middle. I looked out the back window on the sharp curves and saw the fish, red snapper, flounder, sole, all sliding like a wave of water to the outside and I could feel the brake grab to hold us on the curve. I looked at the old man and he smiled and looked down the country road. Hell, we'd make it.

I waved at the station man where we bought our gas. He waved back like he wanted us to stop. West had already taken the corner down toward the bridge but he stopped. And I could see why before I had to ask. The station man came over wearing logging pants with suspenders and rubber boots.

"Say...I don't know how deep the water is there, but no one's come through for quite a while." He looked at West and then me.

West looked across the bridge where the water left only the telephone poles on one side and power poles on the other to show there was a road in between.

"We been gone that long?" I said.

West looked at me and then back at the water. He smiled. "Think it would float these fish away?"

"Shall we try, boatman?"

"She'll be madder than hell if we don't make it. Think we didn't move fast enough to get back before high water."

I shrugged. "Let's live life like we want to."

West turned to the station owner. "I think we can make it," he said. "Thanks anyway."

"I'll watch you and if you get stuck I'll call a wrecker," he offered.

West nodded. He took his foot off the brake and we rolled toward the bridge. Our tiredness left us. We searched the water as we approached, then stopped where the water crossed the road and eased into the murky swirling river that was moving across from left to right. It was slow-moving and bits of wood and a short log floated by. When we started in, West picked up the speed to twelve miles an hour in low gear.

We ground through the water, our grill pushing a steady wake ahead and out to the side of the truck. I rolled down the window. The water was over the running board. I couldn't see our tires going around, just the mud they stirred up amid the slurping noise they made pulling through the water.

There was a bump. We'd hit a sunken log. The speed dropped and the motor coughed once, twice, and then picked up again and the black end of the log surfaced ahead of us, submerged, and bump again, lighter, and it rose up and sank off to our right. West was tight-lipped watching the poles and speedometer.

Water was rising and trickling around my feet with each turn of the tires.

"She's coming in!' I said. I looked at the floor and West scanned the poles and speedometer.

"Can you see any of the bridge ahead?" He said.

I looked hard. I wanted to see it. "No!"

"We don't want to miss it," he said.

I could see us missing the bridge and floating down the channel. In that freezing water, we'd have to get out quick and fight our way through two tons of fish floating around us. I opened the door. West threw a startled glance at me and then looked back to the poles.

"Gonna see if I can see the bridge posts from the hood," I said. He nodded.

The water gushed in when the door opened and poured down my rubber boots. It was cold, damn cold, and my feet felt like logs pulling them up on the fender. We were close to the bridge and no time to empty them out. I strained my eyes for a glimpse of the white posts that lined the bridge. I wanted to see them so badly I almost could see them in a new place each time I blinked my eyes.

The grill came out of water a little and I knew we were on the approach and still I couldn't see the bridge posts. I heard West shout, "Can you see 'em?"

"No!"

I had to see them. Only the swelling water was there with the rain pounding the surface. The truck started to slow.

"Maybe the bridge is gone!" I shouted above the wind. I was edgy.

He stopped the truck and the water closed in around the cab from the wake it had been pushing. The motor conked and then died and when I looked back at West he looked grim. He rolled down the window.

"See 'em?"

I shook my head. Then I saw what needed to be done. I eased myself off the fender to the bumper and the cold water mixed with the water in my boot that was just getting warm. I stepped in with both feet and touched the solid road underneath. The water moved around my groin.

"Colder than hell," I shouted back.

He smiled.

I walked and felt along with my toes on the gravel, hoping to feel the boards of the bridge. My right foot was almost numb. I started using my left foot to feel with and felt a gap in the road. I eased my foot past the gap and found a board. I pushed at it and it held, so I stepped on it. The next plank was there and the next. I crept the length until I got to the approach on the other side.

"She's here but for the first plank."

"How big a hole?"

"Twelve...maybe fifteen inches," I said.

He didn't answer.

"Think we can make it?" I asked.

He shrugged his shoulders. "Might if we can get it started."

I sloshed back to the truck and raised the hood. The water was just below the distributor and about an inch below the spark plugs. West handed me a screwdriver and I pried the fan belt off so the fan wouldn't throw water all over the sparkplugs and distributor. I took my shirttail and dried the plugs at the connection. The points looked dry.

"Give her a whirl."

He stepped on it and the starter turned over and over.

"She's too damn wet!" he hollered.

"She's gotta start," I said.

The wind was picking up and I couldn't feel my legs any more. My feet started to ache. I waited for it to start.

"Keep grinding her!"

It turned over slower now and I looked back at the high bridge where the service station man was standing. I saw him there and waved. Just then it started and I reached for the hood, slammed it down, and jumped on the fender. He took the truck up easy and then rammed it over the gap. I was praying that nothing had changed since I checked it and that the other boards would hold our load.

When we hit the gap the water spread away and I saw the posts. The front wheels bounced over. The back ones would be harder with the load sitting right over them. It hit and slowed and then pulled up out of the hole. We had easy sailing the rest of the way for the road raised and the water level dropped below the running board. We stopped to put the fan belt back on and let the water drain out of the cab.

"Think she'll kill us both?" I joked.

"I doubt it. Not both of us. You maybe, but I'm her husband."

"Yeah. Like that would help. She'll claim you brought the flood on so you wouldn't have to come home."

"She knows I don't have that kind of power."

We rearranged the floatable stuff that had drifted around the floor of the cab.

"She'll blame us anyway."

He nodded. "Probably."

Rose was screaming about the high water when we got home. "I thought I'd have to mail you some money to stay in town. I can't believe you made it. How did you get across the bridge?"

West hung his hat on the nail and I sat down to coffee and cake while he told the story. When I heard him say—"Well, here we are," I knew it was over and we were clear of any charges of contempt. West even had a smile on his face.

The kids had to stay in town because of the high water. That was a relief to everyone. Ralph had gone in to the doctor and he was in town for as long as the water was high and he and the kids kept calling every fifteen minutes to see how things were.

The flu and now a flood, what could happen next?

CHAPTER 14

"Well, we got a lot of calves in today before the water came up, anyway," Rose said.

"How many?" I asked.

"Hundred and four."

"Hundred and four?"

"Yes. And I've got three mink missing—all Platinum's. We need to look for them. Something's going on and I don't understand it. First two and now this one."

West stopped with his sweatshirt half off. "We better kill the calves tonight or they'll be getting out." He finished changing while I warmed up and changed my clothes. He put on his rain clothes and I put on my big cowboy hat; together we fed and watered the mink.

The calves were bawling their heads off. Rose had shoved boxes end-to-end to make a corral and put some of them in there after the main corral was full. Those outside stood drenched and shivering but quiet. Very brave little day-old calves, wet and cold, with no mothers to nuzzle them or let them suckle. Soon they'd have no worries, no empty stomachs, no wet skins.

We finished feeding and watering, cleaned up the cart and the kill floor and washed the grinder and mixer. West steeled his knife.

"You hit 'em and I'll bleed 'em," he said.

The calves were bawling, their lost lonesome sounds covering everything else. The constant noise was nerve-wracking. I picked up the iron pipe, walked into the corral, lifted the gate and led a little wide-eyed calf into the slaughterhouse. I led him back to where West stood hunched over with the blade in his big hand. I lifted the pipe and hit him hard and he crumpled and then stiffened with a shiver as the keen edge laid his throat open and West drove the point into his heart. The bright blood gushed out in jerks and pumps, long squirts at first, and then just little oozes.

A jersey calf had followed us in. I wanted to smash it so hard the head would fall off. I wanted them all to die and stop that bawling. I hit him and he collapsed. West grabbed a hoof and pulled its head over the drain and rammed the knife in, guiding the blood into the concrete ditch.

I pushed two more in and swung on them. When I hit them too hard the pipe crushed their skulls and it made them hard to skin around the head, but they died fast when the bone punctured the brain. No fuss. The old man was good with his knife and he always hit the heart. I wondered if he would ever need to be that good with a knife in any other way.

We had sixty lying on the floor. We had to stop and drag the first ones back along the corridor to the other room. We stopped a minute and straightened up. Everything hurt.

In and in they came. Smash with the iron...down they go, dead. Some I hit badly...too far forward...they stagger, stiff-legged, unseeing, and I swing again and miss, (damn it)...swing and smash behind the head on the neck and they go down and bawl like a dying deer...still bawling when I hit them on the floor like hitting a golf ball and their life stops with a hollow sound. West drags them over...blood runs over his knife handle and stains his cuff. One bellowing with a gurgle...we both look... it's the one just struck...he points and I hit it twice, three times... the head mushy when I stop. Sixty-five...seventy...seventy-one... seventy-two...seventy-three...seventy-four.

I killed the calves. I killed them so hard and so fast that pretty soon all I wanted to do was to kill. I didn't want to stick or gut, but just kill with that pipe. I didn't want to even think about anything but killing. They drop over stiff, I feel good, my muscles feel strong...I swing that iron like an axe and everything plummets into hell with me.

The old man slams the knife in their throat. He doesn't slide it in—he rams it in. The blood gushes over his blade hand and he gets to like the feel of it. We think of nothing but dying . . . and a little of us dies there too, but there is no space in our heads to think of anything but killing.

Each calf gets it special. That's the way it is when you're kill-ing. With one animal—it's all over soon. But mass killing gets in your blood and you can't think. You keep killing as long as there is anything to kill. Then you turn around, your eyes looking for another calf. You're mad at them now; your back is screaming, breath coming in short gulps and you've got your swing down pat—even if they move at the last second, you adjust and the hit is accurate and deadly.

Suddenly it is quiet. There are no more. They all lie dead on the concrete floor.

I straighten up and wince. We look at each other in stunned silence, then look down at our hands. I teeter a few seconds, unsteady, then step over the dead bodies, wash off the pipe, dry it with a rag and hang it on the rack. West stoops and washes the blood off his hands, the cold water running from red to pink to clear and then he scrubs his knife plucking the hair and clotted blood off. He dries it and tucks it up on the shelf. He turns off the light in the killing shed and we walk down to supper in the drizzle. We don't unload the fish. We don't bring in any wood. We sit down in a daze and listen to the conversation but don't enter in. There is food on our plates and we try to eat. We don't do well. In our hearts and guts we're sick.

CHAPTER 15

In the morning my back still hurt. It wasn't raining and I was glad for that. The water had come up in the night and the top of a stump in the meadow we used to measure the rise and fall of the water was barely visible. I went to breakfast with Ladd following me across the road. To the naked eye he had pretty much recovered from the hit West gave him with the shovel but I couldn't roughhouse with him like I used to. If I touched that side he laid his ears back, cringed and slunk away.

"Morning," I said as I entered the house.

Rose was cheery. "Ready for breeding season?"

"Hell no. Are you?"

She stared at me a moment. "What do you mean by that?"

"Well...we've got two tons of fish to grind, a hundred and four calves to skin, a couple dozen pens to make, some mink out and Ralph's in town." I was tired.

West looked at me and I knew he was thinking we wouldn't miss Ralph. I almost said it out loud but checked myself. He knew I knew it. We could tell each other things by just looking now and nobody else saw it.

"We'll put the first two sheds together and then I'll patrol and you guys can finish the skinning. Maybe Ralph can get back tonight," she said.

"The water is up higher than yesterday. How's he gonna get back?" I said.

"He can come over Rainy Fork and probably get through."

West stirred on his chair, his dark eyes stabbing her. "Yeah, but he won't."

Olive looked at him with disgust and went ahead setting the table. Rose could have crucified him on the spot, dirty sweatshirt, chewing tobacco, old man legs and all. I turned my head down and petted one of the cats so they couldn't see the half smile on my face. After all, she had hired Ralph and she only hired people who did right.

We ate. All through breakfast I had to keep sucking air to keep from laughing with West. West wouldn't look at me either. We couldn't afford to be asked why we were laughing. It was that tight for the moment.

The heat coming from the wood stove about knocked me out. After breakfast I stepped outside to wake up. West went to milk and I fed the new whiteface calf Rose was raising for meat. Rose met me at the first shed and showed me how to put the female mink with the males.

"Take only the females on his right as you are facing the nest boxes, up to the next male. If you get a pair that fight, and it's a kit male, take her out and find one that's receptive." She acted like she was laying out the Declaration of Independence and the mink and all mammals' first amendment rights for breeding. It seemed pretty solemn standing there in the mud, the smell of mink musk rising from every male pen. The male mink were very ready for breeding season. The females had to be receptive.

"You should get some mink, Jeff. Be good for you. Help you settle down. I'm gonna have more than I've got cages for and I'll sell you some cheap. What do you think?"

"I'm going back to school. Wasn't thinking of settling down."

"Mink are wonderful creatures. Fun to work with. For a couple hundred dollars you could get started. You build some cages for 'em and I'll let you keep them in here."

"Let me think about it. I need to understand this breeding business first and from what West tells me, there is a lot to learn."

"Don't listen to the old man; he doesn't know blood from tomato sauce about breeding. Just do like I tell you and we'll get it done right. He's always got fancy ideas that turn out like some of his others—no damn good. He doesn't like Ralph either. Did you hear what he said about him this morning?"

"Yes."

"That son-of-a-bitch—he's always making trouble with my help." She frowned. "Ralph's a damn good worker."

"Rose," I said. "Ralph's a hindrance. You count on him to do something and then West or I have to do it over.

She hit her usual line. "I only hire people that can do the work. You and West don't see what Ralph does like I do. He's a little slow, yes...but he works steady."

We heard West open the gate into the mink yard. She threw a quick glance under the roof and motioned to me that he was coming, then busied herself walking about looking at the breeding cards on each pen.

"Don't see any trace of those missing mink," West said. "Don't know how they could've got out."

"They've got to be here somewhere. I don't think they can scale the fence."

"No," West said. "I doubt that."

"We've got to find them before they starve in here. I'll look and you guys work on the breeding."

West took an adjacent shed while I finished my row. I had one fight but got them separated before either got hurt. The male dove at the female I lowered into the pen. He was twice her size but she bit and scratched like an alley cat. He would retreat and then attack again. His social skills were undeniably warped by his existence in a wire pen by himself.

Rose came down the aisle. "Got them all together?"

I nodded.

"Okay." She stopped to check a pair. "You and West start on the skinning and let's not have so many holes in the hides. ...." Her voice droned on. I had heard it all before. I tried to only feel the wetness of the atmosphere. The water was high, the clouds were low, and in between them I existed with lungs to breathe the moisture and limbs to feel the tired aching burden the wetness brought to me with the damp and cold. "...Take your time and do it right but get it done. And don't pile the hides in the corner where the heat will stay in them. Scatter them out."

I turned and walked down the aisle. West met me at the end of the row and we slipped through the gate together.

We walked across the fresh gravel scattered on the driveway, hearing our steps rattle the stones under our feet, paying no attention, trying just to be able to lift our feet and walk straight. We didn't talk. We stopped at the edge of the concrete and looked at the slaughter floor. West leaned against the wall and pulled out a cigarette. He never took his eyes off the floor while he lit it.

He looked at me, his eyes pale and cloudy. Our bodies had an aching anchor, the tiredness sagging and pulling the energy out of them like a heavy weight pulling down on our shoulders keeping our feet smashed flat into the ground, our toes spread out. He didn't say a word, just looked at me. I knew what he was thinking. Hell, what else could he think? What else could he force his mind to do but look and assimilate the known facts and do what he had to do? Not for money, not for love, not for glory, but because he had to. Pride, I guess.

He picked up his knife and whetted the blade like a straight razor, drawing it in an oval motion across the stone from hilt to point, turning it over and pushing it across from point to hilt, always keeping the bevel flat to the stone. I never tired of watching his deliberate movements when it came to doing something. He didn't go about anything like he was killing snakes. His big coarse hands gripped the knife and stone and he blended it all in a smooth movement. I whetted and steeled my blade and drew it across my arm leaving a bare spot of skin glistening where the edge had shaved the hair.

One hundred and four calves lay on the floor, cold and stiff and bloody and wet. I had killed every one of them. Yesterday they were new, sniffing fresh scents, hearing new sounds, tasting water for the first time. They romped with their corral mates and called for their mothers. I herded them into the slaughter house and slaughtered them wanting only to stop the endless bawling and lost some of myself in there. It looked like a Nazi gas chamber after they opened the doors.

West slipped into his rubber boots and pants and leaned over the gutter to let the burned-out cigarette fall but it stuck to his wet lips. He had to blow on it to get it to fall into the drain.

We filled our buckets with water, placed our steel and stone handy and cleared a little place to skin among the dead calves; we'd made our little prison for the morning.

"How long?" I said.

"Three hours. Maybe longer." He said it without looking up and then straightened and looked at me, a twisted half smile on his lips.

I had practiced how he cut and how he moved his knife. I had watched him skin and I had taken a few moves off his pattern, and now I thought I could skin along side of him. I thought my knife was true, that my hand would guide it right

"West—I'll race you. Calf for calf. We shout out any holes we cut."

West shrugged his lean shoulders. He was game. "What's the prize?"

I thought about it a minute and about our conversation in the truck. "A bottle of Jack Daniels. Loser buys but both of us drink."

"Go," he said.

He grabbed a leg and twisted the calf's belly up and started skinning from the throat. I pulled one up, slid the knife down the belly, up and around the bung, leaving an island of it, slipping the blade down the left front leg to the brisket. I dug my nails into the hide and with a long pull of the knife laid a flap of skin loose on the ribs and then from the shoulder and peeled the skin free from the neck meat down to the head, then slipping under the skin, cut around the eyes and through the ear.

"First leg," he shouted as the hoof he had disjointed hit the box. He was ahead but my confidence was still there. I had it figured to catch him at the hind legs with my new cut already made.

I could hear West steeling his knife. I cut the leg off and our hind legs hit the box simultaneously. Now I had the edge. He steeled again—precious seconds.

My knife slipped on the hair and I cursed under my breath, knowing it dulled the keenness. The point caught and I skinned in one smooth movement. I disjointed the front leg, picked the calf up by its stubs and cast it on the floor for the beginning of the pile.

I turned and straightened up fast and picked up the steel. His knife had just found the last joint and he hoisted the calf low along the floor and piled it atop mine. He looked up and smiled. He knew I would catch up someday. He knew that the vigor of youth would catch and surpass the wisdom of the aged. He stopped only a split second to straighten up then steeled and started another. We started together on the second calf. Steeling and bending and cutting and trying to straighten to break the cramps that held us down while we skinned.

The sweat started around my temples and then my back. I could see droplets form on my eyebrows and when I moved, trickles ran across my forehead like little bugs racing across.

I shut out everything but conservation of movement. Making the knife cut clean, leaving the hide without tufts of flesh sticking to it. The pile grew larger and still we were neck-and-neck. Sometimes I would get steeled and begin another calf as he would throw his last on the pile and start to steel. He would steel short and I would miss a joint and he would be steeling when I was finishing.

Back and forth it wavered. Bent over. Blood rushing to our heads. Our backs curved. Holding bloody calf's legs between our knees and bitching to ourselves about the joint-less legs, glued–on hides, sandpaper hair that dulled our blades, and the whole damn ranch, farmers, politicians, and rich bastards. Our backs were hurting, and each calf was heavier.

Rip...steel...rip...steel...pick up the carcass and throw it on the pile, straighten fast. It hurts less. Breathe again and force the smell of blood and torn sour stomachs to go through you and out again.

"Hole," I shouted. (Cut too hard—edge too keen to cut hard, just let it slip along easy like—that's it—hold it easy in your hand and just let it slide.)

Our calves hit the pile together; his slid off and I saw the blood run to his face as he picked it up from the floor. You don't notice how you slow down and how you quit counting the calves or the holes or the legs. Sometimes you don't think. It's like a blackboard; it's got edges but no substance. Like some people's lives, West's maybe, empty except for the edges. He loves the land and what the land will give him but there is no place for it any more, just empty sadness and tiredness that sweeps and drowns the remainder of anything away leaving only the shallow roots of desperation.

What would you do with a marriage full of conflict, two crippled boys spending their shortened days in that house, strangers living on your place and eating at your table? Makes you ponder marriage, kids, and the rest of your life in the whole.

I didn't notice for a moment that West had stopped. When I looked up he was gone. I stood up and felt dizzy and had to lean on the mixer until the wave passed, then I sat down on a bucket. He came back from the freezer room. I didn't hear the motor running so I knew he was defrosting. It's funny how the absence of a sound you've become used to is so noticeable.

He looked down at the pile of calves, bent over the drain and spit out his wad of tobacco and lit a cigarette.

"I wish I had a good drink of whiskey right now," he said.

I smiled at him and his whiskey ideas.

"So who won?" I said.

He shook his head. "Don't know."

"So who buys the whiskey?"

He smiled. "Maybe we split the cost and split the bottle."

"I've never had more than one drink."

"Fine with me."

"Course it would be fine with you."

He nodded. "I bet Ralph's in having one right now."

"I wish Ralph was here breaking his tail over these calves," I said.

West thought. "I'd be willing to bet he hasn't skinned a dozen calves since he's been here."

"Another Jack?"

"Jack had it good here and so has Johnson. His room's free. He's making $200 and Olive's making $100 and the kids only have to pay two bits a meal."

"That's better than he could make on the outside," I said.

He smiled. "But you know...that's good money these days."

I nodded. "He's been off a week now with pay."

"You know—there's nothing the matter with him but those," he pointed to the stack of calves. "He's afraid of 'em."

"Wouldn't doubt it," I said.

He put the cigarette up to his lips and smoked.

"Has Ralph ever said anything positive to you?" I asked.

He shook his head.

"Me neither. Always I guess this or I guess that. I guess he guesses on everything." I drew back my arm and threw the skinning knife across the room. It turned in the air twice and stuck between the ribs in a calf on the wall. I acted like it wasn't unusual. The old man smiled at my acting and I knew he wasn't fooled. It didn't stick every time.

I heard someone running, got up and looked outside. It was Toddy, the youngest of the Johnson tribe.

"The kids are back. How'd they get back with the water up?"

"Probably came through Rainy Fork," West offered.

"Well, they might come, but their old man won't."

He shook his head in agreement.

"He might come but it will take him all day to make it and by then he will have guessed we'd have all the calves done."

CHAPTER 16

Sometimes around 3:30 or 4:00 of an afternoon, after we'd been bent over dead calves all day, West and I would take a break. If the sun was shining we sat on the running board of the truck. He'd smoke or chew, stroke the hair at his throat, and look off in the distance over the river.

I looked over and saw Ralph and Rose feeding in the mink yard. We could hear their voices drifting across the driveway but words were indistinguishable.

I had thought for two days about how to get West talking about the building of the place and had ruled out many opening lines. Finally settled on this one.

"When you got back from logging was this place already set up?"

He turned his head faster than I expected and looked at me eyeball to eyeball.

"Humph," he said. "She tell you that?"

"Not in so many words."

He was silent for a minute. "You know what a Fresno is?"

I shook my head.

"It's a dirt moving contraption pulled by horses. Used to build roads with it before they got bulldozers." His hands showed me the action. "You drop the blade, the horses pull and you scoop out dirt where you don't want it and put it where you do want it."

He pointed toward the mink yard. "You see that cut in the far corner?"

I nodded.

"That whole hillside was the same grade as that piece. I started there and it took me weeks to dig out that mink yard. Before that I cut all the trees down. I fixed it so the water from the hills didn't wash us away every time it rained. You know, that rain on bare ground can really carve a ditch in a hurry."

"I see that," I said. "Where's the water go now?"

"The river."

"All the mink and duck crap along with it?"

"Where do you think it goes anyway?"

"Hadn't thought about it. Always figured it went into the grass."

"Ok. And when it's still hard and water comes along...?"

"Guess it moves along with the water..."

"Right into the river like it's been doing for a million years."

He spit out his chew and lit a cigarette. "Took me a month to fell the trees, buck 'em up and make firewood." He turned to look at me again.

"You know—green wood doesn't work too well in a wood stove. Have to let it season. Green wood will cause a lot of creosote to build up on the inside of the chimney and give you a real good chimney fire one day."

"So you had your hand it in from the beginning?" I said.

He nodded. "I pulled the mink pens over from the other place. Helped set them up and build the fence. Jack and her insisted they build the roofs and set the pens. You can see what kind of job they did. Course Jack could do no wrong so I left them to their devices and built the slaughter house and barn."

"And that house up there," I said.

He turned to look over his shoulder. "And that house up there."

"You gonna finish it?"

He sighed. "I expect. One of these days."

"Before or after I'm gone?"

He turned to me. "You leaving?"

"Not today." I clapped him on the shoulder.

"Hope you stay through breeding season."

"Yeah—well, I signed on for four months and I've been here too long already. I've got the money for school now; I should pack it up and leave."

West reached for a piece of bark and scratched in the dirt carving a small ditch with it. "I worked with a fella like you in a lumber camp up North. He was going to college—saving his money. He hired on one summer saying he needed to make five hundred dollars and the day he had it he would leave. And you know what? he stayed until he had a thousand dollars in the bank. Made him feel more comfortable."

"Comfort is important to some people," I said.

He looked off at the river. "Haven't had a good hand around here 'till you came."

He stared down at his new ditch. I looked at the side of his face. "I appreciate that," I said.

Ladd walked over and nuzzled my hand. I scratched his back and ears until he closed his eyes, sat down and leaned against my legs. He came to me most of the time now and slept in the trailer on his pad. Occasionally West ran his hand over his head when he filled the metal dish but Ladd didn't raise his eyes and look at him anymore since the shovel pounding.

We heard the front door of the family house open. Olive stepped out on the porch, put her hands on her hips and hollered. "Supper."

Ladd bounded away thinking he might be included. West and I rose from the running board and looked around us. The light had changed into a mellow pink and beige hue that glowed above the river when the sun slipped between overlying clouds and the earth and spread parallel beams flat across the land.

CHAPTER 17

The knock started me. I was on page thirty-six of *The Old Man and the Sea* when Ladd jerked awake on his rug. Ralph Johnson stood on the ground about six feet from the door.

"Hope you weren't asleep," he said.

I shook my head. "No—just reading."

"I've never seen the inside of this thing. Wondered how it was working for you?"

"You want to come in?"

"Don't mind if I do." He removed his hat and stepped inside. Ladd nosed his legs and retired on his rug.

"Oh—Ladd lives in here, huh?"

"Sometimes. He comes and goes. It's a good place for him to live out his fantasy of being a house dog."

"Huh?"

"Nothing." I swung my arm around the interior. "Here it is in all its glory."

"Pretty nice for a single guy isn't it?"

I didn't respond. I wondered what was prompting his visit. West and Rose had taken the boys to the doctor, the mink were fed and we had knocked off around 4:00 pm.

When Rose left she said Olive would cook up something for supper, that they would be eating in town and don't wait up for them. I wanted to be polite.

"You want to see the bedroom?" I said.

He craned his neck toward the small alcove in the rear. "Oh, I can see it from here."

"Have a seat," I said.

"Thank you." He sat on the edge of the loveseat that filled the side wall and began twirling his hat in his hands.

"I don't have anything to eat or drink," I said.

"That's fine. The missus is making some supper for us. That's why I'm here. Tell you to come on up about 5:30."

"Wow. Dinner on top of the hill, huh?"

He grinned. "Well—sorta like eating with bums but I think Olive will make something worth eating.

"Oh, I'm sure of it."

There was a moment of silence. Ralph looked down at his hat twirling around and stuck out his lower lip.

"Jeff—I've got something I need to talk about. You and I haven't been close but I figure you can keep a secret, and this has been bothering me a lot." He looked me in the eyes with the first steady glaze I had seen from him. "Can I trust you on this?"

"Why me?"

"I figure we're in this together." He turned the hat faster and glued his eyes to it. "I mean the work and all."

I nodded. What is he going to come out with?

"Don't know how to begin but I can't keep it to myself anymore. It scares me and I'm thinking it might affect us all." He stopped, looked down and keeping his eyes averted started over.

"I've been offered a lot of money to get a pair of Platinum mink. I'm scared. I don't know what to do."

I straightened up. "You mean to steal them?" I was thinking of the missing mink now and pieces were fitting together.

"He just wants to borrow them."

"Who would pay you to do that?"

"This guy who owns a mink ranch south of here." He crushed his hat, eyes running all over the room. "He offered me $200."

"Why doesn't he just buy them?"

"She won't sell them to any other ranchers. She wants to make a big splash at the fur sale with the new color." He actually shrunk in size as we sat there. "I'm scared of the guy."

"Did he threaten you?"

"No." The hat twirled faster. "Well—he did and he didn't."

"So—he made you an offer and you didn't take it and it's over?"

"No—I guess not. I needed the money."

"You could rob a bank and get $200. You wouldn't rob a bank would you?"

"Well—no. Of course not."

"Stealing mink and robbing a bank is the same thing isn't it?"

"Well—I guess so." The hat stopped. "I guess you're right. It isn't stealing if you just borrow them is it? Not like robbing a bank?"

"There's a difference."

Ralph shook his head.

My mind was whirling. "You sure he'll give them back?"

"Says he will."

"Sounds fishy to me."

"Yeah. I guess it does."

"How'd he threaten you?" I was trying to get my mind around this revelation.

"He just said not to come looking for him. He'd find me when he was through with the mink. He followed me out of the barber shop."

"Ralph—have you already given him mink? We're missing some."

The hat twirled faster. He looked at the wall and back at the floor. "I took 'em in already."

I shook my head. "I don't know what to tell you, Ralph."

"I know." His eyes dropped. "You being a college person I thought you might know what to do. I'm kinda worried. I ain't done anything like this before."

I didn't know what to tell him. If he got the mink back would it be stealing? I didn't know. But it sure wasn't the right thing to do.

"Why tell me?"

"It's really bothering me." He shook his head, his eyes narrow, his lips pursed. "Can we keep this just between you and me? I'd sure appreciate it if you didn't tell anybody."

Where do I go with this? "I think we can if you get them back."

He stood up and extended his hand. "Thanks."

It was the first time we had shaken hands since I'd been there. His hand was small and soft. Too much time in the feed bucket.

LADD FOLLOWED ME UP the hill, his tail wagging all the way. When he saw that I intended to go in the building he turned around and walked back. I hadn't been close to the house before so I prowled around the grounds. My eyes took in the water drainage and the open door that I had seen banging from time to time. The siding had warped, pulling nails out of the studs. The cedar wood sheathing had weathered to a pigeon gray. The un-painted window frames were raw wood, the gaps between the window frame and sheathing caulked with rolled up newspaper.

I knocked on the door. Ralph opened it a little too fast, like he had been watching me inspect the house. "Come on in," he said.

Our footsteps echoed in the dark hallway. Ralph opened a door into the kitchen and all six kids and Olive looked up at me.

"Hi," I said.

The kids all said "hi" at once. Olive gave a forced smile. She had a rag tucked in the ties of her apron over a housedress; hair pulled back, and a spatula in her right hand. The smell of pork chops, sauerkraut and potatoes filled the large room. The kids were doing school work on a table of 2x8s sitting on packing crates, the only furniture in the room,. Illumination was provided by a single light bulb hanging from the ceiling dead center of the table. That light dimmed the moment I looked at it.

"Happens when the freezer goes on," Ralph said. "It's hooked up to the slaughter house fuse box."

In a few seconds the light brightened again. Ralph grinned.

"Let me show you around," he said and all the kids jumped up and followed us through a door into the hall. He shone a flash light into a smallish room.

"Was probably gonna be the bathroom," he said. The floor had an open hole about where a toilet would have been installed. The smell gave me a hunch that it might have been used that way on cold nights.

Next he showed me where the kids camped out in a long room with windows on the North side. Bedding was piled here and there on two mattresses on the floor. Clothes hung on nails driven into the wall between the windows. Black plastic sheets partitioned the rooms and were attached to a 2x4 nailed to the floor.

"This is where the kids sleep," Ralph said.

I nodded. "Kinda like boy scout camp isn't it?"

"Yeah. It's cold when the wind blows. There's no light in here except through those windows."

He took me through another door into their bedroom. There was one small window on the North side. The room was cold and smelled of unwashed bodies and sweaty socks that had been worn too long in rubber boots. There was no light in there either.

"Well—I guess that's it," he said.

The kids led the way back to the kitchen. Toddy, the youngest of the clan, picked up his books and papers and ran out of the room. The others followed. That cleared the table for the supper dishes. Ralph and I stood close to the cook stove where there was light and heat.

We both looked up when the light dimmed again.

"Freezer," Ralph said, smiling.

I nodded and counted the seconds before the lights reached full brightness again.

"Where does your sink water go?" I asked. I was having a hard time keeping what he had confessed to me earlier from taking over my thinking. Small talk was all I could manage while his confession ran through my brain.

"Goes into a fifty gallon drum buried outside. I hooked it up after we got here and decided to stay in this place rather than rent somewhere. They wanted first and last months rent for places in town."

Olive chimed in. "We didn't have that kind of money." There was a snarl in her voice that I had not heard before.

Ralph smiled and started over. "They said we could live here if we wanted to while we looked around but..."

"Foods ready," Olive said. Everyone had a chair except that Toddy and Ermaline shared one. Each person got one pork chop, a scoop of sauerkraut, a potato, and a glass of milk.

Ralph gestured at the gallon of milk on the table. "West's cows give more milk than they use so they give us a little for the kids. Not enough for us to sell,"

"Why would he give you his milk to sell?" I said.

"He doesn't use it," Olive jumped in.

"Looks to me like you make out pretty well. No rent or utilities to pay, two salaries, free milk."

"If we had a dirt floor we would be like slaves," Olive said.

I shook my head. "Slaves don't have choices."

Olive squinted her eyes. She looked at me like I had suddenly sided against her whole family. "What choice have we got?"

"You can stay or go."

"Ha," she threw her chin up, slammed down a one layer chocolate cake and proceeded to slice it with a knife like she was butchering it. "You're single and it doesn't hurt you any. Our only choice is to work every day to her demands and listen to West complain about Ralph's work and my cooking. We've had enough of that."

"I don't know what single has to do with it?"

"You being single don't have the responsibility of these kids. This isn't good for them and she could make it a lot better."

I took a new breath. "I've heard her say Ralph is a good worker."

"She may say that to your face," Olive said. "But I've heard her say other things behind his back." She shook her head. "She can't be trusted. The boys tell me things about both of them. They harbor bad feelings about them. Feel they're being kept in prison in that house."

"Not much of a life in there," I said.

"Paul especially. He rants about West every day," she said.

The snus incident on the driveway came back to me in a flash.

"She's got money you know. She could afford to put this place in better condition." She raised her eyebrows and using her apron for a hot pad picked the coffee pot off the stove. "You want some more coffee?"

"No thanks." I pushed back my chair. "One summer I lived on a lookout that was way more primitive than this place. I think you're getting a good deal. Think how much you're saving."

"We're saving enough to get out of here and then you and her can run the place anyway you like," she said.

Ralph held his coffee cup between his hands, head down, elbows on the table. When he raised his head he looked in my eyes and I could almost feel him ask if I was going to hold his secret long enough for them to get out of there.

I walked to the door and turned. "I don't have anything to do with running this place. I work here just like you. Thanks for supper, Olive." She didn't respond. "I'll check the mink yard, make sure every things ok, Ralph. You don't need to come down."

"You're ok with what I told you earlier?"

I nodded. "By tomorrow I'll forget it."

Ladd met me half way down the hill. We walked over the check the yard gates, make sure the cows were settled for the night, and no water was left running or lights on. Instead of a night walk I went back to the trailer and got out my journal.

Olive Johnson said if the floor was dirt they'd live like slaves. It wasn't any worse than my forest service lookout. Course, I had been on the lookout by myself; not with six kids. The smell of dirty clothes and wet socks permeated the bedrooms. It is my firm belief that nobody has ever put a wet rag on any of the windows—inside or out. That they let any light in at all was testimony to the nature of glass. One sink in the kitchen for everything. Pioneer conditions for sure but they are living there free.

I'd like to know how the kids act when they go to school. They are pleasant and well behaved around here but I wonder if they get teased for their body odor and clothes at school. Kids can be pretty cruel.

CHAPTER 18

The days drifted by in a monotonous stupor; starting at five thirty in the morning we put pairs together as soon as it was light enough to read the breeding cards in the gray dawn. We alternated our eating shifts so someone was patrolling the mink yard all the time. Rose and Ralph patrolled all day and West and I drew the feeding and the wood getting in the afternoons until the water went down. Then the wood man could drive through with his truck and dump a double load of peeler core ends on the driveway. West and I moved them over onto the grass. We split some and hauled stove-sized pieces into the house. Olive didn't say anything. We were too tired to notice if she liked the nice new wood or not.

All over the Oregon coast milk cows were having calves and coming fresh. The farmers brought in the bull calves and they kept bringing them in by Rainy Fork because they didn't know the river had gone down. Some calves had the scours so bad they couldn't stand up and I hit them in the head lying down.

Some were frisky and jumped around and butted the others, who bawled endlessly, wanting only the comfort of their mothers' udders.

As the month ploughed ahead with no rest, no time off, straight twelve and fourteen-hour days, skinning, putting mink together, marking breeding cards, salting hides, grinding, mixing, feeding and watering, each of us drew more into himself, thinking only of his own hardships, looking forward to the last day of breeding season when we could let up.

West and I didn't talk much any more except when he smoked. The others were over their flu now but it had left them weaker except for the old man. He plodded along about the same as ever.

Rose was putting in long hours patrolling up and down the sheds in the drizzle; cigarettes and coffee kept her going. She was up at the end of the yard when West and I sat down for a while in the slaughterhouse.

West reached out with his leg and kicked a dead calf that had fallen off a nail on the wall.

"Hurt your foot?" I asked.

"No—but it hurt my back." He lit up. "Heard her talking about raising Ralph's pay last night because of his hard work."

"*His* hard work?" I said.

He nodded.

"What the hell has he done?"

"Nothing," he said.

We both sat there thinking about it.

"When I came here he was the worst worker she ever had on the place. She told me the first day that Ralph was as slow as the seven year itch. And dumb. And Olive was the worst housekeeper this side of the Mississippi. He hasn't changed and she wants to raise his pay. That takes the cake."

"Guess he said something about going to Idaho to work on a chicken ranch or something for his father-in-law."

"And that's why she's gonna up his pay, huh?" I said.

He shrugged and nodded his head.

"Well, if there's any justice on earth, it sure missed this place by a mile."

The old man drew in on the cigarette then blew out the smoke in a slow steady stream. He watched the smoke drift, his eyes following it until it blended into the fog and disappeared.

"You know," he said. "Ever since she started hiring a man, it has been the same process." He looked at me. "He is always good at the start. Then when she starts telling them all those lies about me and they see it isn't true...if they've got any guts, they tell her so. Then she turns against them until me and him have an argument over something and then they become the best of friends and come hell or high water, she sticks to them."

"So you and I shouldn't have an argument? Is that the deal?"

"We see things pretty eye to eye," he said. "Don't figure we'll argue much."

"I don't take to hitting dogs with a shovel," I said.

"I did that of a purpose. Don't like a dog digging."

"He didn't dig much."

"Digging is a bad habit for a dog to get into."

"Would you hit me with a shovel?"

"If you were digging in my corral."

I stood up and brushed my Levis off. That I could stand straight after sitting that long on cold concrete was a testament to my youth. I stuck out my hand. West looked up, a smile forming on his face. With the cigarette between his lips he took my hand and grunted himself off the curb.

WE ONLY HAD THREE calves to go and after I skinned them out and salted the hides we threw 100 calves in the truck and took them to town to the freezer. It was thirty degrees on the pier where the freezer was located, and because of the storm the fishing boats were in. I walked a plank across the water over to the deck of the closest boat.

I hollered down into the hold. "Need any hands on this boat?"

"Got more hands than we got fish," was the reply.

"The hell you say?"

"The hell we don't say," came back.

"Why the long johns, man?" I felt silly now.

"Colder than a well digger's ass down here."

"How would a salt know what that feels like?"

"Used to farm, lad, I know how to dig."

I looked at West and he smiled.

"Got a farmer here says he never saw you before," I said.

"Tell that plow-pusher I dug more wells than he's got hairs on his head."

"I told him but he doesn't believe it."

No answer. He was busy digging out fish, so the old man and I left to freeze the calves. That's what we came there for anyway.

We got back pretty late but since supper wasn't ready yet we parked the truck and sat in it. Rose came through the gate. She pulled the cigarette from her lips.

"My Gawd, it took you all afternoon!" she said.

"Damn near," I shot back.

She looked at me surprised-like, and after holding her cigarette away from her lips for a couple of seconds, put it back in her mouth and walked away. West shrugged his shoulders. I figured out one day he could shrug his shoulders to mean about eight things. It saved him removing his cigarette to talk, I guess. We got out of the truck and went into the mink yard.

Passing Ralph in one shed we walked on down to the last four sheds. West and I started walking up and down the aisles, putting new females in with the males that were ready, separating ones that were done, digging in with gloved hands to tear apart fighters and sloshing through the slippery, muddy aisles, staying on feet that were numb from cold and ache.

Time slowed down when the clouds covered the sun. The day started gray and went through the daylight hours with the same shade and then darkened gray until there was no light at all and our world consisted of what little we could see around us. You never knew where the sun was but you had faith it was still up there. It was generally earlier than the light made it out to be.

That left time for thinking. With all the mink mating going on I got to thinking how long it had been since I had a date with a girl. Man, it was a long old time. You couldn't really call it a date the day Rose shoved me into the farmer's car and sent me to town with that pretty girl. I didn't even get her name. She was pleasant, too.

I sat down at the end of the row. West came over in my aisle and shook a nesting box to break up a fight I didn't hear. He sat down beside me.

He took out his plug of Days-o-Work and bit off a chew. Then he offered it to me. I took a conservative bite. It was sweet and almost refreshing in the cold air. He smiled at me while I chewed and spit.

"Good for you when you're tired," he said.

"What's happening to me? I didn't drink, swear, or use tobacco when I showed up here and now you've got me doing all."

"Not much. This plug would last a year at the rate you take it."

I wiped my chin. "That's about all I could stand. Do you swallow it?"

"Not often. Can though. When I was working where I couldn't spit I'd swallow it." He shook his head. "It isn't bad. You get used to it. I knew a guy that put in a big chew of an evening when he went to bed and left it there all night."

"Was he married?"

West nodded.

"And his wife put up with that?"

"Guess she did."

I shook my head and spit out the remains in the aisle. "What's that girl's name that Rose sent me into town with?"

"Rassel. Rassel Swenson."

"She live close by?"

He nodded down river. "About a mile that-a-way."

He got up and moved across the open aisle to his shed and I sat there a moment longer.

I ducked my head as I walked through the low shed and emerged into the rain, listening for fights. I checked the two sapphires on the end but nothing was doing so I separated them and threw the old boy another female. He chased her around, she snarled a little and bit him twice. He stopped to lick his hurt paw then caught her against the water can. She would have his kits.

Rose walked over, a wet cigarette dangling from her lips, looking serious. I tensed inside and tried to relax my breathing.

"You know Olive's gonna quit Friday?" she said.

"No," I said.

"I gotta have somebody in there with those boys," she threw back defensively.

"She's quitting because the kids heard what you and West said about Ralph in the slaughterhouse and they came in and told her. That's gotta stop!"

I straightened up under the shed. Slowly I dumped my thoughts out. "I didn't say anything that wasn't true, and I'll say it to anyone who wants to hear it again. I'm getting a little tired of doing all the heavy work and him just patrolling up and down the rows."

"He's doing exactly what I tell him to do!" she said.

I raised my voice. "Well, then don't look at your watch when we pull in at 5 o'clock after putting a load of 100 calves in the freezer."

She switched her tactics. "Ralph is a good worker, a little slow, but a good worker." She drew again, and let the smoke drift out her nostrils. "The old man has always caused me trouble with my help, him and his black bastard mouth. Someone ought to beat the hell out of him. Jack did it once and someone should do it again!"

I snorted audibly. She turned with a sneer and walked away in the rain. I watched her back as she walked away. Looks like a man. Billed hat, short gray hair, storm jacket with a hand in the pocket, Levis and knee-high, rubber boots. She's tough on men—their clothes, their strength, their manner, their hands, their bodies, their heads, brains—but she dresses like them.

Can't she see that we all are working from dawn to dark to make the ranch work? We've got three guys, and a dog here and two boys, who should have been men by now inside the house, and she's one of two human females on the place. But it is her place. Her ranch, her mink and her life that is being spent in this hell hole cut out of the side of a hill. Day after day she works at pushing us apart. To what end?

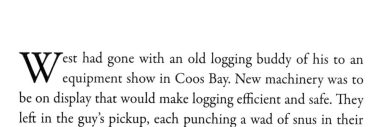

CHAPTER 19

West had gone with an old logging buddy of his to an equipment show in Coos Bay. New machinery was to be on display that would make logging efficient and safe. They left in the guy's pickup, each punching a wad of snus in their lower lips as they rolled down the driveway, and laughing like two teenagers about to pick up girls and go to a movie.

Rose and the Johnsons had each gone to town in their own car to do different things and were not going to be back before supper. Olive Johnson had made a meat loaf that I was instructed to put in the oven at 4:00 pm.

Ladd came in from a deer run and looked a mess. I decided to give him a bath so I could stand him in the trailer and probably on my bed when I wasn't looking. I tied him up in the slaughter house with a chain to his collar. That gave me a measure of control because he did not indicate he would take kindly to soap and water. I got him wet and lathered and then he sat down and resigned himself to the indignity of the bath. I couldn't find anything to dry him with and I couldn't leave him to his own devices or I'd have to give him another bath. I took him in the house to dry out.

Paul heard me come in. "Is that you, Jeff?"

"Yup."

"You smell like a wet dog."

"I've got a wet dog with me."

"Mom doesn't like him in the house."

Ronny giggled.

"Well—your Mom isn't here right now and I need to get Ladd dry before he comes into the trailer."

"She'll smell him when she gets back."

"We won't be here that long. Have you got any rags or an old towel that I can rub him with?"

"You could use Ronny's towel."

Ronny's left leg and arm rose in unison; his head went back and he gurgled out a laugh. Paul let out a snort.

"No—I don't think I'll do that. Nothing else?"

Paul shook his head. "You can put him by the stove."

I walked Ladd over to the stove and let him turn around several times while I held on to his collar until he lay down and started licking himself. He seemed contented and it worked for me.

"Jeff—what are you gonna do this afternoon?" Paul asked.

"I didn't plan anything. Just washed Ladd. I think he must have rolled in a dead deer carcass or something. Boy, he smelled."

"Let's take a ride."

"A ride? Where? In what?"

"The truck."

"The truck?"

He nodded. "We'll be back before everyone else."

"Back from where?"

"From where we're goin'."

I thought about that a minute. I had not been given permission to drive the truck but I hadn't been told not to drive it either. I had been with West in it several times and knew how it shifted.

"Paul—you've been thinking about this haven't you? You and Ronny have been in here scheming and you're about to get me fired."

"No. Mom isn't going to fire you. We'll only be gone a couple of hours." His sightless eyes were crinkled at the edges and the smile he wore was broadening to open his lips.

"Where you thinking of going?"

"Seven Devils Road."

"Sounds like a neat road to take you two guys on and lose a truck over the edge. The farmers that came over it during the flood said it was a dangerous road."

"That's only if it's been raining. Come on we're wasting time."

"Is this what you do for fun?"

Paul laughed out loud and Ronny squirmed and giggled on the couch. "Come on. You a fraidy-cat?"

"How about Ladd?"

"Bring him along."

I GOT THE KEY off the nail by the freezer door, checked the gas level and pulled the truck down to the doorway of the house. The emergency brake wouldn't hold it so I put it in reverse and turned the engine off. That held it. Then I carried Ronny out and set him in the middle of the seat. Paul had worked his way out to the porch and I helped him in the passenger side to wedge Ronny in. I closed the door and pushed down on the door lock. I didn't want to lose those two guys on a corner somewhere on Seven Devils Road.

Seven Devils Road was named by the early log truck drivers who carried the big coastal firs out to the mill. There was a series of turns—and maybe there were seven—that could cause the scalp to tighten on a strong man coming down with a load of logs. I didn't know that at the time. I found out about it that afternoon.

Neither Ronny nor Paul could see anything but I wasn't a hundred percent sure. Paul rolled the window down using both hands and laughed about it. Ronny laughed at everything. It didn't make any difference if we stopped or I missed second gear and the transmission growled or I honked the horn at a cow in the road. Several times his left arm, which rose when he was excited and laughing, hit the rear view mirror and I had to readjust it.

Paul grabbed his arm and held it down. "Cut that out." He said.

Ronny laughed so hard I thought we'd have to stop and help him catch his breath. Paul had his other arm out the window playing the flat of his hand against the wind letting it rise and fall. Playing it like a bird.

We drove along the river for a ways then the road began to rise. Even unloaded I had to gear down to get up the hill.

When we hit the top of the grade I could see why they named it Seven Devils Road. You know that kind of feeling you get when you're in over your head? When you have to decide whether to turn around or go forward? You may have made a hundred decisions already that day but this one keeps coming up 50/50 and you don't know if the reward is worth the risk.

Paul jerked his upper body forward and slammed the flat of his hand on the dash board. "Come on. Take 'er down." He was pumping his body back and forth from the waist up.

"It looks pretty steep."

"You can do it. Take 'er down."

I pushed in hard on the brake and it sank to the floor. I pumped the brake pedal several times and it gained length. "Paul—I don't know if this truck can make it."

"Sure it can. Come on—take 'er down."

I put the truck in first gear and eased off the clutch. It started down the hill as I checked the range of play in the steering wheel trying to figure out how much turning I'd have to do to make some of the upcoming curves. The boys felt the truck pitch downhill and they opened up all stops. The yelling I'd heard in the house before was nothing like what they were doing now. I rolled down my window. I wanted to be able to get out of the cab if we didn't make it and their yelling was so loud I was having trouble concentrating on the road.

I didn't take my eyes off the road but I suppose we were doing about twenty miles an hour when we took the first switchback. Ronny leaned against Paul and that threw them into uncontrolled laughter. As the truck picked up speed on a straight stretch I pumped the brake and glanced at the speedometer. We were going almost thirty miles an hour and my hands were gripping the wheel so hard I could see the tops of my knuckles turn white.

"Let 'er go," Paul yelled.

"It's going," I said.

"Let 'er go."

"Hang on. We've got a sharp turn coming up."

I pre-steered into the turn using up all the free play in the steering wheel and making sure we got the front end of the truck in the correct position coming out of the turn and inside of the outside edge. Those switchbacks were designed for fifteen mile an hour turns for logging trucks. We hit it at almost thirty. The empty truck didn't have the load to hold us on the inside and as it drifted through the turn the rear wheels bounced on a drain ditch and threw us toward the outside edge. I could visualize how far down the hill the truck could roll if we left the road and I didn't see how any of us could survive it.

The dual rear wheels bit into the hard dirt surface as we came out of the turn and shot us back into the center of the road. I pumped the brake and let the front wheels skid a little toward the inside of the next curve coming up. Then the gravity of our forward movement took us low into the curve and I felt like a race driver letting the front wheels slide while goosing the gas a little to shoot us through it.

My adrenalin was pumping. Paul and Ronny had not stopped laughing since we crept over the top of the hill. I was getting the feel of the truck now and was able to set our angle of attack into the curves with some accuracy, hitting the gas as we entered at the right angle forcing the truck to maintain the angle I had set which shot us out into the next straight portion. There was one straight portion for each curve so if I could maintain control through the curves I could feel better about the straight section and get ready for the next curve.

I didn't think anyone could laugh as long and as hard as those boys did while we were negotiating the downhill truck run. It might have lasted only five minutes. I don't know. I didn't keep track. I steered that truck the best I could and although I can't recall any specific prayers I am confident that there was a constant prayer in my heart.

We rolled out at the bottom and had a long straight stretch where the road widened by an old log deck. I pulled over and stopped and turned the engine off. Paul and Ronny had laughed themselves out. Their faces wore smiles that crinkled up their cheeks and the skin around their eyes. Paul was shaking his head from side to side.

"I told you it would make it," Paul said.

"We're not home yet," I said.

"Don't worry. This old truck will make it."

"It'd better. We're twenty miles from home."

I kicked the starter and turned the truck onto the road. We headed back to the farm on the river grade road at a leisurely twenty-five miles an hour. Neither boy spoke or laughed or grinned. They sat in the seat like they sat in their wheelchairs, oblivious to the world that went on around them.

Paul was right. We got home before anyone else. I got them both in the house, turned on the meatloaf and took Ladd up to the trailer. Then I put the truck back in its rutted parking place. I slammed the door and walked around it to see if anyone could tell it had been on a wild ride. Looked natural to me. Even looked like it had a smile on its grille but I knew that couldn't be. The engine clicked as it cooled down, the only clue to having made the Seven Devils run. I patted the hood. It had gained a personality with me.

The meat loaf was done and smelled good. I cleaned and cut some celery and put peanut butter in the groove of each piece, poured some milk and we sat down to eat.

Paul ate several bites and swallowed. "That was fun. Thanks, Jeff."

"You're welcome. Just thank God that we made it back here."

"I told you it would make it. That old truck has a lot of life left in it."

"Yeah—well—it about took the life out of me."

Ronny snorted and Paul threw his head back. He had a stick of celery in his hand and he waved it like a band director.

We heard the cars drive up. Johnsons apparently had eaten in town but West and Rose showed up and joined us for supper just as we were finishing. They were each full of new information about what they had seen and done during their day. I looked at my plate and hoped Paul would hold his tongue.

After Rose got through disclosing her day's activity she asked, "What did you boys do today?"

"I washed Ladd," I said.

"Paul—Ronny?" she said.

Ronny started with his deep throated gurgle pointing his arm at the door. Paul interrupted him.

"We didn't do nuthin," Paul said. Then he grinned and looked in my direction.

Nobody else saw it.

"Well—it's time you got out some. Next time I go to town I'll take you with me."

Paul nodded his head.

CHAPTER 20

Things were quiet after supper. I asked West again where that pretty girl lived and Paul laughed. Paul ended up telling me exactly how to get there. It wasn't far and I decided to take a walk down there if it wasn't raining.

I showered and changed my clothes. Ladd lay on the floor with his eyes looking at my every move.

"What?" I said.

He wagged his tail but kept his eyes on me.

"Going courting. Tired of just you for company. When did you ever rub my back or pop popcorn or make the bed? You do kiss me when you get the chance—I'll give you that."

Ladd slipped out the door, his eyes asking where we were going. He took up a position on my right side and walked at my pace when we left the trailer, turning his head every few seconds to see where we were going.

"We're going to Swenson's dairy. You know the way?"

Ladd dropped his lower jaw, let his tongue hang out and walked faster down the driveway. He turned right when we got to the road and I almost believed he could understand human talk. He couldn't read signs though. He walked right by the Swenson's Dairy sign.

I turned up the driveway and then stopped and thought about what I was going to say. Then she opened the door. The light from inside back lit her figure as she stepped off the threshold and came out to their car. When she opened the door, the dome light showed me standing there. It startled her at first but she didn't say anything, just walked up to me slowly and stood there, inches from me with her hands at her sides.

For the past week I planned my opening conversation with her in my head. While I was skinning, feeding, moving mink, I thought of the first sentence and pictured how I'd say it. But at that instant, with her standing there looking into my eyes, that really good plan went out the window.

I put an arm around her, pulled her against me and kissed her. She moved into me easily and in that instant I remembered the difference between a life and an existence. A heart beat I could hear and short breaths puzzled me. Wow—had it been that long? She smelled so clean. I took her hand and we walked down the road toward the river. Ladd trailed behind. We walked along the bank for a ways and then sat down on a washed-up log.

"So you are Rassel Swenson?" I said.

She smiled. "Rassel," she said. "With the accent on the el. And you're Jeff?"

I nodded. It was bright when the moon came out from behind the clouds.

"What kind of a name is that?"

"It's an old family name. One of my mother's favorite aunts. I got tagged with it as the only girl in the family."

"Do you end up explaining it a lot?"

She nodded. "It takes some getting used to for people." She looked at our hands with fingers entwined. "Do you like working there?"

"Wow—that came out of nowhere. What makes you ask that?"

She shrugged. "I don't know—just that so many men come and go from there, that's all."

"How many have you counted?"

"I don't know—seems like a new one comes and goes every few months. They're good neighbors and all but their hired hands don't seem to stay long."

I reached down and petted Ladd. "Did you ever hear of one of her hired men by the name of Jack?"

"Yes. He was the drinker. They say he had quite a soft spot for Rose but I never saw it. Just rumors." She pet Ladd. Ladd was getting more action than I was. "He left one day and no one knew where he went or why he left or anything. Just left outta there. Not that I'd blame him."

"Why's that?"

"I don't mean that in a bad way. It's just that working at that place has always seemed like the least fun on earth. Not that this dairy farm is all that nice and easy but we don't slaughter new born calves or kill mink to get their hides."

"You sell your day old calves to her to be killed, ground up and fed to mink."

She winced. "I know." Ladd got more action.

"Really—what is it that bothers you about it?"

"The killing and the smell, I guess."

"That bothers me too. But the bull calves are not wanted. What are the farmers going to do with them—raise them as veal? Then what? They get killed a year down the road with the same result."

"I suppose," she said.

"I can look at those soft round eyes in a day's old calf and get all welled up about it, but the fact is, they're unwanted. They are feed for mink." I moved a foot down the log. "Think of the bears and wolves who take day old sheep and caribou and moose. Think of the lions that take day old animals in Africa. A certain number of day olds are feed for the rest of the food chain. I try not to get sentimental about it. I couldn't do the work if I did."

Rassel squirmed but kept hold of my hand. "When you put it that way I can at least understand it. I suppose you get used to it, huh?"

I nodded in the dark but when the moon came back out from behind a cloud and lit up the recently flooded field in front of us I felt like I hadn't told the whole truth. Killing calves every day had gotten to be routine and I suppose I had relegated it to the unconscious part of my brain. But a lot of killing filled up that portion and it was spilling over into my attitude. Sometimes I found myself yelling at people and harboring resentments. What I'd told Rassel was rationalization. Pure rationalization. It put me where I wanted to be in my mind and I had given that to her as a label. But even though I knew it wasn't wholly true I didn't want to revisit it here and now.

Rassel quit petting Ladd and lifted her head. "Let's talk about something else," she said.

"Let's talk about you," I said. "I already know about me."

"Okay. What do you want to know?"

"Can I kiss you again?"

"No." She put her palm against my chest.

My jaw unhinged. "For crying out loud—we've already kissed. What's the matter with another one?"

"Get serious. You wanted to know about me. I'm willing to answer reasonable questions but kissing will block out my memory. We can kiss anytime but we don't have many chances to get to know each other. I want to get to know you. See if I like you and if you like me."

I looked at Ladd. He was no help.

"First question: are you going to college?"

"Yes. University of Oregon in Eugene. Think I'll like teaching but I might switch to nursing or counseling. Next question."

I frowned and smiled at the same time. "You know what teacher's make?"

"Not much. About $3,200 a year but you have the summers off and you can help kids and learn a lot yourself."

"That's not much more than I make on the mink ranch."

"I know but I'm not doing it for money. I'm doing it for love. The money will follow later." She sat silent, an expectant look on her face.

"Have you got a boy friend?"

"Not so's I'd notice."

"Nobody from school?"

"There was a guy I was sweet on but he couldn't stand the pressure of school and joined the Navy. Said he'd be back but that was a year and a half ago and he's been to all parts of the world since then. Doubt he wants to come back to a farm girl now."

"Even one that smells sweeter than fresh cream?"

She smiled. "Cream sours if you leave it out too long."

"Is that a hint I need to take you back?"

"Well—I did just go out to the car. My folks might be wondering about me."

"I would if I were them."

"Yeah. The last kidnapping we had around here was in 1902 when grandpa kidnapped a neighbors pig and held it for ransom for two weeks until they paid for his uprooting a row of carrots. I believe the ransom was five dollars. Carrots were pretty pricy that year."

I took her arm and pulled her to me and kissed her lips. My gosh—what I had been missing and didn't even realize it. Intelligent conversation with a pretty girl and necking thrown in for good measure. I was alive again. The blood racing around inside made my fingers and toes tingle. I could hear my heart beat. Who ever hears their heart beat? My hand rubbed the softness of her young back, feeling the bra straps. She liked to kiss and she was good at it. Even practiced, I'd say. I relaxed. Pretty soon the mist got so thick the air couldn't hold it and released little drops that beat on the leaves like a distant drum.

We walked back to her house. She stepped up on the front porch, turned and put her arms on my shoulders. I kissed her while she stood on the step, her arms around my neck. I was soaking up the soft warm moist feel of her lips. That was a fun way to kiss her. I didn't have to bend over.

When will I see you again?" she said.

"Any time I don't have to work."

"How will I know you don't have to work?"

"I don't know. I don't know that myself."

"You're crazy—do you know that?"

"Not totally."

The porch light came on and her mother opened the door. "Oh there you are," she said. "And the young man from the mink farm. Dad and I fell asleep in our chairs and I just woke up and you weren't here. I thought I'd check."

"Hello, Mrs. Swenson. I'm Jeff."

"Yes—I remember you."

"I was just leaving."

"It is pretty late. Don't know what comes over us to fall asleep in our chairs like that with the radio going full blast."

"Farmers get up early."

"Well—yes we do. Are you coming in, Rassel?"

"I'll be there in a minute, Mom."

"Okay dear. Goodnight Jeff. Oh by the way, we saw a white mink down by the culvert under the road. Think he must be yours."

"Thanks. I'll tell Rose about it. Good night, Mrs. Swenson."

She turned and closed the door but she left the porch light on, a bare bulb that turned everything the tint of clay.

We said our goodbyes and I walked home in the drizzle. Ahead I could see the big house on the hill, gray and ponderous in the poor light.

I saw a quick flash of white fur. I ran up to where it was. It must have been our white mink. Where it had been there was a dark object on the road. I turned it over. It was a dead chewed up mud hen.

Well, at least it can provide for itself.

I kicked the bird off the road and walked on up the driveway. Ladd followed me to the trailer, shook himself and beat me to the bedroom. He was on the bed when I got there. I took down my journal, got comfortable, stuck the pencil between my teeth and thought.

Rassel Swenson is her name. Beautiful sweet girl lives down the road a half mile. A dairy farmer's daughter. She's attractive, smart, good conversationalist, aggressive, and easy to kiss. She nailed me on how I feel about the mink farm work. I thought I knew but I couldn't verbalize it very well. I may not have told her the full truth. Here's what I think. I think I told her the way I wanted to feel about it because I hadn't taken the time and effort to decide how I really feel about it. And right now I still don't know for sure. I can see the process; see the motivation of the dairy farmers and Rose's need for mink food. Someday they'll find a use for day old bull calves on dairy farms but not this week or this month or this year. Could be part of a future novel.

I closed the journal and got ready for bed. When I went to pull back the covers Ladd was on my side of the bed.

"Down, Ladd. Beds are for people—dogs sleep on rugs on the floor."

I had to say it twice. He didn't believe me the first time.

CHAPTER 21

The radio was blaring when I came through the front door. Paul had his wheelchair parked in front of it and was leaning his head toward the speaker.

"Paul—are you deaf?" Rose said. "Turn that thing down a little."

"I want to hear the hog report."

"I know, honey, but turn it down. You're killing us."

Paul fumbled with the volume control and lowered it by several decibels.

Dinner was still being prepared. Olive was making a casserole that was one of her mothers' recipes and kept saying how much we'd like it. I could smell bread baking too. West had separated some cream that morning and talked Paul into turning the butter churn. Paul would do almost anything for fresh butter and it gave him a good half hour of exercise turning that crank. He would get frustrated as the butter got thicker and was harder to churn but I'll give him this; he stayed with it until it was done and Olive could paddle it out of the churn, squeeze the buttermilk out of it and put it in the refrigerator to cool and harden.

Paul cleared his throat. "Jeff—what do you know about hogs?" he said.

"I know less about hogs than I do about mink. And I'm just finding out about mink."

"Do you know how fast they grow?"

"All I know is, we get bacon and pork chops from the little critters."

"Well—they grow up pretty fast. Ronny and I have been planning on starting a hog business. I've been thinking we can feed them the food off the top of the mink cages that the mink don't eat. We've been throwing that away."

"Yeah."

"That won't be enough but we can supplement it with other stuff. Garbage from the house. Maybe they'd eat the calf insides; the liver, heart, lungs and stuff. Think they would?"

"Maybe if you ground it up and put something with it."

"Like what?"

"I don't know. Meal of some kind."

Paul raised his head in the direction of the kitchen. "Mom—do you think a hog would eat the same food as the mink?"

"Honey, I don't know anything about hogs. I suppose they would. They both eat meat. You're the one studying it. Find out those things."

"Ronny—what do you guess we could make on this?" Paul said.

"Yeaaahhh," Ronny said. "I doonn know." He laughed.

"You see," Paul turned to me although I don't know how he knew where I was in the room, "Ronny and I have saved up some money and we're goin' into the hog business."

"So I gathered," I said.

"I think we'll get rich—don't you?"

"I have no idea. Why don't you stick with the mink?"

"They've got mink," he said waving his arm to indicate Rose and West. "I think we can do pretty good with hogs."

The wheelchair squeaked as he turned it back to the radio. The stock news was over and he turned the radio off but not his enthusiasm for hogs.

"I think they grow real fast. You can market them all the way from six months to a year."

"Who's gonna take care of them?" I said.

It was silent in the room for a minute.

"The Johnson kids," he said.

I looked at Olive. Apparently she had heard this already because she didn't wince.

I thought about the older boy salting hides and sharpening his knife. I didn't see a lot of hope for good hog economics in that tribe. "Well—there's enough of them to get it done," I said.

Paul laughed. "We'll pay them a percentage of the gross sales."

"Who's gonna figure that out?" I said.

Why was I slamming their pig deal? Here they had saved the money, helped design the hog farm, and made a decision to do it. They listened to the stock report twice a day and knew a lot more about hogs than I did.

"Listen," I said. "This using left over mink food and stuff that we just throw away is a great idea. Start small and when you prove your theory then you can become big time hog farmers. I think it's a good idea."

West looked at me with a noncommittal expression. I expected him to say something but he was silent. With both hands he lifted his cup of coffee and sipped it and returned to staring out the window.

AFTER DINNER, WEST KNOCKED on my trailer door. Ladd lifted his head. I opened the door to see him standing there still in his working clothes.

"You wanta take a ride with me?"

"Where you headed?"

He nodded his head in a downriver direction. "Pick up those pigs for the boys."

I thought about it a moment. I wasn't doing anything that couldn't be stopped. "Sure."

We picked up some rope and the side boards, threw them on the truck and got in. He looked at the steering wheel a moment, then inserted the key and after letting it warm up a few seconds he put his hand on the wheel and let the clutch out. The truck started a turn to the right. He stopped it and looked at the dash board.

"Somebody's been driving the truck," he said.

"What makes you say that?"

"Wheels are turned. I always leave the wheels straight when I shut it down. And the gas is a bit lower than I left it."

"Hmm" I said.

We went down the incline of the driveway and turned right along the river and past the Swenson farm. I was thinking of confessing that we had made a Seven Devils run with it but decided to not volunteer anything not knowing how big a deal it was one way or the other.

We talked about the weather and the pigs and that was the end of the truck bit.

THE PIGS WERE LITTLE and pink.

"They're Yorkshire pigs," the man said.

"They look healthy," West offered.

"And they are, sir. Overall a very good pig for raising." He stuck both hands in his pocket and like a born salesman asked the buying question. "You're going to take the whole litter aren't you?"

West shoved the hat back on his head, put one hand on his hip and aimed a finger at each pig as he counted them. "Six. But that one's a runt isn't he?"

"I'll let you have him for fifty-cents if you take the lot."

"How much are the others?"

"Three dollars apiece."

West nodded, reached in his pocket and pulled out the money Paul had given him. He counted out fifteen one dollar bills, looked in his other pocket and thumbed a fifty-cent piece into the man's hand.

"They old enough to eat solid food?" West asked.

"Sure. If they balk at it at first, give them a little milk in a bottle or pour some milk in a pan with the food in it. They aren't bashful about eating."

We got them in the truck, put up the side boards and the tailgate and started toward home driving about ten miles an hour. I kept my eye out the rear window to make sure we got home with all of them. Going up the driveway was a hoot. First one, then two, then all of the pigs slid down the truck bed with their feet and legs splayed out, snouts in the air, and smacked into the tail gate. No injuries. We put them in the small pen Ralph Johnson had made out of hail screen and 2x4's.

The scratch and clunk of Paul's wheelbarrow reached my ears above the grunts and squealing of the piglets. The entrepreneur made his way to the pen, turned and sat down on his seat with all the majesty of a sitting king. He cocked his head and listened to the sounds of the six pigs exploring their new home.

"Could you hand me one?" he said.

I reached over the wire and picked out the runt and handed it to him. It was kicking and squealing. Paul brought it up as close to his face as he could and moved his head around like he was examining it.

"What do you think, Paul?" I said.

He turned his head toward me but didn't answer. I thought he acted disappointed.

"Here," I said. "Let me give you another one." I took the runt and handed him one of the larger ones.

His face broke into a smile. "This is better. That other one was kinda small wasn't he?"

"Yeah. He's the runt of the litter."

"How many did you get?"

"Six."

"Does that include the runt?"

"Yeah."

"How much?"

"Paid fifteen dollars for the five and fifty-cents for the runt."

"That's a good price." He handed the pig back to me. "Give me the runt again would ya?"

He held it like you would hold a puppy you loved dearly. The piglet looked up into his eyes while Paul held a bottle to its hungry mouth. When it was full the piglet fell asleep in his swaying arms. Paul had a touch of the mother in him. Perhaps he had been occasionally spared the harsh side of this place.

He reached the piglet out into the air for me to take. "Gotta let Ronny know about our new herd." He turned his wheelbarrow around and got half way to the house when he stopped and looked back. "Why don't you bring one down for Ronny to see?" It was more of a command than a request.

Ralph Johnson came down from the house on the hill and slid in next to the pen with his arms hanging loose and staring at the six piglets.

"They look small don't they?" he said.

I nodded. "They're just babies."

He picked one up and cuddled it. Then he held it away from him. "Something's crawling on it." He held the piglet in one hand and picked something off it with his other and examined it up close. "It's some kind of bug."

"Probably pig lice," West said. "You need to de-louse them."

"How do I do that?"

"I don't know. You took on the job for the money. Maybe you need to find out."

Ralph picked them each up and examined them. "They've all got lice."

"They've been living together," West said.

"I guess I'll do it in the morning when it's lighter. They'll be alright here for the night."

"Ronny's wanting to see one. Why don't you take one down to him," I said.

"With these lice on it?"

"Sure. A pig farmer has to come in contact with pig lice sometime. Just as well be the first day he gets them."

Ralph hesitated—standing there holding the pig at arms length—the pig with his ears perked, snout moving, eyes blinking—then he started toward the house with the pig in his outstretched arms leading the way. He backed through the partially open door and we heard the commotion.

Rose chased him out of the house with the pig still at the end of his arms.

"You get rid of those bugs before you bring anything like that in here again."

West and I smiled.

I guessed it about right. The next morning Ralph had his hands full de-lousing the pigs with some flea and tick powder West used for Ladd, getting them fed and getting a small shelter for them to gather in when the weather was too hot for their skins or to cold for their little bodies.

West and I finished the morning's work and made it to dinner a little after noon. Paul was listening to the Chicago stock report. He and Ronny cheered every time they heard the hog report. It didn't make any difference if the radio announced sow's bellies, or hogs or pork sides—they took it to mean their own enterprise and even though the piglets were still suckling on a bottle half the time, they were a future they had never had before and they whooped and hollered. Paul threw his head back and pounded on the wheelchair arm. Ronny yelled something and jolted his left arm and leg into the air. It didn't take much to set them off when it came to hogs.

West smiled at me and I chuckled.

"Maybe we can buy in," West said.

"They selling shares?" I said.

CHAPTER 22

The calf season was closing out and it was a good thing. West and I had our knives honed down to thin strips of metal. We kept up with the skinning pretty well, but we had over two hundred hides in the freezer that we hadn't had time to salt. Rose hired Johnson's oldest boy, Robert, to salt them. While his folks were gone to Astoria to visit Olive's parents, he stayed home from school and salted hides.

The boy sharpened his knife in preparation to cutting off the tails and ears. He made violent motions with the stone and ended by striking the steel with the rusty blade a few times then ran his thumb down the edge and grabbed a hide. West looked at me after hearing the knife strike the steel so hard.

"The boy is learning to sharpen his blade," I said.

West smiled. The kid looked at us but didn't change expressions. He was about fifteen years old and thought he was pretty well versed in the ways of how to do most everything.

He grabbed the ears and sawed with the knife through the hair until he had worn them away from the hide. His next assault was on the tail, which he eventually won.

He had salted about ten when West said, "How much you getting to salt?"

"Ten cents," the kid said.

"A hide?"

The kid nodded.

West turned to me and shook his head. "She show you how to salt?"

"Yeah," the kid said.

We went back to our skinning and out of the corner of my eye I saw the kid watch West sharpen his knife and then try to follow it. But he still sawed the ears off and it was getting the best of him. Even day-old calves have thick hide on the head.

"I'll cut the ears and tail off for a nickel," I said.

The kid smiled. "Give you two cents."

"Two and a half?"

"No."

"Wait till you get up tomorrow morning and you'll make it two and a half," I said.

He sawed some more.

"I'll sharpen your knife for a dime," I said.

"Okay."

He handed me the knife. While West smoked, I put an edge on the old knife and steeled it so fine that it shaved hair on my arm with the first pass then handed it back to him.

"I think you could make more charging him a dime every time you sharpen his knife." West said.

We were finishing the calves that lay on the floor when a truck drove up with eighteen more, bawling, bumping into each other and scared. It backed up to the corral gate and a heavy set middle aged farmer with a protruding stomach covered by his overalls got out the drivers side and climbed up into the bed of the truck. He picked up a calf by the flank with one hand and a leg with the other and threw him off the truck.

"Hey," I yelled. He raised his head. "Don't be throwing those calves off the truck like that."

"Why not? You're gonna kill 'em anyways." He had a wide grin.

"That's right but we'll do it our way."

The grin left his face. "And I'll unload them my way."

He threw another calf to the ground. It landed in an awkward way and tried to stand. Its left front leg was broken. It cried in a small voice as it struggled to stand on it and stumbled each time it gave way.

"I told you to stop that. Now knock it off." My neck felt hot.

"You want these calves or don't you?" He pitched another over the railing.

The boy had gotten out of the front seat, his hands jammed in his Levis and he walked over to the edge of the floor. I was wiping the blood from my wrist and between the fingers. He pursed his face.

"If I couldn't find something better than that to do I'd be a bum," he said.

I wiped the blood off my knife and instead of returning it to the sheath at my waist, grabbed the point between my thumb and first finger and with a sideways flick of my wrist, sent it flying toward the shed wall. It turned once and stuck in the wood behind the winch handle. The kid could have touched the handle without moving. I wiped my hands. My breathing escalated.

"You crazy sonofabitch!" his old man hollered. "Watch what you're doing or I'll ram that knife down your throat!"

I looked up, my blood hot from his treatment of the calves. "You and who else?"

"Just me, punk!"

"You're a little old for that kind of stuff, aren't you, fatso?" I dug it in hard.

"Why, you little..."

He jumped off the truck and I walked to meet him. The blood rose in my neck. I wanted to bust his brain in with the kill pipe. We met across the calves and his first swing caught me thinking about decking him myself. It was hard enough for an old man, but it didn't hurt me. I let him have one in the belly and drove it in and at the end I pulled it up into his diaphragm. His body didn't move but his stomach did. There was a whoosh sound as air erupted from his lungs. He made one more swing and I hit him in the heart with another right. He didn't go down but he stopped. I backed off and saw the kid reaching for the knife in the wood so I hit the old man again, a good one, and he went down in a sprawl across the calves.

The kid had the knife and was looking at his Dad on the floor breathing hard. West handed me his knife. We looked at each other trying to determine how far this was going to go and then the kid stuck the knife in the wall and helped his old man up. They left with the kid driving.

I handed West his knife.

"You shouldn't have done that," he said.

"I didn't like him throwing the calves off the truck."

"They were his calves. We hadn't bought 'em yet."

"I don't care. That's no way to treat a calf."

He motioned with his outstretched arm at the many calf bodies lying on the concrete floor at our feet. His eyes and silence begged me to see the irony in my statement.

"Ah, hell—it all started when I stuck the knife right where I wanted it." I said.

"You couldn't do it again," he offered.

"A bottle of beer on it?"

He nodded.

I retrieved the blade and stood about where I was before and let it fly. It hit handle first and bounced on the cement.

As usual after I made a bad display of manners it came back to eat on me. I couldn't for the life of me figure out why I had flipped over the edge with the young farmer and his dad. He was acting badly with the calves, in my opinion, and then I escalated it into a brawl that didn't make sense for any of us. I looked for reasons and found them all around me.

CHAPTER 23

We finished skinning the new calves and sat down to rest. "I'll take my beer now," West said.

"Yeah—right," I said with a chuckle.

We sat and he smoked until Rose called us to dinner.

It was a lousy dinner. Rose was doing the cooking while Johnsons were gone and while we all knew she could cook up a storm, she claimed she didn't have time to do any real cooking. She peeled carrots and put on a loaf of bread and some lunchmeat and that was it. West opened a can of tomato soup. The soup was hot and we ate our sandwiches in silence with just the muted sounds of eating and Paul's incessant foot tapping to remind us we were all there in a room.

After the short dinner, West and I walked out together.

"She offered to sell me some mink, cheap," I said. "What do you think?"

He shrugged his lean shoulders. "If you can get anything cheap I suppose it's a good deal."

"I mean—what do you think about the business?"

"You know how I feel about the mink, Jeff. If they're run right there's money in them. But if you run them like this place is run," and he gestured to the old house with the roof sagging and the pile of tin cans weather-beaten behind the house and the ugly mink sheds and the muddy driveway, "why, I wouldn't get them."

"Yeah, I suppose." What had started out as a short spell to make some money and not spend it on luxuries was turning into a convoluted life choice. If it wasn't for the joy I got out of working with West and the occasional mental wrestle with Paul, I'd leave in a heart beat. Especially if they'd let me take Ladd.

I looked at the mink Rose had offered to sell me. They were small females bred to good males and could promise some fine kits. Buying them meant anchoring me in the same place for a spell. I thought about the green hills I had come over and the whip of sea wind at my neck and the bubble laden froth blown off the wave crest and then about staying put in this place. Eating and sleeping in this place every day—same people, same scenery, same sounds and smells—it wasn't my life style.

The old man went down to the barn, the one he had built by himself. It was standing proof that he could take raw lumber and nails and concrete and design and construct a building that served his purpose. I left the mink and flailed through hordes of flies all the way to the slaughterhouse.

The sunshine had brought the flies out of wherever they had been hiding to survive the rain. I felt slow in the fresh heat. I took off my shirt and hat and splashed a little cold water behind my neck. My blade was still sharp so I only steeled it and dragged a calf over to skin.

I looked up and saw Rose standing at the edge of the kill floor tapping a cigarette on the back of the package, looking at me with eyes squinted and a partial smile like she knew a big secret.

I straightened up. She put the cigarette between her lips and reached under the sweat shirt for her matches.

"What's the matter between you and the old man?" she said as the short smile crept over her face. The match flared and she looked away from me as she touched the flame to the tobacco and took a big draw. I waited for her to blow the smoke out before I answered. I had to think about this one.

"Nothing," I said. I picked up the steel and moved the blade across it twice. "Why?"

She assumed a superior let-me-tell-you-something attitude and her face took on a half smile. "Came in last night saying you had accused him of being the father to Jane Wyler's kid. He was drinking pretty heavy."

"Me?" I said. "I don't know anything about a Jane Wyler or her kid."

She went on like she hadn't heard it. "I know he wasn't the father of that kid. I know genetics too well for that." Her cigarette burned smaller.

"You don't understand. I don't know anything about a Jane Wyler."

She went on, "Two blond, blue-eyed people don't have a brown-eyed, dark-haired kid. I saved his face over that one. Mrs. Wyler called me up and said she was getting tired of doing Jane's work for her while she and my old man were out in the barn. It got so that every time my phone rang everybody on the line picked up their receiver." There was a perceptible shift in her voice. "Tell you what I'll do, Jeff. I'll give you a Platinum male if you convert him."

I didn't want to look at her but I did—watched her eyes grow hard.

"Number one," I said. "I've never heard one word about Jane Wyler. I don't even know what you're talking about. Number two, I haven't been a Christian very long myself. Number three, I don't think I'm equipped to try it."

She went from jovial and self assured to demanding and convinced. She leaned forward and in a harsh tone said:

"Oh you know well enough. Go ahead. Make him confess his sins. Make a Christian out of him and then you'll learn the dirty filth he pulls on his family."

Her vehemence took me off guard. She looked quickly down at the house and I heard the Buick car start, loud without the muffler on it. A cold blue cloud of smoke settled in the driveway area as the car disappeared down the hill. She turned back to me.

"Where's he going?" I asked, hoping I wasn't going to be alone all day with Rose in this type of mood.

"He never tells me where he's going," she said.

Her eyes bored into me trying to find the answer or a spark of belief for her story and I wondered what I showed to her. After what seemed like a minute she lifted her head, crushed out her cigarette and blowing out the smoke walked away to the mink yard. I began to breathe again and my gut relaxed like cold honey flowing out of a jar.

What kind of a buzz saw was that? She had run West down many times but she hadn't hissed and sucked in air—and her eyes—they looked like grapes being squeezed. How come I was always in the middle? I never heard Ralph talk about being in the middle. I hated it.

I skinned and the calf pile grew. The flies buzzed while I tried to get my mind around Rose's latest accusation. As I pondered the new Jane Wyler twist the Buick swung up the driveway and stopped and West got out, lit a smoke, and walked over to me.

"Hi," I said, and he nodded.

His hat set down low on his head and I couldn't see his sideburns or any hair at all. I grabbed his hat and lifted it off. His hair was there but what was left must have been left purely for seed value. His smile drew clear across his face pulling up the slack skin on his jaw and we laughed together.

"Kinda close," I said.

"It's the only hair-cut I'll get for a year so I told him to make it a good one." He took back his hat and set it on his skinned head. It slipped down to rest on his ears. "Got something else."

"Something else?" I said, thinking he may be ready to confess on Jane Wyler.

He nodded. "Bought a bull."

I straightened up and started to smile. "A bull? What kind?"

"Hereford."

He put on his apron while he was talking, pulled on his boots and set his hat on a sack of feed. He took his knife from the shelf and started steeling it.

"What do you want with a bull?"

"I think there's pasture enough now to raise a few more cows. A good bull will save me money. I can rent him out to others too."

"Where is he?"

"Guy's gonna deliver him in a couple a days."

I shook my head. "Isn't that something?"

West stretched to pick up the whetstone.

"I hear tell that you need to be a Christian," I said. "And you need to quit messing with Jane Wyler—whoever she is."

His lips parted. "She tell you that?"

I nodded.

He kept smiling and stoned his knife pushing it away from him on the stone and then drawing it back.

"I'm more of a Christian than she is," he said. "As for Jane Wyler," he shook his head. "I don't know how long that story is gonna live."

"Probably live as long as there is life in it..."

He butted in..."Jane's been over here a time or two. Always to pick up some extra milk or bring us a few vegetables from her garden. I think her ole lady started that rumor for something to do."

I took on a lawyer's persona. "So, for the record, you are stating here and now that you are not the father of Jane Wyler's child, is that true Mr. Helner?"

He caught the tone and raised his right hand. "True your honor."

"And that you are not now or ever have been in consort with Miss Wyler."

"What does consort mean?"

"Diddling. Have you diddled with Miss Wyler?"

"What does diddled mean?"

"Oh for crying out loud..." I said.

Rose hollered from half way up the driveway. "West, Ronny needs you."

He laid up his knife, dried his hands and walked down to the house, shuffling, shoulders bent, arms swinging.

She took his place and I could feel her eyes on me. She was nodding her head when I looked at her. "I've tried to get him to go to a psychiatrist. He's unstable." Those words hung between us." Three prominent people told me to get my things in order, that there is some skullduggery afoot." She glanced down the driveway.

"You know you hear a lot of things about Jack from the old man but the real reason the old man hates him is because he bought a saw and some tools to help with the pens. If you did that he would turn against you the same way."

I straightened up. "Do you think Jack will come back?"

"I don't know," she said. "Sometimes I think the old man killed him. He just disappeared. West says he's wanted on some check charges or something but he always paid everything in cash. He doesn't have a checking account."

"You're talking present tense there."

She laughed. "Guess I am, aren't I? Well, he's probably somewhere."

Down at the house the door slammed and you could hear the shuffling sounds of West slogging in his rubber boots up the hill to the slaughterhouse. She stood there a bit longer then turned with a scowl and sauntered over, opened the gate and evaporated into her mink yard,

She had to see that her pounding me with West's perceived faults were not taking. That he and I worked well together shared each other's chores and enjoyed the company. It seemed like she was poking her sword toward me trying to find a chink in my armor. Maybe I was flinching and she thought she had scored a point or two. But to what end?

West looked back over his shoulder at her. "What did she tell you now?"

"Said you need a head doctor...a psychiatrist."

He expelled a short burst of air that I could barely hear. "Like I've said, I'll go when she's ready to go with me."

We laughed and he finished honing his knife and we skinned together with the faint scent of the new cherry blossoms drifting in now and then with the fresh breeze that began from the west then shifted to the east, crazy wind, shifting, unsettled.

CHAPTER 24

I thought about buying mink for a week. There were arguments on both sides and Ladd heard them all. So did Rassel. Rassel had some good points on why not to do it and Ladd had no opinion at all.

When I'd start talking to him he would be very animated, lift his head, smile, wag his tail and look at my eyes like he understood everything I was saying. He would only do that for a minute or so and then he must have concluded that what I was saying wasn't worth listening to and assume his usual resting position with head on paws, jaws shut and eyes half closed.

The arguments were ones I had made since the end of college. Being stuck in one place wasn't a fun energetic thing for me to think about. This mink business was seven days a week and long hours during breeding, kitting, and pelting. There was the occasional 100 calf day thrown in to see if you could take killing that many new born calves even though you knew they were doomed whether you killed them or not. Also being bent over for hours, hands and feet covered with blood with a constant prayer in your heart that you would be able to straighten up again later in the day.

Then there was the financial part. With only six mink I couldn't sell any the first few years to recoup expense money. I'd need to save them all to be breeding pairs. And what if some of the kits weren't really good breeding stock? Pelt them and go to market with five or six mink skins to sell; a waste of time and money. I'd have to get Rose to take them with hers to make any sense at all.

And of course, the emotional part of being here. I'd be tied in with Rose and her shenanigans for a few years. Nuts. Yet—the figures that West and I put together in our heads and scratched on the ground during breaks looked good. There was an outside chance that given four or five good years of breeding and keeping the kits alive to adult- hood I could have a nice annual income that would support me while learning how to write. And if that didn't work, I could always sell the live mink to another farmer, take the proceeds and do something else. That gave me a window to leave early if I really didn't like it.

But in spite of the negatives I had come to love the little animals. They had a positive attitude. They knew what they were about and with no hesitation pursued their life wherever they were. The fact was they lived in the moment. They were always interested in what you were doing near them. There was no history to ponder, no future to consider. If they bit you on Monday they forgot it before Tuesday. I thought I had those same qualities until I started working here and writing in my journal.

In the end I justified to myself that it was only delaying my return to college for a short while. Enough time to get the cages built, the mink started, doing it right with West's help. It was exciting—to think about having my own mink.

Dwelling on the lock-in of having the mink soured me so I quit thinking about it. I looked ahead to the increase in my herd and the financial boost they would give me. Being able to go out every day and walk around my mink—healthy, happy, breeding, bright eyed and bushy tailed. I believe whoever thought up that phrase must have been looking at a mink when he coined it.

In the end after days of debate with myself, Ladd and West, I bought five females and one male from Rose on the agreement that she take out $25 per month from my pay check until they were paid for; I would build my own pens and surrounding fence with an entry gate and all; and pay five cents a day each for their feed.

"What do you think?" I asked West.

He nodded his head. "Sounds fair."

"That's what I thought." I scraped the mud from my boot with a piece of shingle. "You want to teach me how to build a mink cage the right way?"

He lifted his head and the smile started. "The right way? I can do that."

I settled on a name for each of them but decided that would make it too tough at pelting time.

ON OUR NEXT TRIP to town with a load of calves for the freezer we stopped at the lumber yard. While I was counting the $100 I had brought with me, hoping it would be enough for the wood and wire, the yard man led West and me to the piles of lumber that would best work for the cages. He left to do other work while West picked through the pile and laid the ones he wanted aside in a neat stack. I watched.

This was work he enjoyed. He was always busy running his hands up and down the wood, squinting his eyes along the edge to see if it was straight, bending it to see how flexible it was. Then he would stack it in our stack or put it back in the pile.

"How many cages do we need, Jeff?"

"Six."

He nodded, counted the wood stack, stood back and assessed it again. "We got it."

We hauled the lumber back to the cashier, picked up the wire and staples and a few steel posts and loaded them in the truck.

All the way back to the farm, West had a smile on his face. "We can build some right good pens with this material."

"I sure hope so. I'll never hear the end of it if my mink get out."

He nodded. "We lose several every year."

I swallowed knowing about several that were missing. I hated to know that and not be able to tell West. I had promised Ralph that I wouldn't say anything. And he might have gotten them back. There had been no more mention of them missing.

"How long will it take us to build these...doing it in the evening?"

He thought a minute. "About a week. Maybe could do one a day."

"How much am I going to owe you for your journeyman labors?"

"A six pack of beer and a bottle of Jim Beam." He turned his head towards me with a half smile creasing his face. "That fair?"

"I guess."

WEST AND I HAND shoveled a level place that would hold the six pens and allow room enough to walk on all sides of them. I drove the steel posts in each corner and strung the wire and by the end of the seventh day we had a first rate enclosure that would be the nursery for my up and coming mink ranch.

Paul had worked his way over to where we were with his wheelbarrow. "What you going to call your mink ranch?" Paul said.

"Jeff Baker Furs," I said.

"Humph. Sounds kinda snooty don't it?"

"I hadn't thought about it. What's this place called?"

"Helner Mink Farm."

"I like furs better than farm. I'm gonna leave it."

Paul snorted then took a couple of minutes to get a pinch of snus in his mouth, working silently until his tongue had moved the tobacco where he wanted it and his uncoordinated hands had pressed the lid back on the can and deposited it in his overalls pocket.

"How many did you get?" he asked talking around the snus.

"Six."

"That's not enough. You should have gone into the hog business with me and Ronny. That's where the money is. If times get bad you can always eat the pigs."

"I'll grind up your pigs and feed them to my mink."

He laughed. "I doubt you'd do that."

West was standing off to one side looking at the completed cages and fence. "Now don't those beat anything you've seen in there?" He lifted his chin toward the mink enclosure.

"Sure do," I said. "But they're brand new. We'll see how they look in a year or two after the mink have been chewing on 'em and the weather has had its way."

"They'll still be good. We built them the right way." He put one hand in his pocket and looked off to the hills. "I reckon this means you'll be around for awhile longer."

I took a good breath and looked at the sky. "It does say something about that doesn't it?"

He turned to me and smiled. "I'm glad."

"Yeah. Me too."

I clapped him on the shoulder, letting my hand rest there a moment. The three of us were each looking at the new cages with our own eyes. West who designed them, cut and mitered the wood, and instructed me in how to fit the wire over the frame; Paul who really couldn't see them but knew enough about it to consider their utility, and me. I was happy to have it done and to move the mink in. I admired the way the old man had stuck to building them what he called the right way. A couple of times I would have opted to short cut some of the gluing and stapling but West kept me in line with our original plan.

After supper, Rose came out and inspected them. She stood back and crossed her arms over her chest and smiled. "They look real good. Real good. When do you want to celebrate?"

"Celebrate?" I said.

"We can move the mink in the morning but we should celebrate now. I brought the celebration materials. They're in the house if Ronny hasn't gotten into them."

Paul snorted and rose up off the wheelbarrow. Everyone started toward the house and I followed. The supper dishes had been cleared away, the Johnsons had gone up to their dwelling and Ronny was holding a bottle of beer in his better hand. He had a smile on his face that I had not seen since the Seven Devils Road trip. He waved the beer at us, then found his mouth with the neck and took a swig. He belched. Paul thought that was the funniest thing since the mouse ran over his legs on the couch.

Rose opened the refrigerator and took out a six pack of beer. She set it on the table along with the bottle opener. Then—as I was trying to make sense out of this—she reached into a cabinet and brought out a bottle of Jim Beam whiskey.

"A little celebration," she said. She handed down some glasses and opened a tray of ice.

West took off his hat, put it on the hall tree, smoothed his hair and sat down. I sat down opposite him. I wanted to see his eyes and face as this celebration went on.

"West told me what you promised him so I just picked it up when I was in town yesterday." She handed me the sales slip. "Didn't think you'd mind us sharing it."

"I sure don't mind," I said. I looked at West. He was concentrating on pouring a half glass of Jim Beam over two ice cubes. Paul had a beer opened and was pouring a little whiskey in a glass. He was going for a boilermaker. I knew that drink from the motel work and it could take a good man off his feet in no time. Rose poured an inch of whiskey in a glass and swirled it around.

"Here's off to a good start on your mink, Jeff," she said.

She lifted her drink and the four of us clinked glasses. I turned to Ronny sitting on the couch in the living room.

"Ronny—here's to your success getting that beer down."

He raised his left arm and leg and laughed. It was a good thing he had swallowed the mouthful of beer before he did that or it would have gone all over him.

The whiskey was something new for me. I sipped it and let the sour mash taste spread over my tongue and gums. The first swallow made my head and shoulders shudder. "Wow," I said.

Paul laughed. "Jeff—do you like it?"

"I don't know. I'll let you know when my head comes back on."

"You'll get used to it," he said.

West took one swallow at a time seated back in his chair, legs crossed, with a smile on his face. He was staring out the window into the dark night.

The talk was about mink, the fur market, what to expect from the summer fur auction. We played a few hands of hearts. West had to take Ronny to the bathroom after he drank his beer and Paul went to sleep in his wheelchair after downing his second boilermaker. Rose, West and I played cards until I couldn't keep my eyes open and headed for bed about 10:30.

Ladd was under the trailer waiting and as soon as I opened the door he was in for the night.

"I gotta teach you to open the door," I said. "That way you could get in here and get to sleep early. Be ready to go fetch the cows in the morning."

He was on my bed turning in a tight circle getting ready to flop down when I caught him.

"Down," I said, and pointed a finger at him. He regressed to puppy tricks to deflect my displeasure. He rolled on his back with his feet in the air, grinning and crinkling his eyes and turned up the corners of his mouth. His tongue lolled out over bared teeth. He was a parody of all subservient human beings who have had to be persistent to win.

"This is not negotiable," I said in my most authoritative voice.

His response was to lie on his belly with his head between his front paws, his rear in the air, tail wagging. Each of us having stated his position, we remained thus with his tail ticking like a silent pendulum. I was defeated. He clearly understood my reluctant "Ok," and finished his curl, tucking his tail under his chin and claiming his portion of the bed. He chose well as I found that I could, by positioning myself across the bed from corner to corner, sleep in comfort with his assured warmth on one side.

Bought six mink. Good and bad. Means I'm here longer than I'd planned but it could give me a financial boost when I move on. Ronny, Paul, West, Rose and I celebrated with Jim Beam and beer. It was a small riot. Two handicapped kids drinking reminded me why ancient tribes brewed beer to lighten the load of living.

CHAPTER 25

About two weeks after our night of drinking and card playing the day started pretty well. The pressure from the old
pump was lousy in the morning but it had enough oomph to
squirt on my legs when I moved it and when that cold water hit
my pants I felt like tearing the hose apart with my hands. Rose
was talking baby talk to the mink as she wire brushed the old
dried meat off the top of the pens. "Nice mommy...don't bite...
that's a good girl...where's your hay? Poor mommy, no hay for
her." She finished one side and came over where I was watering.

She hadn't said a word to me yet that morning and I didn't
feel like opening the conversation.

She started with a sideways glance, eyes narrow and a swing
of her head that I disliked. "Ever see a man dying of thirst?"

"Booze or water?" I said.

"Well, booze."

"Plenty of them."

"You should have seen the old man last night. He was about
to die of thirst until I told him to go ahead and have a drink. He
opened some beer and never even offered Ronny some."

"Ronny's really going after that beer, isn't he?" I said.

"He likes liquor to stop his pain. It keeps him quiet if he drinks a little, but he's afraid of it. Won't take any pills either unless he knows what they are—afraid of becoming a drunkard or a dope addict."

"Ronny seems to have gotten worse since I've been here," I said.

"It's the ole man makes him worse!" She picked a string of rotten dried meat off the pen top. "I wish you could have been here last night. If you could believe one of his dirty lies after that...him and his damn dirty mouth. Wouldn't help Ronny off the bed until I called him the second time."

"Really?"

She looked at me trying to decide whether I was serious or making fun of her. "You damn right. My attorney is gonna write him a letter. A peace bond. That was the last straw. His mother said when I married him not to wait on him and by gawd I'm not going to any more. If he breaks his leg again he can just lie there and die for all I care, before I'll wait hand and foot on him again."

She stopped and I shut off the water and moved to the next aisle. That left her alone scraping pens and I could hear the scrape...scrape...of her brush. She was hating West and learning to hate me. Hating me because I wouldn't believe. And I had started to believe—but it was West I was believing.

There had been no time to just work and get to know the people. They were shoved at me from day one. I took naturally to West. They were both competent people in their work yet she banged on him every chance she got with me. I never asked Johnson if he got the same treatment. In fact, Johnson was a second stringer who only got sent into the game when he wasn't sick, wasn't in town, and there was something to do that he knew how to do by himself. Neither West nor I wanted to work with him.

The pump didn't improve the pressure and it took three hours to wash out the pans and fill them with fresh water. I walked down to the pump house to turn off the water. The grass was getting thick in the pasture and I wondered when West was going to turn the yearlings out.

A small garter snake slithered out of the grass and wiggled across my path. I drew my skinning knife, mentally counted the paces between us, compensated for the twisted blade of the skinning knife and threw it with my wrist flexing, giving the blade a good twist. The knife turned and stuck catching the crawling snake at mid-body. It kept wiggling but remained fixed in place. I bent and pulled the knife out. Blood and strings of innards squirted out of the slit. The snake coiled up with his little black tongue spitting out at me and threatened to strike. I wiped the blood on my pants and threw again. The point hit the snake behind the head and pinned him there, separating his head from his squirming body. I walked down and turned off the pump and came back for the knife. I pulled it out and sheathed it watching the dead body writhing in the sun on the green grass.

They say snakes don't die until the sun goes down but it didn't move after two o'clock. I began to feel bad about it. Garter snakes helped around a farm. They ate slugs and toads that you didn't want in your garden.

Sometime I had made a choice to enter into this killing game. From the calves and mink and fish and now a harmless garter snake. I had hunted before and knew the brief hunter's thrill of taking a rabbit or deer. And I ate them. I didn't eat these things; I just killed them for something else to eat or to take their pelts.

I found that hard to square with how I felt about life. My years of trapping, when I would skip school to check my traps hidden in the hills, were always half thrill to have caught a rabbit and half shame to have killed it. We ate the meat and I tanned the hide. The two seemed to balance out but always the thrill of jumping an animal in the hunt was matched by the depression of seeing it hanging dead, stripped of its hide and horns, chest propped open with a pine branch to cool. I decided I wouldn't kill any more snakes. But then I flip-flopped and thought my knife was a fair weapon to kill a wiggling small animal like that.

West was skinning when I got back from shutting off the pump. He looked up and smiled.

"What you smiling at?" I said.

"Johnsons are leaving..."

"Really?"

He nodded.

"I'll be damned. I didn't think they'd ever leave."

West just smiled.

"Where are they going?" and then as an afterthought, "Her Dad's?"

"Yeah."

We both felt real good about their leaving. Rose always said he did more work than the two of us and now with his leaving she'll have to see that we were doing all the work while he was here.

The gut truck pulled up the hill in compound gear and backed up to our barrels which we had filled with calf guts and feet.

The driver slid out of the cab. "Howdy, boys,"

"Hi."

West stepped over. "How about you coming a little more often in these warm months with these maggots?"

"They bother you, do they?" the bright-eyed driver said.

"Get to smelling up the place," West said.

"I think we can make it," he said. He nodded at me. "You learning the business?"

"Oh, yeah. Even bought some mink of my own."

Rose opened the screen door and called up. "Ronny wants you, West!"

I helped the driver lift the barrel of guts and dump them into a box in his truck.

"What do you know about this place?" I said to him.

"Why?" He said, a perpetual smile on his face.

"Just wondering whether anybody feels the way I do or not."

"How do you feel?" he said.

"You tell me first."

He pushed his red-billed cap back on his head and took a drink out of the hose, wiped his mouth and smiled. "Well, at first they all said the old man wasn't worth a damn. Heard it from Paul and the old lady and Jack. I didn't meet him for quite awhile. He was logging somewhere around."

"Yeah, he was logging out back," I said, pointing up into the hills.

He shrugged his shoulders. "So I figured the old man was no good. Now that I know him, I think he's the only one that's worth a damn." He flashed his smile again.

I chuckled. "What do you know about Jack?"

He turned on the hose and washed his hands. "Jack was hard to figure. Sided with the old lady all the time. Likeable guy though. "

"You any idea where he went?"

He shook his head. "He just disappeared. Some guys say they've seen him in town but I've never seen him again." He coiled up the hose and hung it on the wall hook.

"You don't have to stop talking when I come up," Rose said. She had walked up quiet while we were talking and we hadn't seen her.

I turned. "We just happened to be through, Rose," I said.

"Jeff," she looked me squarely in the eye. "My hearing's too good to know you just stopped. You heard me and quit talking and you know it."

The driver just smiled at her.

"You're crazier than hell, Rose. We were finished and we didn't even know you were there!" I said.

She gave me that look I had seen her reserve for kin folk. That burn-you-in-a-wagon-full-of-hay look. Then she walked away, a cigarette dangling from her lips.

"She gripes me," I said.

"Don't let her get you down," he said as he stepped on the running board.

"Yeah...easy for you to say."

"So long." He let the truck slide down the driveway and popped the clutch to start it.

Something was coming over me. Before I came here I didn't sass people back but now I was learning how to do it with a swear word or two thrown in for good measure. There was a time that a false accusation would have rolled off my back. Even getting jailed on the coast when I knew I wasn't a vagrant or wanted for something hadn't teed me off like her suggestion that we quit talking because she was approaching.

I took a deep breath. I was forgetting my roots in this place. Whether I stayed another week or finished my commitment of four months, I could sell my mink and go down the road. Yet the idea of having an income was firming up in my plans and raising mink was something I could do while writing, in or out of school. I had grown fond of the little critters, considered

myself a mink rancher, and looked forward to seeing West every
morning.

THE OLD MAN AND I exchanged glances a couple of times at
the supper table. Rose caught our last one and threw a burning
look at West. The Johnsons were talking about their trip and I
didn't want to listen, so Ladd and I left the house and walked
up on the hill behind the place. We went quite a ways in the
evening light and standing on the last high hill, we saw the sun
drop into the ocean. In the fading twilight we turned around to
trace our way down over the trail through the new trees past the
corral and into our yard.Ladd was with West during the day a
lot more lately. The old man sort of worked on him. He would
kick him and hit him, but he always had a free hand to pet him
and the dog started getting the cows sometimes. It looked like
maybe there was some understanding between them on the
farm work now that the new dog had come.

CHAPTER 26

West came out and we finished the calves. I threw the bodies down on the concrete hard.

West looked up. "What's the matter with you?"

"Oh, she as much as called me a liar!"

He straightened up. "You know what she said last night?" He didn't wait for my answer. "I was carrying Ronny to bed and Paul said something about Johnsons leaving and she said, 'Now Jeff will have to work'. I told Ronny, by gawd, Jeff was working."

"The hell!"

He nodded.

"Listen, West. "Next time she tells you anything I said, check with me. I'll tell you the truth. She's trying to drive a wedge between us with tales of what the other said. We can beat her at her own game."

He nodded again, his head bobbing through the collar of his blue work shirt.

In a couple of hours Olive called us to dinner and I went down even knowing I couldn't eat. Rose calling me a liar and implying that I didn't work had my stomach tied up like a net full of rocks. Rose acted like I wasn't even in the room. That suited me fine. I had no courting to do with her.

"No appetite?" West said.

"Hell no." I pushed the plate away and went out.

"Now what's the matter with him?" I heard Rose say as I went out the door. I spun on my heel, stomped back in and stood with my hands gripping the back of the chair, shaking like a young kid. Blood was pounding in my neck, my breathing, short and shallow. I exploded.

"In my entire life I have never been called a liar. If you think I'm a liar you should fire me now... right now!" I slammed my fist on the table rattling every dish. It startled Paul. He flinched and looked up at me. Everyone else found another place for their eyes to rest.

Rose began humming and removing the food items from the table. Bit by bit the others took up their utensils and returned to eating. The humming continued as if she was alone in a garden somewhere completely removed from the present situation. I stood, awkward, not thinking about my next move.

Paul put down a carrot and chunk of meatloaf he had in his hands and started to clap. His smile, slow to start, twisted his lips upward and grew until his palms began to meet regularly in front of his sightless face and his feet lifted and fell on the thin wooden floor long scared from chair legs, wheelchairs and dog claws, creating an overpowering din of clapping and foot stomping. Ronnie joined in from the couch. His gurgling yell, mouth open, yellow teeth exposed, blended until it sounded like an indoor football rally.

Rose halted for a moment, her back to the table. When she turned around she took charge. In two steps she was behind Paul and grabbed his wrists, one in each hand, and slammed them on the table breaking his plate, pushing her chest against his back, her weight trapping his arms. Paul's smile vanished.

Her weight on his back forced his head down until his nose rammed the table.

"Gawd dammit...cut it out," he said.

West looked over but didn't move.

She was silent, her face tight. The determination that had built the ranch was showing in her. With all the years that Paul had pushed his wheelchair I thought he had the strength to resist. He struggled, arched his back and pushed with his legs, but with her weight on his wrists he couldn't move them. Defeated, he stopped moving his feet. Ronnie, with no vocal support from Paul, ceased yelling and in that split second the walls absorbed everything. Paul turned his head until one eye was above the table top. He struggled twice and then rested on the table. I could see him relax, surrender and give in.

That was all it took. Rose was back in control and life would go on as it had before. I went outside, apparently unfired.

West came wandering up and down the aisles looking for me.

He sat down on the cart, pulled out a cigarette and took a deep puff before he talked. "Hungry?"

"No."

He rolled down a sleeve and buttoned it. "Nice try in there."

"Didn't do any good."

"Maybe not. But you didn't get fired either."

"At least I had Paul and Ronnie on my side."

"Yes, and that's making it hard for everybody—this choosing sides."

I scraped dried feed from my fingernails. "Not my problem."

"It could be. With Johnsons leaving there'll only be us to pick on."

Suddenly an idea hit me. "Let's get out of here, West. Let's hook up that trailer and go fishing somewhere."

He snorted. "And what would you do with your mink?"

"Turn 'em loose."

He snorted again and flicked the ashes from the cigarette. He let my suggestion die. It wasn't a good one but it was an honest one for the moment. We sat looking toward the river.

"Ralph's going into town this afternoon so we'll have to finish in the slaughter house," he said.

"That's alright with me," I said. "Who gives a damn?"

He smoked like he had a year to finish one cigarette. A cow bellowed in the barn and he looked in that direction like he could tell from here if there was any reason for her to call.

"Guess I'll turn the yearlings out in the pasture tonight. Looks like it's going to be spring now for a while. Grass is good."

"Yeah, real good," I said. "What are you going to do with the bull?"

"I need to build him a better pen. The one I've got may not hold him. May need to go up and cut some logs to make it pretty stout."

"How big you gonna make it?"

"Couple dozen logs ought to do it." He was looking at the hills as his cigarette burned down to his fingers. He dropped it at his feet and stamped it into the ground.

"Let's get at it," he said.

I chased him in the cart.

We went down to the gate. I rode the cart, switched to full power, and rattled down to the slaughterhouse. He stopped behind me to pick up a hide that one of the dogs had dragged out. We suspected King but we never saw him and you couldn't punish a dog for something until you caught it in his hand, or mouth as was the case.

"If you ever catch him with a hide, beat the hell out of him with it," West said.

I nodded, knowing that was the accepted way of breaking dogs of doing something people didn't like them to do. People

and dogs...people and bulls...chickens, hogs, ducks, geese, cats...
do what the master says.

He threw it on the hide pile and I started putting the
grinder together. Everything smelled like fish. There were so
many flies that their humming provided a background noise for
everything we did in the slaughterhouse. The hides were covered with the little black, shiny-winged creatures and when they
flew off they left a coating of minute, cream-colored eggs. The
eggs turned to maggots in a few days and then the whole place
crawled.

Some flies hung suspended in mid-air then moved about
like hummingbirds to hover somewhere else. West sprayed
water through the air trying to get rid of them but as soon as he
stopped spraying they were back.

I put the grinder together and looked up to see King grabbing another hide in his puppy teeth and starting out the door.
West threw a loop in the hose and using about six feet of it like
a club, swung it up over his head and brought it down across
the dog's ribs. King yelped, dropped the hide and limped off.
The old man smiled. I didn't say anything. Just sat there on my
haunches wondering why everything had to hurt around there.

I BROUGHT OVER A calf, the flies buzzing out of it as I moved
it from the nail. I could see the liver was almost eaten away and
a large blob of eggs was about to hatch on the kidney. West
didn't look at the calf as he ground it.

The second calf didn't smell good to me and I laid it across
the grinder. West pulled the front legs apart and what we saw
almost turned our stomachs; the whole insides eaten out and
thousands of maggots infesting it from the lungs down to the
bung...piled on top and eating each other. I threw it out on a
box. The pile on the box grew to three before we finished grinding.

"Price of meat gets high at this rate," I said.

He looked up at me and said, "I've seen calves lay there and rot when Jack was here. He'd haul them down to the river and throw them in, hides and all. She won't admit it, but I saw it." He looked at me like I didn't believe him.

"We pay too much for them anyway," I said.

"The fella here buying hides..." West hoisted a bag of meal to his shoulder and dumped it in the mixer..."He said we shouldn't pay more for a calf than the price of the hide." He looked a bit questioning.

"Counting the labor and all," I said. "Wouldn't be cheap meat even at that."

He smiled. His smile always meant something to me. It was his way of saying, "What I say is right, don't you think?"

Maybe it was. Sometimes the old man was a hard guy to figure. He would sit with smoke half closing his eyes and pet a dog and then he would hit him with all his might with a hose and brass nozzle. He would tell me how he would run the ranch and then forget he had told me and tell me again the next time the subject came up and I could never bring myself to tell him he was repeating it. Maybe it was so prevalent in his mind that he forgot that he had ever told it because it was always there, and each time it seemed new to him.

He would thank me for building pens for the few mink I had bought because, as he said, "Jack never built a pen or a nest box as long as he was here and I held that against him and if you wasn't to build a pen or nest box then she could say that right back at me." Then the next day he would make me mad for having mink when I said, "Why don't you put a pump down on the river bank and use that water if you get so short for mink water?" And he said, "You and her is the ones that got the mink, why don't you do it?"

Funny old man. So alone and passed by. In the logging camp he had been part of a group of men who worked together, drank together, and daily put their lives on the line knowing the other man would do his job and keep them from harm. It was his family six days of the week. Here, he shuffled through the day doing the best he knew how and satisfied himself that that was enough but never satisfying her. His day began and ended with choices dictated by the needs of others as though his independence was suspended until such time that he could satisfy them all. I didn't want to add to that burden.

We finished the grinding and mixing, loaded the cart and fed. It took a long time to feed because we gathered up all the old feed and fed it to the hogs. Of course, I wasn't involved in the hog business, but it seemed to me that we spent a lot of time saving the left over mink feed to feed to the hogs; time that really wasn't returned in the growth or profit of the mink.

We used to throw the old feed on the ground. And under our feet, the cart, and the usual rain, it got stomped into the soil where it came from in the beginning. Occasionally we had rats and mice in the mink yard going for what we threw down but they had to beat the rain to it. The rain took everything.

I watered and finished out the last two rows of mink feeding. We killed all the calves but one roan that West wanted to save to suckle on his fresh heifer.

He tied a rope around the calf's neck and started out towards the barn letting the rope unwind until it reached the end and jerked the calf off its feet. The calf looked around, its large infant eyes unperturbed. West backed up and pulled on the rope. The calf skidded over the gravel a little but wouldn't rise. The old man leaned into the rope but couldn't budge it so he wrapped it around himself once and bent over, planted his right leg, and with his arms straightened out behind him, pulled hard. He sic'd the dogs on the calf and they commenced biting, snapping and barking.

"Come on Ladd, sic'um, boy."

The dogs snarled and bit the hind legs. The calf jumped up, planted two feet out front and jerked backwards with all its might. The rope that West had wrapped around himself proceeded to unwrap like a string on a top. He spun around twice and fell on his side.

He smiled without letting the cigarette fall. He got up and, facing the animal, pulled hard on the rope, which he knew and I knew and the calf knew, was no good at all. At the precise instant West was pulling the hardest, the calf relented, and sprinted past him. Unbalanced, his arms shot into the air, one leg straightened and rose off the ground. He struggled, fell backwards, but hung onto the rope. When the calf reached the end of the line he bowed his head like a Brahma bull and pulled West past the old Plymouth car that was sitting on blocks.

"Hang on, West," I shouted.

What a day.

CHAPTER 27

Last night's rain dried up today and the mud cracked along old lines. The sun washed the hillside clear and green and a turkey buzzard swung back and forth across the evening sky, tracking for dinner.

I looked down again at the three calves almost crawling away with maggots. Rose had given me instructions to bury them. "Too far gone," she said. It seemed to me that the maggots should have carted the calves away so I wouldn't have to bury them.

Made me look around, think about the whole farm. I looked around for a place to bury three rotting calves while we added pigs and cows and a bull to the mix. I wondered if the maggots could crawl out from the grave I would dig and then I thought of something they wouldn't crawl out of.

I pulled the box with the calves and maggots behind the slaughter house and piled it on top of the paper sacks and wood scraps that had accumulated there. I drenched everything with two gallons of gasoline, stood in the doorway and threw a lighted match at it.

There was a whoomp. The explosion hit me in the chest like a linebacker and about knocked me out of the doorway. The whole pile of dead calves, paper sacks, wood scraps, green and dead grass and limbs of nearby trees were enveloped in fire. I watched the maggots writhe, turn brown and shrivel; the dead calves broil, bubble and spit, then black and char. A jaw fell off. One carcass burned in half. The smell was sickening—sweet, bitter, repulsive.

I watched it, punishing myself by inhaling the acrid air swirling around the perimeter of the fire. They had rotted on my watch. I wasn't any better than Jack. Ladd had bolted when the pile exploded and now I went to look for him to take a walk in the cool evening and purge my lungs of that smell.

THE NEXT MORNING IT was all burned out, just jutting skulls with bits of charred meat clinging to them, skeletons scorched a black with little wisps of smoke curling through the eye sockets. I smelled them smoldering away for days.

It rained but I watered the mink anyway. The rain was dripping off the brim of my black hat turning the water dark in the mink cups. The rain didn't stop and neither did I. I heard a truck labor up the driveway but nobody called me so I didn't go over.

Rose came up the aisle through the drizzle and I saw her motion me over inside the shed. She was shaking mad all over.

"Did you clean the water pans?" she fired at me.

"Those that were dirty," I said.

"Did you put penicillin in that sick female's pan?"

"Of course I did." Something else was on her mind and I knew it would burst out any minute.

She sputtered like she couldn't control her speech. "Did you hear what West said to that farmer just here?"

"No," I said. "Too far for me to hear anything."

"He said, 'can you help a man that's starving to death?' He meant that sexually!"

"Come on, Rose. I don't get that out of it."

"Isn't that a hell of a dirty thing to say?" she said.

"Yeah—but I don't think he meant it that way. Why would he..."

"Because he would. He did. He's no damn good."

I shrugged my shoulders. She had it all figured out in her head anyway. She shook the droplets of water off her shoulders, readjusted her rain hat and was off, her feet stomping in the mud, wrath dripping from her mind to her mouth.

By the time I finished watering the rain had stopped and I looked up at the clouds moving fast across the hills with little blotches of blue sprinkled with gray and black. King let out a little bark and I saw him dashing back and forth between a couple of old discarded pens and then I saw him and Ladd playing with something that moved.

As I walked over, I noticed a small starling huddled against an empty box. "Get, King," I said and sent a kick his way. He ducked and laid his ears back. I picked up the bird. Its lower beak hung loose and disjointed. Left leg and wing were broken and the little black eyes glistened as I took my finger and pushed its lower beak up to meet the other. But it fell back and the little eyes blinked. I could feel it hurting.

I cuddled it in my hand and for the first time since I had become an adult I felt a growing compassion for a small living thing. The bird's heart rate subsided and its eyes half closed. I had the power of life and death over this creature, but somehow it trusted me.

This is crazy. We've got a hundred of these starlings around here and none of them do us any good. I kill a hundred calves a day and grind them and feed them to the mink and here I am debating about the life of a starling that is so wounded it is going to die in a few minutes.

I walked through the slaughter house to the back wall, said a small prayer for the starling who looked at me with that lower beak hanging like a broken hinge, and hurled it against the wall. It hit with a fluff of feathers and left a blood spot on the board. I picked up the dead bird and felt the broken creature. I threw it hard against the wall again. My pity gave way to my daily occupation of killing and it was just as real, just as far down inside me, to let my blood race when I struck calves and before long I was hitting them in the head without even full awareness of what my hands are doing.

My breath came in jerks and I felt weak. I had the power to take life from animals like God has the right to take our lives. Am I a God? But it was in pain...broken up...better dead...oh merciful one...healer, benefactor, and gracious killer. Hell.

I went back in and picked up my knife. My thoughts were about the bird on its back, wings unfolded like a small fan, eyes closed, lying on the earth where moments ago it had soared above it.

Finally, I laid the knife on the shelf, took a shovel and walked back outside and found a clean grassy knob where I turned over a spade full of dirt. The bird lay at the bottom of the wall where I had thrown it.

It hurt to feel again the warmth in my palm, the silk touch of feathers on his breast; all the dead gentle wildness that but moments ago were his. I laid him in the hole, arranged his legs and wings and put a small stick under his broken lower beak to hold it together. The blades of new grass waved with the ground breeze like a hundred small green flags. I tamped down the edges, took a deep breath and left the burial ground.

ROSE CALLED ME TO supper and I left ten calves un-skinned.

"What ya been doing, Jeff?" Paul asked as I stepped in the door.

"I buried a dead bird. King found it on the ground and the dogs worked it over pretty good."

"It die?"

"I killed it. It was pretty well beat up."

"Wish you would have brought it in for us to see."

"I'm sorry, Paul. I didn't think about it."

"Well—maybe next time."

"I hope there isn't a next time."

It was pretty quiet during supper and I worked hard at forgetting about the bird and the calves and everything to do with this place.

Paul started his sales talk as soon as the supper dishes were cleared.

"Well, Jeff," he said.

"Well, what?" I tallied.

"When you going to buy a razor?" He looked sightlessly in my direction.

"Strictly a straight-edge man, Paul, no electric razor for me."

"Those are old-fashioned. You need a new one." He persisted.

"How much?" I said.

"Twenty-four dollars."

"Can I trade in my safety razor and my straight edge?"

"I don't know if we can take them or not," he said.

I laid my hands on the table and stood up. "Well, if you won't I can't afford to buy one."

"I'll find out..." Paul said.

"Okay," I said.

I NEVER HEARD ANOTHER thing about buying an electric razor although he sold Ronny a new one and for awhile he thought about adding that to his growing hog farm business.

The idea of having a dual career was energizing for him but when he only sold one electric razor he decided to stay with the hogs and go back to punchboards.

"Where's that punchboard that wasn't finished, Mom," he asked one day.

"I don't know," she said.

"I have to get those punches sold or give back the people's money that already punched," he said. But he never did find it and he never sold any more punches. He sent away for some all-occasion cards that he would sell for a dollar and a quarter a box.

Guessed I had come to the end of my time there. My thoughts couldn't come together and my feelings—my feelings were all over the place. I had to corral them from time to time to avoid going crazy. Rose was pretty normal during breakfast but before going to work I had to have a talk with myself to steel me against what might come. Had to be ready for anything It was like walking on egg shells. More uncomfortable now that I had my mink to consider.

CHAPTER 28

She yelled and backed away. "Hold on to him!"
The young male mink jumped from my grasp and now hung by his tail from my left hand, reaching for anything he could grab with his front feet. I grabbed his back with my right hand and pressed him tight against my apron. She maneuvered her hand between his flanks.

"Gotta feel his testicles to see if they've dropped. If they don't drop he'll be sterile."

I nodded, feeling strange about this woman massaging a male animal's parts while I was holding him.

Her glance skirted the area around the pen while she felt his testicles. "The old man's a sex fiend. He'd blow his top if he heard me say breeding or testicles to another man." Her eyes looked away from me when she said it.

"He's okay," she pronounced and I stuck him in his pen.

A man walked up the driveway with a calf in his arms, a young calf— legs longer than needed and wide eyes taking in the new sights and sounds. Another man followed him up the slight hill with a smaller spotted calf cradled in his arms. Rose laughed at the sight of a man carrying a calf from nowhere, and I followed her over.

West stepped out of the freezer.

"Where do you want these critters?" the man asked, a little winded.

"In the corral," Rose said.

The man dropped the calf and took a big draw of air. West offered him a chew of tobacco. The man took the plug, looked for a corner that hadn't been chewed off, and bit down.

"Thanks."

West nodded and returned the plug to his pocket.

"Hey, how'd you get here?" I said.

"Took the boat across the river. If I go by road it's about fourteen miles." He was a big, lean man and beneath a day's growth of whiskers his jaw muscles flexed as he moved the tobacco around. His eyes landed on West's Plymouth sitting in the weeds.

He turned to West and pointed at the gray wreck beyond the fence. "What do you want for your old Plymouth car?"

West stroked the hairs at his throat. "How much is it worth?" he said.

"Oh...ought to be worth ten dollars."

"Who wants it?"

"My hired man needs some part off it."

A half smile broke over West's face. Memories of where he had been with the car, people who had been in it and his eternal dream of getting it running again must have gone through his head while he maintained a rhythmic stroking of the white hairs that grew haphazardly from the skin on his neck. The stroking, like a pacifier, served to promote good thinking, decision making, quelling of dreams long ago abandoned to reality.

"Yeah, it ought to be worth ten dollars," West said.

"It's got the wheels and motor on it, doesn't it?" the man asked.

"Got the wheels, but no motor."

"No motor?"

West shook his head.

"Well, hell...then it isn't worth ten dollars," the man said and that ended the talk on cars because he could see that West didn't want to sell his old car. He wanted it around, like the big, gray house that frowned down on the valley with shuttered windows and doors that were warped and swung in the wind. It was his estate: the unfinished house, the old Plymouth car, a few cattle, one bull, and his pasture.

"I heard you shooting those mud hens yesterday," West said.

"Those damn things," he said. "They eat every blade of grass on forty acres if a man lets them."

West nodded. I pulled up a chunk of wood and sat on it enjoying hearing the man and the conversation.

"We killed about a hundred," he said.

"Eat them?" I asked.

"Hell, no. Don't think they're fittin' to eat, do you, West?"

"Oh...if a man was hungry enough, I guess they'd do."

"I suppose so."

"Ol' Baker calls them government chickens. He shot a couple hundred on his place and the state cops were out there threatening to arrest him and he told them by gawd if them government chickens was gonna eat his pasture out he was gonna shoot every last one of them."

West nodded.

"Well—gotta be getting home. Got some fence to fix up."

"She'll pay you when you go by the house," West said.

"Okay...so long. Thanks for the chew."

West nodded. He sat there with his legs crossed and his hand still at his throat pulling long white hairs, chewing tobacco, spitting on the mud. Time stood still as the men drifted out of our sound range. We could see them at the door and see Rose pay them, but the sound was gone. The buzzing of flies in the slaughterhouse was the only noise we picked up. It was like a total cessation of the day. Maybe the sun stood still as well, I didn't look at it. When the men walked down to their boat and Rose let the door slam and the dogs lay in the driveway with their heads on their paws the thought occurred to me that I would never get any older. Time was over and so was my life. No sooner had that thought come to light than I wanted to get the hell out of there.

"Let's take a load of calves over to the freezer before dinner, huh?" I said.

West looked at me and then turned on his seat and looked at the calves hanging on the wall. "How many full of maggots?"

"I don't know, but they all will be if we don't get about fifty over there.

"Okay."

I loaded the calves while he went in the house for something and I was ready to go when he came out. He took the wheel and that truck really moved down the road. He wrapped her up to about sixty when we got on the highway. I kept looking in the mirror to see some blue Chevrolet police car streaking behind us but the old man was lucky that way.

He stopped and backed the truck into the freezer room entrance and we sat looking across the street. In the bar across the street, visible through the window, a black man was playing the pin ball machine. That was the second time we'd seem him when we came in with a load of calves for the freezer.

"He seems to be playing pin ball every time we come to town," West said.

"Maybe that's his line of work," I said.

We both stared through the windshield across the street, neither of us moving.

"She'd probably blow her stack if she knew we were sitting here like this," I said.

"Yes, and her and her old drunk would go to town half a day and let the calves rot and then throw them in the river," he said.

He paused. I waited because I thought he was going to go on. I was right. He continued.

"She told me the other night that three prominent business men had told her to get her things in order, that I was trying to get the mink."

"She told you that?" I said.

He nodded.

"She told me that too and for me to keep my eyes open because there was some skullduggery afoot."

"She can't see that her drunks is what got her in debt and that my chasing them off kept her from going so deep she'd never get out," he said. "One guy told me I'd better get a pistol and carry it 'cause Jack said he'd get the mink if he had to kill me." "Course her stars tell her Jack is a good man," I said.

He smiled. "You know—she usually reads me my horoscope for the month and it's usually no good and then she reads the good about her. I didn't hear anything about the stars last month so I looked around and found the horoscope and you know what it said?"

"Probably that you were the greatest," I said.

"Hers said, 'let your mate have more say in affairs and his judgment is often better than yours.'" He smiled. "She reads only the good stuff on her and only the bad stuff on me."

I shifted my weight on the truck seat and put my foot up on the dash board. "Nobody ever heard from Jack again?" I said.

The look in his eyes when he turned his head threw me for a minute. "He's dead."

"Dead? Really?"

He nodded.

"For sure you know that?"

He nodded. "Alcohol killed him."

"How do you know? Other people have been saying he just disappeared. No one's seen him or knows anything about him."

"He's dead." He looked out the windshield and pulled on his neck hairs. "I know it."

"Well I'll be damned." My curiosity got the better of me. "How'd he die?"

He looked at me, his steel gray eyes hardened with the talk, then looked away. "He choked to death on his own vomit."

I shook my head. "How come nobody else knows this?"

He pursed his lips and shook his head from side to side.

Must have been several minutes before either of us talked or moved. Finally I opened the door, stepped out on the running board, grabbed my gloves and opened the freezer door.

We stacked the calves in the freezer and closed the tail-gate of the truck.

"You want a beer?" I said. "I owe you one for my missed knife throw."

"Okay!"

WE LEFT THE TRUCK parked in front of the freezer door and walked across to the bar. It smelled soft and punky, and of spilled beer. The black man we had been watching put two beers on the wooden counter. They were in frosty mugs.

"Been watching you play the pin ball machine," West said.

"Oh," the bartender said.

"We were loading stuff in our freezer across the street."

The bartender tossed his head in understanding.

"Can you make any money doing that?" West said.

"I can't. We've got a guy who comes in here and claims he's ahead fifty bucks but I doubt it. He drinks so much I don't think he could keep track."

The phone rang and the bartender went to the other end of the bar to answer it.

West took some time nursing the first half of his beer. Then he tipped it up and downed it in one good, long drink. His smile stretched from his lips to his eyes, the skin crinkled in around the edges from sun and wind and age. He looked like he felt good. So did I.

Seemed like a good time to get another question resolved. "Ok—who's Jane Wyler?"

He smiled but didn't change stroking his neck. "She's a neighbor. Over beyond the Swenson Dairy."

I stuck my tongue between my lips and waited. He turned toward me, "Why?"

I shook my head. "Nothing. Just heard about her the other day. You friendly with her?"

"Hardly ever see her. They used to bring calves here when they were running cows but I haven't seen her for years."

"Were you friendly then?"

"Enough to say hello and goodbye."

"On the driveway or in the barn?"

He smiled. "What are you gettin' at?"

"I think you catch my drift."

"Oh—her kid? I did take her in the barn once to show her our milk cow. We were only in there a couple of minutes. I couldn't have undone all the buttons on my overalls in that time. No—I think she got that kid from a logger on their place. Looked a lot like him anyways."

"Another beer?"

He shook his head. I paid and we walked out into the hot sunshine over to the truck.

We hummed out of town and raced down the straightaway. He slowed down to cut the noise level some and asked, "Does your Pa take a little whiskey or beer now and then?"

"Used to," I said.

"All my family does," he said. "And there ain't one of us a wino. Oh, I've got a brother that drinks whiskey, a bit in the morning and when he comes home at night, but nothing to get drunk about." He shifted down behind a logging truck on an uphill grade.

"Feller told me once, he has a drink or two on Saturday and that's all he needs for the week, but if he don't have that one drink on Saturday, he's no good the next week. It relaxes him so's he can rest proper." He looked at me and smiled. "I like a beer or two in warm weather, and now and then I like a drink of whiskey in winter time. But I'll go sometimes two, three weeks, maybe a month without even thinking about a drink."

WHEN WE GOT HOME Ralph was salting hides in the little shed. He looked up when we came in but didn't say anything.

I killed twenty calves and West and I skinned, throwing the hides in to Ralph. The winch motor pulled them off fast and they piled up higher than the door and faster than he could salt. I saw him look at us once out of the corner of his eye. Somewhere a kid screamed. West straightened up and stepped bent-legged to the front of the slaughterhouse.

"What you kids hollering at?" He yelled.

No answer.

Ralph's voice came out hollow from inside the salting shed. "Haven't seen a kid yet that didn't holler."

"Well, they ain't gonna holler like that around here," West said.

"I know I made a lot of noise when I was a kid," Ralph said. West let it drop.

We heard her call above the whine of the winch. A big, coarse, "It's on." We washed up and stepped out of the cool shed into the hot day. All the way to the house we walked with our legs spread, straightening our backs and letting the tingle work out of our bones, letting the bent nerves quiet down.

CHAPTER 29

The house was stuffier than usual. Not a draft of air. A curtain hung over the living room window giving the room a gray pall. Olive hadn't cleaned up yet so I washed my hands over a plate of carrot and potato peelings sitting in the bottom of the sink.

West and I sat down. Paul was already eating and Ronny, for the first time since I had been there, had a plate with meat, cucumber, and a half an avocado on his lap. He sat in one corner of the davenport—his blind eyes revealing nothing. His mouth revolved slowly, masticating the meat he had bitten off. There was grease and gravy on his new beard and mustache. It was like watching a zoo animal that had just been fed.

When Ronny took a big bite of the avocado, I couldn't watch anymore and let my eyes drift down to my plate. I could hear him chewing. I put potatoes on my plate, the steak, bread and honey, corn with little red and green peppers, and poured milk. I tried to pray while other thoughts raced through my mind.

I couldn't think of a prayer. I could only listen for Ronny to breathe...(breathe, Ronny...now...now...NOW) 'Our Father, bless us this day...(breathe, Ronny...for God's sake, breathe) 'bless this food to our bodies...(aren't you ever going to breathe?)...

Ronny started crying his low, body-twisting, heart breaking cry, the avocado oozing out between his lips in a green, bubbling mass that slowed and crawled into his beard as he writhed around. He coughed and spit the green ooze on the davenport and across the rough floor.

I knew he wasn't trying to breathe and I couldn't do anything but sit on the edge of my chair waiting to see if he would choke to death. His face grew darker and he bent forward. Rose rushed out of her chair, spilling her coffee. She grabbed his left arm and lifted it high and pounded him on the back with her other arm.

Slowly his head came up and he coughed again, spitting bits of meat and avocado over the floor. She raised his arm higher and he sucked in a quick breath. There was a long second before he expelled it, then he let out a long, loud cry. He sucked in another short breath, still crying.

"I want to die!"

"What's that?" Rose said.

Ronny took another breath. "I want to die!"

She flung his arm down and yelled in his face only inches away, "Cut that gawd damn nonsense out—you hear? Just shut that up right now!"

My guts drew in tight. I stopped chewing the bread in my mouth. I didn't want to swallow it. I never wanted to swallow anything again as long as I lived. I was sure I could feel an ulcer beginning. My mouth watered and I tried to breathe in a simple unforced rhythm but the breaths came in irregular hitches and gasps. West twisted in his chair and looked at Ronny sitting on the davenport not breathing, green mouth, harsh eyes, pulling his knees up to his face and wanting to die, wanting never to wake up in this world again, wanting with all the power that remained in him to destroy himself.

West poured some coffee. Then he stood up and slammed his spoon down. The spoon chipped the plate and bounced to the floor. He started to pick it up and looked at me like he wanted to say something, then smashed his boot down, flattening the spoon, turned and walked into his room. I could hear the springs squeak as he lay down. Judas, it was hot in there—hot air—hot breath—burning. Ronny sat stone still, his curled up body looking for all the world like a flesh colored mannequin.

Rose picked up the newspaper and sat at the other end of the couch. Paul ate on, turning his head after each bite of food toward the window and chewed, looking out with dull eyes.

I tried to swallow that one bite. The problem was that I needed to think about it enough to swallow it. I finally washed it down with milk. Everything was stone quiet and I began to wonder if I had dreamed the whole episode.

Paul looked at me and started a conversation like the world was in its ordinary state. "It won't cost as much as I thought, Jeff,"

"What?" I asked.

"That ham radio I was telling you about."

"Oh."

"I thought it was five hundred..." he paused waiting for me to answer.

"How much is it?" I said.

"A little over four hundred for a good set. If you want to go overseas, you have to have a DA."

My stomach relaxed. I could feel the knot unraveling. There wasn't much I knew about radios, but I was willing to talk about anything else, anything at all.

Paul and I talked about ham radio sets. In the living room it was like nothing untoward had ever happened. West came out of his room and I stood up and took the opportunity to follow him out through the door into the yard.

I caught up with him. "Ronny wants to die?"

"Yeah," he said.

He turned away and walked into the freezer. I wished I could believe that he really didn't want to die. I walked over to the little pool that filled a hollow in the grass and lay down beside it. Ladd followed me.

I lay there petting Ladd when West came out of the freezer, looked my way and then came over and sat down. He lit a cigarette. We sat that way for quite awhile. Ladd moved over to him and West petted him. They were getting closer. A man like him just takes to the free love of a dog even if he has to whack him from time to time.

"Rose says I gotta get rid of Ladd," he said.

I jerked my head around. "Why?"

"Chasing sheep."

"Can't you break him of that?"

"Tried. It doesn't stick with him very long."

"Man—I'd hate to see him go."

"She thinks King is a better guard dog." He looked at me with a half smile on his sad face. "She wants to guard against someone stealing the mink, I guess."

"I haven't seen anyone sneaking around lately, have you?"

"We are missing three mink."

I looked at the ground and pulled some grass. Didn't want him to see my eyes.

His left hand worked at rubbing King's ear.

I put my arms behind my head and looked at the sky that was trying to stay clear of clouds—a tough job for an Oregon coastal area. Being young and free had a lot of advantages. I could hardly put myself in West's position. How much time did he have left in this world? What would the next ten years bring for him? I tried to imagine myself at his age until my thoughts crossed trails so many times it just blurred out.

"What do you figure on doing with your time?" I said.

He looked at the hills and took a deep breath. "I don't know. I look for Ronny to die in a year or so and then I'll leave. Go somewhere I can hunt and fish when I want. Take that little trailer and Ladd. I got some money in the bank—enough to do that." He was looking at the river below, just talking—just thinking.

"You like the coast?" I said.

"Yeah, I like the coast. I'm getting too old to work alongside a young fella. My feet are too slow. They won't hire an old man when there's younger fellas." He sat still and smoked. He could sit so still you'd think he was formed out of some kind of clay that looked human like, something other sculptors had not found yet.

That afternoon we went to work later than usual. Rose didn't come out of the house until late and then she went to town, and we just did what needed doing. I hauled manure from the mink yard to the pile outside. I made a game of seeing how many wheelbarrow loads I could get to stack up before the pile collapsed and tumbled down.

I had just emptied the wheelbarrow, when a fog of burning rubber drifted out of the slaughterhouse to overpower the fumes rising from the manure pile. West whirled—pretty fast for an old man's feet—and turned off the power to the mixer. Ralph frowned at West. "Gotta mix that kelp in there real good."

I ran to the mixer. There wasn't enough material in there to wet the big spoons.

"You got any cereal?" West said.

Ralph took two steps backward. "No, but it's coming."

"Then leave the damned thing turned off until you get it!"

Ralph untied the strings on his apron and threw it on the floor. "You can mix the feed then for all I give a damn," he said and walked off.

I looked at West and shrugged.

"He's leaving tomorrow anyway," West said.

"For sure?"

"For damn sure!"

Well, that was good news. It made me feel real good on several accounts.

A car drove up with calves. I went in the house to get the money.

I said "Hi," to Paul.

No answer. I turned to Ronny.

"How you doing, Ronny?"

"I'm still alive," he said. He talked better this afternoon.

"That's good."

"I don't think so."

"What do you mean?"

"I'd rather be dead."

"Don't be crazy. You don't know anything about it."

"Ha...I wish I could die."

I took the money from under the clock and closed the door behind me like I was leaving a church. It was as quiet inside as a confessional.

Rose drove up with the cereal. We finished mixing the feed, fed and watered the mink and went to supper. It was over none too soon for me. I went to the trailer and read. My reading kept getting interrupted by thoughts of the old man and his land and the new bull he was getting. The moon was coming up when I quit reading and wrote a short note in my journal.

Ronny saying he wanted to die brought a new focus onto the farm. Instead of it growing and living it started to feel like it was not

*meeting the needs and goals of the people on it. His day has to be less
than good. How does he move out of that cage and have any kind of
life? Then look at the burden for Rose and West. Now—a new bull
coming and Rose wanting to get rid of Ladd. It is not good to get
attached to things.*

I PROPPED THE DOOR of the trailer open the next morning
and took a good look at the new day. Little tails of mist were
drifting up from the wet ground through the trees and dis-
appearing into the pale, blue sky, the sun playing peek-a-boo
behind light clouds.

King wiggled his tail and hind end while he walked up the
little path toward the trailer, his lips uttering little whimpers. I
patted his head and he laid his ears back and snuggled up closer.

I didn't see Ladd anywhere. I walked over to breakfast.
Halfway through a pancake, West looked out the window
toward the house. "Thought I saw Ladd coming," he said.

"You really gonna get rid of him, West?" I said.

He looked at me, but Rose answered. "Maybe he won't have
to. Maybe somebody did it for him."

"How's that?" I said.

West stuffed another bite of pancake into his already-full
mouth.

I waited for his answer.

He chewed with patience. "I sent him for the cows and he
went right on past and headed for Bill Freck's place. A little bit
later I heard some shooting," he said.

Rose cut her pancakes in small bites. "That damn dog does
no good here now. King guards the place better than he does."

I REMEMBERED ONE DAY when we had worked especially hard
and were taking a five minute break sitting on the boxes outside the slaughter shed, West lit a cigarette and Ladd nuzzled

his hand. Slowly he scratched his ears and the dog closed his eyes and leaned into the hand and knee. The smoke curled up around West's face and his eyes wrinkled and his hand moved in slow dragging circles around Ladd's ears and head.

Another day Ladd came in hungry, his legs matted. West knew he had been running deer and he cursed him for it. Ladd lay down, his eyes searching for understanding, flickering back and forth from West to me. West cut a big chunk of meat from a calf's hind leg and laid it in front of Ladd.

ABOUT NOON WE HEARD another shot and our eyes locked. We went to dinner with no sign of Ladd and I wondered and waited. Then I didn't wonder any more because I saw him standing on the hill looking down at the house. He moved in a painful hobbling walk.

I ran from the dinner table out to meet him. There were little tufts of red dyed hair on his shoulder and left side. I saw where one shot had torn his mouth and looked inside to see the lead planted between two teeth and sunk deep in the gum. Two other shots had gone through his lip but missed his teeth and went out the other side.

My pocketknife was sharp and he didn't whimper. He just sat still and trusted. I pulled back his lips and picked at the imbedded shot, dug at it with the point of the knife until it came out and fell into my hand. Ladd lay down and licked my boots. He knew, somehow...I don't know how, but he knew.

I leaned back against the peeler wood. Sweat was running down my forehead. Ladd lay very still until we heard a shout in the house, muffled by the thin walls, then the door swung open and Rose walked out with a rifle in her hands. She came straight toward Ladd and me.

"Get away!" she yelled to me.

"What for?"

"I'm gonna kill that sheep-running dog!"

"Like hell you are!"

"Don't interfere in my affairs, Jeff. He's my dog and you got nothing to do with it!"

West came out of the house behind her faster than usual. As he moved toward her she lifted the rifle.

"No!" I yelled. I raised my arms and rushed at her, my eyes focused on the muzzle.

Ladd was limping towards the trailer when the blast smashed my ears, a fireball concussion that kicked me off my feet. I rolled and felt my chest to see if I was hit. I sat up. She levered in another shell. West stopped some feet behind her, his arms hanging straight down, shoulders hunched, jaw agape, staring. She fired again.

The old man balanced on his skinny legs for a few seconds with a look of puzzlement on his face. His chin sunk to his chest and he turned and shuffled up to the barn.

I went up to Ladd. The muscles quivered under his skin, then he stiffened, his legs going out straight, toes separating. He opened his eyes when I spoke to him but closed them again and panted in short wheezy breaths. He whined once and opened his eyes. His panting stopped. I stood up.

West was coming from the barn with a shovel over his shoulder. I stepped back. He stretched out his old man arms; his knees bent out to the side and picked up Ladd. He adjusted the weight between his arms and looked at me, tears running down his cheeks. I watched him until he reached the open gate of the corral. It was a tough climb for him carrying a dead dog that hung over his arms.

I went to the trailer and pulled out the blanket that I had used for Ladd's bed, took it outside and shook it. My eyes began to water and my nose plugged up. I folded the blanket and put it on the floor of the closet. Then I lay down on the bed, my mind a jumbled mess. I tried to think about each thing one at a time but I couldn't pull it off. Pictures of Ladd popped into my head like a dandelion releasing its seeds. They just rose and disturbed whatever I was thinking and I couldn't settle down to it again. Him chasing deer and drinking out of the pond up on the hill; lying on the blanket under the bed; the look in his eyes when he was on the bed and knew he shouldn't be; how he closed his eyes and laid his head back when West stroked him. It was hard to write in my journal but I felt I had to do it.

Rose shot Ladd today. She could have shot me and West too for that matter. Things die around here all the time and I'm part of it. I could have stood in front of Ladd but I didn't. My mind is so jumbled up right now I don't know who I really am or what I'm doing here—or anywhere for that matter. Things have to clear up.

I don't know if I cried or not but my pillow was damp.

CHAPTER 30

After breakfast West hovered over Paul's wheelchair. "Paul—you wanta go to town with me?"

"What for?"

"Need some lumber for the stanchions."

Paul sat silent, probably remembering the incident over the snus. With a lift of his head he said, "Yeah. Get my jacket will ya?"

Ronnie began moving on the couch. He made some sounds with his agitated movements.

West looked at him. "You can't go, Ronnie. I gotta take Jeff with me to help load it and there isn't room in the truck for four of us.

Ronnie deflated like a balloon and returned to the inanimate skeleton of a human who lived his life on the couch and in bed.

Going to town was a break for Paul and me. No calves to process for me and some new sounds and smells for Paul.

West backed the truck under the roof overhang at the lumber yard. He took a bite off a tobacco plug, put it back in his overalls pocket and slid out of the front seat.

"We won't be long, Paul. You OK?"

"Yeah."

West closed the truck door and moved toward a stack of lumber in the yard. Fresh cut lumber smells drifted across the gravel driveway: fir pitch, pine tar, a faint odor of turpentine. The pleasant orderly stacks of lumber reminded me of sawmills along the coast and I breathed it in.

West stopped in front of a short stack of 2x4s, stooped and curled his big hand around one end. He lifted it to eye level and glanced down it while running his hand along the edge. He turned it over and bounced it to check its flexibility. A large knot halfway down the stick negated its flexibility and he laid it back down. He picked up another, using the same process. When the piece bowed in rhythm to his flexing a faint smile formed on his lips. He set it aside.

"Think I'll need about twelve, don't you?" he said.

"Don't know, West. What are we building?" I said.

"Stanchions. When I get the bull I need stanchions for the cows. They won't stand still with him around the barn."

"You're serious about a bull?"

"Yes, I am."

"What else do you need?"

"Some 2x8s for the top and bottom. Probably eight ten footers."

"They're over here," I said.

He finished sorting the 2x4s then began on the pile of 2x8s. Same process but many more discards. After he had separated eight of them that met his criteria he stacked them together and called the yard man over.

"Hi, West. Whatcha need?" he said.

West nodded at the pile of 2x8s. "Need those eight 2x8s and that stack of 2x4s over there," he said inclining his head toward the other pile.

The guy lifted up the top two boards and grinned. "West—you high graded me on these. You took the best boards out of my pile."

"Need 'em for stanchions. Can't be rickety."

"I know, but I can't let you have the pick of my crop at the same price as the sign there says. I'll have to charge you a little more."

West nodded at the sign. "Price doesn't say for which boards."

"Well—that's true but it's for the pile. You high grade all the good stuff out of here and I'll have to sell the left over's at farmers' grade. Doesn't work out for us very well."

"I'm not in the business of making it work out for you. I'm wanting a board that will stand a six hundred pound bull ramming into it without breaking at a knot."

The yard man took the pencil from behind his ear and wrote on a pad he took from his apron pocket and we all listened to the pencil lead scratching. When he finished he checked his figures and stuck the pencil back behind his ear and showed the pad to West.

West chuckled. "I guess that's not so bad." He reached into his back pocket and took out a can of snus. He opened it, twisted off the lid, and held it out to the yard man. After they had each deposited a pinch of snus—which I declined—in their lips, they went into the office to settle up.

Paul was chewing snus and trying to get the window open to spit when I got back to the truck.

"Hell's fire, Paul. Let me help you with that."

"I can do it."

"Well, you're sure a long way from getting it over the running board."

"Just wanta get it out the window."

As I was rolling down the window, he spit. It hit midway on the glass and oozed down in a brown stream.

"See," he said.

I shook my head. He couldn't see it. I went into the office to the bathroom, got a paper towel and wiped it off.

We loaded the lumber on the truck, tied it down, and West started her up. I hopped in the right side. "Move over, Paul."

West looked over at me. "We own it now." He said a big smile on his usually dour face.

"Yes—I guess we do."

We rolled out the gates and onto the highway and I had to say what I'd been thinking. "You know she's gonna be mad spending this money on good wood for your bull."

"My money. My bull."

"I know, but..."

"How about we pick up some ice cream?" Paul said.

"Ice cream?" West said.

Paul nodded and turned to me. "Would you like some ice cream, Jeff?"

I looked at West who was looking straight ahead through the windshield. "We don't have any money for ice cream," he said.

"You had money for wood, why not ice cream for me and Ronny?"

"We just don't and I don't want to hear any more about it."

Paul crossed his arms, sat silent a moment, and then in a slow exaggerated explosion spit his whole wad of snus on the windshield.

I took a deep breath. The nerves in my back shivered and I put my head against the back of the cab holding the tension at a level I could handle as I waited for either to speak first, thinking West might swing a fist and smack Paul.

West paid no attention to the spittle running down the glass and into the air vent on the dashboard. He continued driving like we were on our way to a picnic.

I felt for my wallet thinking I might spring for some ice cream but I had left it in the trailer. There would be no ice cream.

She would be mad about the lumber. Of that I was sure.

I turned my head toward the side window. My side of the truck smelled like wet snus.

CHAPTER 31

The Johnsons left with a big honk of the horn from their car with the heater and the radio and white sidewall tires. Stuff was piled high on the top of their carrier with a gray tarp roped down over it. They stopped for coffee and cake at the house with Rose before they went and she gave them their check and a mink pelt for a present.

West and I didn't go to the coffee party. We skinned calves. He would step over the carcasses and look to see if they had gone yet while he steeled his knife. And then he'd come back in and I would ask him if they were gone and he'd shake his head no and then we'd skin five or six more and he'd look again.

But we heard it when they left; the goodbyes being shouted back and forth and the write-us-a-line stuff that people always say. Rose went back in the house and West and I took a break. He went to the freezer and brought back two bottles of beer he had put in to cool in hopes they wouldn't freeze before the Johnsons left.

He pried off the caps and handed me one. I wouldn't take his smoke, but I took a chew of his tobacco. We laughed and snorted and had a grand time. We even finished skinning the calves before it was time to feed and water.

I helped West clean the barn and get ready for the new bull that was coming tomorrow. I could hardly wait to see a good, heavy, white face bull up close and touch his meaty body. I thought about raising some good cattle myself that night, but with the mink and the anchor they provided to mobility, it didn't make sense.

Somehow musing about the bull made me think about Rassel. I hadn't thought about her for weeks. She only lived a mile away, but I was bushed after working long days. It was difficult to clean up to go meet her. The weather had been tough. I had 90 reasons but I think the biggest one was that the tension around the ranch drained every emotion I had. Plus I had thought my stay was going to be short and attachments could prove difficult during a three month period.

On the other hand, what I had seen of her, I liked. The short time had not hindered me when I worked at the motel last summer. Different situation though. We had every meal together, and every night with no commitments other than to find something enjoyable to do. It had been easy to enjoy female company in a resort town; it was clean, washed by sea air, plenty to do, and money to do it with.

Now I was committed for the rest of the year, through breeding and kitting. The more I thought about Rassel, the more I wanted to see her again. Talk to someone other than this family. Hold her. Kiss her. With the reality of the season stretched out ahead of me, I promised myself to make a stronger effort to see her.

WE ALL KNEW THE new bull was coming but nobody seemed excited but me.

"Where's the bull coming from?" I asked Rose.

"He never tells me what he does. You know that, Jeff. What he does with his time and his money is none of my business."

"I wonder if they're having any trouble with him." I said.

We started dinner and still the truck had not come. I threw some potatoes on my plate and just then we heard the shifting of gears and the slow pull of the truck up the steep driveway. I jumped up and ran out through the open door and stood there waiting in the bright sunlight for the new bull.

West drove right on by me and up towards the barn. I took off running behind the truck, feeling the closeness of the new bull, his smell of green grass and clean hair, the proud but frightened look in his wide eyeballs. When the truck stopped I climbed up on the rack and looked at him.

"What a magnificent bull, West. Where did you get such an animal?"

"Down around Banks," he said without looking up. He threw his lasso out on the ground and began coiling it around his hand and elbow.

It was a big two year old white face with curly hair on his forehead and heavy horns that started at right angles out from the side of his head and then curved towards his eyes, light-colored at the base and then a dark brown running to black towards the tip. What a beast he was, heavy and meaty, with wide shoulders that held that magnificent head, every pound a good bull.

West handed me the rope. "I want you to take this rope around his horns and then you hang tight on it but don't pull unless he gets away from me."

I fixed my rope and waited. West, with a yank on his rope, pulled the massive head around and the bull started out of the truck, hooves slipping on the wood bed, then gaining purchase, slipping again and then in one big leap the bull jumped out of the bed to the ground and took off. West skidded to the ground with the rope burning through his hands.

When the bull tightened the slack in the rope West held, he stopped and turned. West started walking toward the barn and the bull followed, looking back at me now and then like he was wondering what I was supposed to be doing. I followed them both and when West reached the open door he stepped inside. The bull went just to the door where he planted his two front feet against the jamb and pulled back hard. I could hear West sliding across the barn floor.

A stream of muttering came out of the barn but I couldn't understand it. West threw the rope around a post and pulled. He pulled but nothing moved except the bull's head which went nose high when West pulled and nose down when he relaxed. I walked up behind the bull and planted my boot just below his tail and up and over the jamb he went. I heard West curse.

I had a good hold on my rope and trailed the bull into the barn at a run. The bull had a mind to go through the unopened door at the other end, dragging West with him. He smashed into the door and West glanced up at the roof.

The whole barn shuddered. The door rattled on its rollers but stayed connected to the barn. The bull backed up two steps, looked at the door and hit it again, his horns splintering the wood. West looked at me and I yanked on the horn rope and gained a surprise that spun the big boy around facing me.

The next thing I knew, I was reeling him toward me and he was coming right on. West took two quick steps into the milk parlor and yanked on the rope but it had no effect on the bull.

He stopped dead in front of me and I grabbed his left horn and threw my whole body weight into it which turned his head. West pulled and I pushed and the bull walked up the ramp to the milk parlor and then stopped. I got behind and pushed but he wouldn't take the last step.

"Does a bull's leg bend like a horse's?" I asked.

"Yes," West answered.

I grabbed his right front leg and lifted, bent it up like you would if you were shoeing a horse, and set his hoof up on the top step. He stayed like that while I went around and did the same with his left front leg. Then I took hold of his tail and twisted it and up he went. West had him tied before the bull knew where he was.

We stood there looking at him with our breath coming hard. He was beautiful. He was puffing, too.

"Can he make a calf?" I said.

West spoke through his smile, "He looks like it, doesn't he."

"Yeah, man...what an animal."

While we were admiring the panting bull, a cow in the adjacent stall, bellowed low and sorry. West looked over.

"I want you to help me with that cow...she's got to get up or she's gonna die and lose her calf."

"What's the matter with her?"

He shrugged his shoulders. We walked over to her as she lay on her side in a hole on the mud floor. I reached under her hindquarters and West put a rope around her neck and we pulled and pushed and grunted but she did no more than roll onto her stomach. West spit out his cigarette and stamped it into the manure.

He hunched over and shouted. "You gotta want to get up to get up!" He kicked her in the neck with his rubber boot. She didn't budge.

We got her hind end up. Then West tugged forward with the rope and pulled her up on her knees while I held her hind end up. She was too heavy. I dropped her and she fell again.

"Dammit, cow, get up!" West said, and he kicked her in the face and neck and on her nose again and again, pounding with his fist on her head and neck. She stirred but didn't try. "Again!" he screamed while be beat her with the end of the rope.

I lifted hard and he kicked her on the nose and pulled with the rope. She stumbled to her feet and stood swaying. She stayed up. He patted her on the head. We were breathing hard, but over it we could hear the bull puffing harder, a sort of sneezing sound.

We jumped over the hay and saw him down on his knees, the rope around his neck choking him. His eyes bulged in the sockets. His head was in a stanchion and the rope was too short for him to be on his knees.

West tried to back him out of the wood vise but his horns kept catching. He couldn't back out. He was choking more all the time. West untied the rope from the post and we tried turning his head sideways but he couldn't figure what we wanted of him.

He braced his front feet, snorted and tried to back out, his horns pulling on the stall, milking pipes, electrical extension cords and all. Fortunately, he couldn't get enough slack to rip them out, but when he backed up his little eyes squinted, his shoulder muscles rippled, and back he came, West trying to hold him from hitting so hard, like a rubber tire bumper hanging over the side of a boat.

West reared back and kicked the bull square on the snout. I backed up expecting to witness a new hole in the side of the barn but instead Toro just stood there while the old man doubled up the end of the rope and started lashing him across his tender nose.

Every switch made my stomach crawl and I could tell the white face didn't like it either. He suffered a half a dozen swats then turned his head a quarter turn and backed out into the parlor like he knew the combination all the time. I felt a bit easier about the beating.

"Damn bull," West muttered. He tied the rope short enough that the bull couldn't do that again. He backed up to lean against the stall, and removed his gloves, his breath ragged.

We stood for several minutes looking at the panting bull, spread-legged, wide eyed and nervously quiet. West reached over and patted the bull on top of his head, digging his fingers into the curly hair and running his eyes over the ridges of muscle visible beneath the clean hide and curly hair.

"Lot of meat," he said, admiring the definition and strength it implied.

We cleaned up and walked over to the house for supper.

"Judas, what an animal," I said as we entered the house. No one replied. We sat down and ate. I didn't mind it being unfriendly. We had just put a new bull in his new home and it felt good just to handle the rope on such an animal.

The supper was cold.

THE NEXT DAY WE built new pens all afternoon and after we had finished the last pen and ground the feed, West and I fed the expectant fathers and the very pregnant mothers. It would only be a day or two now before the first kits would be born. West went to milk his cows and I turned on the pump and watered. The water barely trickled out which meant I had to go check the pump.

I stepped over the electric fence making sure I didn't touch it and get a shock. Sometimes, if you were standing in water or your pants were wet and you touched that wire it could give you a jolt to remember.

As I walked down the cow trail rutted with last night's hoof prints, the pump sounded like it was on its last legs. The rubber belt frayed and the burning rubber smell drifted over the whole mink yard. Water backed up and shot out the piston end where the old leather washers leaked. I opened the cutout valve and checked to see that it was putting some pressure behind the water, closed it, and headed back across the electric fence.

West was in the barn and I could hear the scurry of the cows' feet as they rambled over the board floor in the milking parlor.

Funny how cows know their stall every time.

I crawled over the back fence and jumped into the mink yard where Rose was equalizing last night's feed. Suddenly we heard the unmistakable whack! whack! Whack! of a board against a body and the scurried scramble of hooves on wood.

"That sonofabitch is beating a cow again," Rose said. "Someone should beat the hell out of that bastard."

I walked over to the water faucet, concerned, but unwilling to do or say anything. "If Jack was here," she continued, "He'd beat the hell out of him." I turned the faucet on and heard the whack, whack, resounding from the barn carried by the cool air along with the stamping of feet.

Yeah, I wondered, so what would Jack do?

"He beat him up once," she said. I filled one water can. "He beats all the animals." I filled another water can. "If Jack was here, by Gawd, he'd teach him a lesson." I washed the green algae out of the water pan. Now it was bothering me.

Whack! Whack! Whack! Whack! Whack!

I'd had it. "Sonofabitch!"

I threw the hose down and got to the fence in four steps. I went up and over the fence, down the muddy stairs and jerked the sliding door open.

"West!" I yelled. His back was to me with his arms raised and he brought the board down hard on the rump of the bull just dashing out the rear door and down the ramp into the green pasture. Straining for breath, he looked at me, laid the board against the wall, and locked the cow in her stanchion. He was puffing hard as he leaned back on the upright post. I stood frozen with my fingers gripping the doorjamb while he pulled a cigarette from underneath his sweatshirt and lit it.

He drew in on it and blew out the smoke. "What do you want?" he wheezed.

"Nothing." I stood ashamed standing there making judgments from the noise only, and not from what actually was happening. "I just wondered what the noise was about." I turned around and pulled the door closed feeling like a fool. I walked up through the grass, wet with droplets of dew, feeling the adrenaline seeping out of my body and picked up the water hose.

"Well?" she demanded.

I cleaned out one water pan trying to think how to tell her. "The bull got in the milk barn and was mounting a cow."

A strange look of confusion spread over her stern face and then she said, "Well—he has beat a cow just to be beating it. He's gonna have to cut that bull. That animal will tear apart everything I've built here if he leaves him a bull. Breed the cows then cut him."

I watched her lifted brows. Her statement rambled around inside of me while I tried to understand whether West would ever cut that bull. Whether to believe it or not. In the end I discarded it. Isn't that a hell of a way to be, I thought, a ping pong ball between two paddles?

To see a Hereford bull up close is to know that he was built for beef. Huge flat back on wide spread short legs. Heavy sides. So different from a range bull. He is something to look at and I think he likes being looked at. He stands still with only his eyes moving in their sockets. He has eyelashes that would make a cheerleader envious. Don't know if West is going to name him or not but think I'll make up a short list of names.

We had a rumble with the bull in the milk room today cause I had met my limit with animals getting beaten around here and was ready to take the ole man on—urged on, of course, by Rose. Bull was where he shouldn't have been and was asked to leave to the tattoo of a 1x6 board. It sounded way worse than it was and West was in the right to get the bull out of there.

CHAPTER 32

The first mink had their kits on a warm May day. I saw one mother having hers on the hay she had scraped out of the nest box onto the wire. She had three while I watched and then I had to go salt hides. There were only a few kits born that day.

Two women drove up with calves in the trunk of their car. Rose paid them—I took them out. The women stood talking with Rose for some time. She was talking loud.

"Everybody knows me and knows I don't lie. They know I wasn't having an affair with Jack. He was awful good to the boys and a good worker."

I peeked between the cracks of the boards from inside the salt shed.

"When everyone tries to run you down you know there is some skullduggery afoot!" She looked my way.

The women smiled and moved unnaturally. The younger of the two got in the car behind the wheel and the other, still smiling, walked around and got in. They laughed their good-byes.

I salted with a smile on my tired face. Sometimes I couldn't smile but today, even with all its heat, I could smile. It felt good. I wondered how good I could feel with tension rising out of every conversation lately. She was pushing me to take her side and I didn't like it. Was it just man stuff or the fact that so far in my life I had had problems with bossy, middle-aged women? I thought of the desk lady at the motel where I had worked: middle aged, fat and domineering. These women acted as if, because they weren't men, they should be disrespectful, hold the high ground at all costs, disallow any thinking that I might have independent of what they ordered. And that woman who managed the YMCA camp that summer. She wanted me fired for allowing the kids to pin up a petition on the bulletin board to go swimming in the river instead of the city pool. She got her way. The Director of the YMCA came down, sat opposite me on a picnic bench and just like that, fired me for insubordination.

It felt like the great desert the next day and the whole mink yard shone like a mirror that beamed the heat up under my pant legs and drew the starch right out of me. My eyes squinted from the bursting light that glanced off the aluminum sheeting.

Everywhere the mother mink were taking their kits out on the wire to escape the smoldering heat of the nest boxes and everywhere they were falling through the wire, crying their piercing monotone cry. The mothers raced back and forth across the pens with their heads down looking through at their babies helpless on the hay and manure below. We walked up aisles picking up kits, letting the mothers sniff them through the wire and if they licked their long, red tongue out we eased the kit through the wire. The mother took the kit in her mouth and pulled it in, licked it and put it out on the wire again. Maybe it fell through again and maybe not.

Always we wiped our hands clean after handling each kit to erase the smell of the last kit. Occasionally you couldn't tell which nest the kit came from. If you put a kit in the wrong box the mother could smell that it wasn't hers and would sink her fangs into the little body and drop it through the wire to die.

I had a sick feeling in my stomach to see a kit warm but dying when just seconds before I had it alive squirming, crawling and nosing in my palm. Blood oozes out of its wounds and it lies very still. I pick up another, a bigger one this time, and hope and pray I am putting it in the right nest. The mother licks—you lower the kit's head and she opens her jaws and takes the head while her little black darting eyes cover you as she pulls it through the wire and ducks under the cover of hay to deposit it, and come back to hiss at you as you bend and pick up another one.

It took an hour to go up three sheds; mink kits fell all over the yard. I didn't have to wait for one to cry; everywhere they were out and crawling together, alone, down into the drain ditch to wallow in the mud and drown, out down the aisle, across the aisle, everywhere but under their own nest. I had to guess where they came from and sometimes I could tell by the color and size of the kit and then again I couldn't tell anything and I threw the dead away when the female killed them.

What a stupid waste. Small wire on the bottom of the pens would keep them in and you wouldn't lose so many.

I walked down to the end of the shed where West was standing, stooped, cigarette hanging, shirt open to catch the faintest breeze. He lifted a double handful of dead kits in front of him... nine, ten, eleven kits. I looked up and our eyes met saying all the things we thought and he lifted his shoulders in a little shrug, dropped them at the end of the row, turned and walked down, crossed the ditch and started up another shed.

I took the last shed. At the first pen there was a kit on the ground making the loudest crying I had heard and squirming like an earthworm. I picked him up and he stopped crying. I lifted the nest lid and the old female got very nervous. The best thing was to lower it slowly so I put its head a half inch from the wire. The mother crouched and hit the wire like a diamond-back rattler. I lowered it again and she sniffed and flicked her tongue in and out like some giant salamander. I thought she was the mother and it would be ok.

She took its head in her jaws and as I lowered the lid she snapped her teeth tight, one fang going through the kit's head and ear, the other through the shoulder. And then, with me sick that I had misread the female, she ate the kit. I held the box lid and watched her chew the little body until there was nothing left and I hadn't the sense or strength to lower the lid; I just stood there and watched her lick and chew until she swallowed the last of it and turned and hissed at me and I lowered the lid like the last viewer lowers a coffin lid.

I stood for some time watching other kits in the shed crawling loose on the ground and wondering how many would die if I put them back in. Tired and desensitized I reached down and picked one up and opened the next box and lowered him to the wire. She took him. I noticed that I had been holding my breath. After that I began to breathe again.

I finished the shed with no more deaths and then at the last pen I stopped. A big kit lay still under the shadow of the post and I didn't want to pick him up because I could see the two holes in his shoulder and stomach. Everything went mad inside and I grabbed him, still warm, and walked down to where Rose was bending over a nest box.

"What the hell kind of ranch is this that kills forty mink a day?" I said.

She didn't even look up.

"Why don't you do something about it? Buy wire for the pens or boards or something to keep them alive!" I shouted.

She gave me a calm look and drew on her cigarette. "I lose kits every year. We can't raise them all." She stood ten feet from me, insolent and imperial.

"You haven't got the brains to run this ranch!" I said and with a quick step I threw the dead kit at her. She turned to avoid the flying kit, walked right by me and started up another shed.

I stood in the row between squealing kits and hissing females weakened by my anger and not knowing how to fight it...her...or anything. You can't fight a woman—you can't hit— you can't talk her into a wall because she won't talk. You can't do anything but take it in your guts. Beside the dead mink, other things roamed through my mind. My throat still choked back any talk about Ralph and his traitorous behavior of borrowing the mink—which he hadn't returned. Ladd and his last moments stuck there too. I sat down on a chunk of wood and felt my pulse.

I blinked a few times, took a deep breath and walked over to the slaughterhouse, picked up my knife and the stone and burned away my anger in the round and round and round turning of stone against steel.

I skinned out what few calves were there and ground the feed early because I wanted to get done before dark. West came over and I told him what she said to the women who had brought the calves the day before. His face looked blank. He watched her going up and down the aisles. He didn't say anything.

We fed early and I watered, getting done before it was supper time. Rose hadn't made a move towards the supper preparation. She was the cook now so we ate poorly, not because she wasn't a good cook but because she couldn't or wouldn't put any time into it. It was getting late. I could salt hides and wait it out, but I went over to where she was cutting wire for pens. I stopped at the shed. She didn't look up.

"What do I get this month?" I asked her. She was cutting wire and I didn't know whether she was going to answer or not.

"Same as last month."

I stood there. Should I tell her what I think or just say I quit? What do I do to get inside her head? If I fight with the old man she'll be number one on my side. But West and I had forged an understanding; a friendship.

"How long do you think I'll stay on that?" I said.

She shifted her weight, cocked her head, narrowed her eyes and said in a spiteful voice, "As long as you believe the BS the old man puts out."

I didn't know whether I wanted to get mad or not. Usually I don't think fast enough to answer real sharp when I'm mad. I try to slug my way out and that's no good when you're in a battle of wits. I thought about it enough to slow me down and the answer came out.

"Who told you I believe the old man?"

"Actions speak louder than words," she said.

"Yeah," I said. "I believed him about how to build cages and I didn't lose one kit through the wire. You must have lost forty, maybe fifty."

She leveled those narrowed eyes at me again. "I see you sneer at me just like the old man does. You're getting just like him; it's a crime."

"When?"

I waited for her to answer, but she hummed to herself.

"When have I sneered at you?"

"I've seen you a couple of times."

"Facts, Rose...when?"

She hummed to herself again. I changed the subject. "Seems funny that what I believe or don't believe has to interfere with my working here," I said.

"Well, it does."

"Why should it?" I said.

"Anyone who works with the old man gets nothing done. When they work with me we get work out!" She was getting mad now and put us on a level playing field.

"Rose, don't be a fool...go look at the stack of calves in the locker...you helped count the hides. Almost three thousand since I came here and West and I gutted and skinned damn near every one of them. You and Johnson didn't skin two dozen of them. We built the shed and the pens and helped breed."

"You didn't help very much with breeding!" She said louder now.

"We helped in the morning and skinned sixty, seventy calves in the afternoon, and you know it!"

Silence again. She cut the wire and put it on the stack and pulled another length out to cut.

"Funny," I said, "that you and Johnsons became such bosom buddies right after that fight Ralph had with the old man and before that you couldn't say enough bad things about them."

"I never said anything bad about the Johnsons. The old man has been feeding you a lot of BS again."

West had arrived behind us with neither of us knowing it. "That's not true," he said.

She turned and looked at him but said nothing.

He wiped his face with his sleeve. "I have only told him the truth from day one. You were down on the Johnsons all the time and everyone knew it but the Johnsons and you."

I chimed in. "You told me that. Standing right in front of me telling me what a lousy worker Ralph was and how Olive couldn't keep her kids or the house clean."

"I never said that."

"The hell you didn't!"

"You ought to talk to some of West's friends down on skid row if you want to know the truth," she said.

West expelled a burst of air in a snicker and turned aside.

"What has that got to do with it?" I said.

"Well, you just listen to what he says and don't get the facts."

"I talk to West and Mel and Charlie and Ed and they all tell the same story on Jack, you, and everything else. And only you and Paul tell me your side. That's pretty slim evidence because Paul believes everything you tell him."

"You're a Christian; you shouldn't listen to all the BS the old man puts out."

"Rose," West said, "You're acting like a crazy woman. You can't call me a liar in front of people who work here."

I took a step closer to her and lowered my voice. "What do you want me to do? Close my ears? Put on ear muffs?"

She got silent and tried to whistle a little and then turned to humming.

We had her in a corner, maybe.

I decided to keep on it. To spill out all the things I had been accumulating, empty that locker for today. I didn't care if she fired me or I quit or she tried to shoot me. Nothing held me back.

"How about the time you told me Ralph was on his toes?" I said.

"I don't believe I ever made a statement like that," she returned.

"Oh, Rose . . . Judas priest, I was standing right in front of you asking for a raise when you said it!"

She hummed again.

"And when West asked the guy if he could help a man who was starving to death and you came up to me and said he meant that sexually."

West stared at her with a look in his eyes I had only seen once before.

"I never mention the subject of sex...that is something the man has to bring up."

"Why, I can name three times you mentioned sex to me without me saying a word about it. That time about him meaning it sexually, when you said West doesn't like for you to mention sex or testicles around the hired men because he is a sex fiend. And when West accused you of having an affair with Jack."

West's face wrinkled in pain. "You said that?"

She was humming and it was getting on my nerves. She didn't act like she was listening, but still I knew she was. She couldn't help it. Maybe she was lying to herself again.

"It makes me pretty mad," she began, "when a rancher asks me if I hired a worker for the ranch or a character investigator."

"You told me to see what West was saying about you down town when I first came here so I've done a little asking around."

"Nobody knows anything about me!" she snarled.

"I even saw the sheriff..." I kept up.

"He doesn't know anything about my business!"

"He knows your gun license expires in June."

"That's all he knows!"

West was shaking his head at Rose. "I can't believe you would do this behind my back."

"Behind your back? You know what's going on. You're part of it. The biggest part!" I watched the color rise above her collar up over her face.

I picked up my shirt. "Since the day I got here you've been running West down in my eyes. Jack was better. Ralph was better. I'm no good if I believe West and not you. How in hell do you expect to keep decent help if you treat them to crap like that every living day?"

I took a deep breath and caught the stench of the mink carcasses that had rotted under the workbench. We had forgotten to throw them in the garbage. I left Rose and West standing in the aisle, picked up my shirt and walked over to the slaughterhouse.

It was cool inside out away from the dusty whirls that the breeze threw up and tumbled across the driveway.

It was a painful supper for me. I sat silent and so did the others. West simply stared through the window. He didn't have his smoke at the supper table but went outside. I couldn't eat dessert. I got a drink of water but even the cool well water didn't go down very well. I went out.

"Leave the door open," she ordered.

I left it open and walked over to where the old man was splitting some kindling. I sat down on a piece of peeler core. I looked at the place in the fading light.

The house looked much older in the last light. The tin cans behind the house didn't shine. The sheds stood silent in uneven lengths. A flap of sheeting whipped in the gust of breeze that crept along the yard. Ladd was gone and I felt a hollow spot for that animal. The prevailing smell was there. I closed my eyes. It seemed like ages since I came over that hill and looked down on the lazy scene. Another couple of months and I'd have enough money saved up to move on. To go to the University and get a masters degree. If I could survive this place that much longer it could be worth it.

The shit hit the fan today. We all got dirtied by it. It might have missed Paul and Ronny but it sure covered the rest of us. With Johnsons gone we are all working longer hours. Rose hasn't made any effort to find a replacement for me or Johnsons as far as I can tell. We must have lost 40 or 50 kits this week. I didn't lose any of my young probably due to the way West taught me to construct the pens. The test now is to avoid losing my mind until I can finish up the kit season, sell my mink, and be off.

CHAPTER 33

Walking down the road toward Swenson's farm I had a growing need to talk to someone who wasn't involved with the mink farm in some way. When I thought about it, the only people I had talked to lately worked on the farm or were coming and going from the farm.

I hadn't had a thinking conversation since I arrived: one where ideas were discussed, solutions sought, alternatives brought up. Learning the mink business, especially now that I was raising my own, was taking a lot of my thinking time. It seemed like a luxury to ponder any other problem but one that was facing me that day.

Thanks to West, I had made some improvements in my cage construction so I only lost one kit and he was a runt that got through my smaller wire. My five females had produced twenty-five kits. My stock was growing fast. Pretty soon I'd need more cages. Every day I was getting sucked into this place like a piece of drift wood headed downriver to a whirlpool.

My knock brought Mrs. Swenson to peek out the short curtain that covered the window in the front door.

She opened it and stood in its opening. "Good evening, Jeff."

"Hello Mrs. Swenson. Is Rassel here?"

"She's on the phone but I'll let her know you're here. Would you like to come in?"

I stepped inside and she closed the door with both hands and readjusted the curtain in the small window. "Have a seat and I'll get her."

"Thank you, Mrs. Swenson." I looked around their living room. Quiet was how I'd describe it. Two large overstuffed chairs, a three cushion couch, a wooden coffee table with cup rings stained into the top, a fireplace faced with river stone and a large radio that stood against the wall. One wall was covered from the wainscoting up with family photos and the short wall near the door to the kitchen featured a large Regulator clock with prominent numbers and hands. The tick tock, tick tock was the only sound in the room. Then there was a slight click and a grinding sound and the clock struck the half hour. The sound pealed through the room, was absorbed by the furniture, then gave way to the tick tock tick tock.

I could hear Rassel talking and laughing. In a couple of minutes she came out.

"Hi, Jeff. I didn't expect you."

I stood up. "No—I'm sure you didn't. I needed someone to talk to who wasn't a mink, a calf, or a Helner."

She laughed. "So I drew the short straw, huh?"

We had already kissed in our relationship but it felt awkward standing in her house and I didn't offer anything other than conversation at that moment.

"You want to take a walk?" I said.

"Why don't we stay here? We can pop some popcorn and I'll try and give you decent conversation."

"I didn't mean that as any putdown," I said.

She shook her head and her pretty hair swung across her shoulders. "Just give me a minute."

She was opening cabinet doors and banging things around in the kitchen. I sat on the couch and thought about how I had been maneuvered into staying in their house. It wasn't hard. It was letting someone else make the decision and going with the flow. Isn't that what I'd been doing since I arrived in this valley?

My dream of having enough money from the motel work to go back to school for a masters degree and become a writer had faded with the trip down the coast at the end of summer. Now I was stuck in a menial job, trapped by my growing mink herd and all the things I thought worthwhile about me were being twisted into someone I was having a hard time living with.

The sound of corn popping gave me a comfortable feeling and the smell of it brought a smile to my face. Took me back to Sunday evenings at home when Dad would pop up a big batch and, always wanting things a little sweeter, drizzled crystallized sugar water over it.

Rassel came in, sat on the couch and set the wooden bowl of popcorn between us. She handed me a napkin.

"Think I'm going to get messy?" I said.

She smiled. "Just don't get it on the couch."

We munched popcorn for a bit, each with our own thoughts.

"So—what kind of talk do you need that you can't get from Ladd?"

"Ladd was shot."

She straightened up. "Who shot him?"

"Rose."

"Rose?"

"Shot him while he was standing right beside me. He'd been chasing sheep she said."

"Chasing sheep?"

"That's what she said just before she pulled the trigger."

"I never knew Ladd to chase sheep."

"Someone had shot him with buckshot. I picked a couple out of his jaw, but he would have made it okay."

"Some farmer probably."

"She thought it was Bill Freck."

"He might do it if Ladd was chasing his sheep."

"Well somebody did. West buried him in the corral."

She took a popcorn kernel between two fingers and put it in her mouth. Then she shook her head. "That's so sad."

"Everything's been sad around there. The calves rotting, the kits dying. I'm raising my own mink and Paul and Ronny—they've got a miniature hog farm going. It seems like the whole place deals in death. We're killing calves to feed mink that we will kill and skin. Raising calves to kill for beef in a year or two. Hogs the same. Everything happening there takes something dying all the time to keep it going. Shooting Ladd is about my last straw."

"How did West take it?"

"Ladd?"

"Yes."

I swallowed. "Haven't talked to him about it yet. He seems okay."

We sat silent for awhile with just the tick tock tick tock marking the parts to our lives that were being lived and passed through.

"Are you writing this all down so you can get it in a book?" she said.

I nodded.

"You should, you know. Writers write about what they know."

"Yes."

She looked at me. "You know that. Look what Hemingway's writing about—what he knows—bull fights, war, the old man and the fish."

"You're right."

"Jeff—you were pretty on top of things when I first met you. Seems like you have been beaten down into someone that doesn't match the person I first saw. Do you feel okay?"

I took a deep breath, held it a second and exhaled. "No." I stood up and walked to the door. Rassel stayed on the couch. As much as I wanted to talk about it with someone else, I froze up. It circled around inside me but failed to surface and I suddenly knew that I had to leave the comfort of her house.

"See you," I said and walked out into the night that was now lit with the first quarter moon peeking through misty clouds.

At the end of their driveway I started jogging and within 100 yards I was pouring it on. I hadn't run for over a year but with each step I got faster. My arms pumped, fists clenched, and then I eased back into a miler's pace, getting my breath and regulating my speed for the longer run.

The moon gave enough light to miss the pot holes and I coasted along like I had in college; head up, arms swinging across my chest, feet reaching out to take a longer stride, and adjusting my breathing to my pace. I had to burn it all out if that was possible.

When I reached the ranch driveway I stopped running and walked down to the bridge and back collecting my thoughts, putting them into some files, trying to make decisions. Some would have to wait.

How do you explain to someone that you don't know for sure where your head is? Rassel seems so steady. It's so lonesome without Ladd and sitting with her is a good feeling. I don't know how West is going to be tomorrow. Rose—I can guess. I should be writing this stuff down but I don't see how I can forget it. It is seared into my brain, what there is left of it.

The smells, the killing, the ritual, all the things that farmers and ranchers do to provide the furs and meat that the public buys. And when they buy it they get soft good smelling furs and bright red skinned, gutted, beheaded, trimmed steaks or further indefinable hamburger patted into rounded mounds in a paper container covered with waxed paper. It all starts here and I have taken part in all of it.

CHAPTER 34

West and I were getting ready to mix the night's feed. I brought in a sack of meal on my shoulder and he had brought several trays of ground meat that he had thawed.

"I'm gonna put that new bull with the cows tomorrow," he said.

"Oh."

"I been thinking with all the mink being born he should start contributing to the population around here."

"Just as well. That's his job."

"She wants me to cut him after he's bred the cows." He shook his head. "Not gonna do it."

"You could've hired a bull cheaper than buying this one if you cut him."

He nodded. "She don't think of those things. That's why this place is losing money."

We heard the kitchen door open and then the screen door slam against the side of the house. Rose screamed. "West! Fire!"

He was halfway down the driveway before I dropped the sack of feed and got going. He disappeared through the open door. I stopped at the doorway and gripped the door frame.

Thick, solid smoke was rolling across the floor and pouring out of the doorway. Someone was coughing. I couldn't see anybody but I could hear someone. Rose appeared out of the smoke hacking and gagging, her hands covering her eyes. She took a couple of breaths and I reached for her but she shook me off and turned back into it. I grabbed the kitchen chairs and threw them toward the wall away from the door. I heard a body fall on the floor, then a grunt and another stumble.

"West?" I yelled.

No answer.

I saw his white head appear. He was crawling on the floor on his hands and knees. His upper body convulsed with choking. I put my hands in his armpits and lifted. He was lighter than I expected. He half rose and looked up into my eyes. His mouth hung open, his eyes red and wet rolled back into his head.

He squeezed my arm. "The back bedroom...the boys."

"I'll get them." I pulled him outside and tried to prop him against the wall but he slumped down on the ground.

He grabbed my pants leg. "No—too much fire."

I shook loose, took a deep breath and pushed into the smoke which was billowing out of the kitchen. I couldn't see anything in the black interior of the smoke. My left foot hit something soft. I reached down and felt an arm, tightened my hand around it, and backed up towards the door. I hit a wall and turned slightly to my right, my lungs pleading for oxygen. My heel caught the threshold. I stumbled and fell backwards out into the yard. I let loose of the arm when I fell and shoved my nose into the grass and breathed in fresh air.

West was lying a few feet from me, his chest convulsing as he coughed hard. The arm I had pulled on was Rose's. She lay unconscious on the ground.

I stood up and ran to the other side of the house. The bedroom windows were blackened. I looked for something to break open the window and finally kicked it in. Hot smoke shot out the broken window. It seared my face. The bedroom was entirely enveloped in flame and curling twisting grey-black smoke pushed out the window like a serpent.

"Ronny. Paul," I yelled. If they said anything it was drowned out by the roar of the flames.

I uprooted a cedar post and smashed at the window frame, finally knocking it into the room. That gave me a hand grip on wood that wasn't on fire. I stuck my head in through the smoke, opened my eyes and held my breath. The smoke curled into my eyes and they closed involuntarily. I backed out and sat on the ground trying to regroup.

Then the smoke and the house and the propane tank and the tar-paper roof exploded in unison. The windows erupted showering hot glass into the yard. Fire shot out in every direction. I ran back to the front of the house.

"West—get up—move," I yelled.

He came up on his hands and knees, eyes looking at the inferno in front of him. Shards of glass fell off his back, some leaving burning marks on his shirt. Tears ran down his face. He stumbled to his feet, wavered a second and backed up. I took a hold of Rose's arms and pulled. She was conscious and asked for water. We moved in fits and starts across the driveway and collapsed on the wet ground. West sat down. I got a pan of water from the slaughter house. We turned to stare at the fire, the heat scalding our faces. Fire was everywhere. There was nothing that wasn't burning. Green grass around the edges turned brown and coiled. The few trees that had grown close to the house were scorched black, leaves curled tight. Small sounds of glass and light bulbs breaking, a sudden rush when the fire found something especially volatile in the sugar or flour bins. Flames rose high from the corner of the kitchen when the wood pile caught fire. And the noise rose like a symphony as if it had a life and a purpose to perform. We sat stunned as the volume climbed and peaked and declined. Various parts of the house caved in scattering flaming debris in all directions. We sat unable to move or make any rational thoughts come.

A car spun its tires, throwing gravel and a cloud of dust in the air startled us as it bounced up the driveway and stopped. Mr. Swenson flung the door open and jumped out. He stood for a moment looking at the burning pile of the house.

"My gawd!" he said. "Everybody ok?"

He stood there looking at the three of us nodding his head up and down as if to reassure himself that everybody was ok.

Then Rose pointed with a blackened arm and whispered, "The boys are in there."

He looked at the huge fire, eyes wide, mouth open, and shook his head. "I'm so sorry. So sorry." He went to get some water for us to drink. My throat felt like sandpaper.

CHAPTER 35

The fire truck arrived about an hour later. Mr. Swenson had gone home and called them. West, Rose and I sat on the slaughter shed floor looking down on the smoldering mass that was almost flat now. The fire had burned everything except the bathtub and the wood stove which stood as blackened remnants, the only things higher than the foundation. The cast-iron frying pan was intact; the aluminum pots and pans were melted flat and welded together. Each window, blown out, lying on the dirt, was just a pool of melted glass or blackened shards, the wooden frame an outline of ash around it. It was the most complete fire any of the volunteer firemen had ever seen.

The medical examiner was going to come out tomorrow and retrieve the bodies of Paul and Ronny, if he could find them. The fire chief wanted to know what started it.

"A candle," Rose said. "Ronny was throwing his arms around and knocked over a candle that we burned once in a while." She dabbed at the corner of her eyes with a Kleenex.

The fire chief nodded. "A candle?" he said.

"Yes."

He wrote that down on a clip board he held in his left hand. "Candle," he said.

"He liked a candle. Didn't like the dark."

"I understood he was blind?"

"Yes. He is—was."

The fire chief cocked his head.

"He was blind but he liked a candle burning?"

"Yes."

I left West and Rose to finish with the firemen and walked up to my trailer. Inside it smelled remarkably clean. I pulled off my smoky clothes and put them outside in a tub, threw in a cap full of Clorox and poured water on them. Then I climbed into bed naked and tried to sleep.

"West! West!"

I awoke and listened. Sleep drugged me but it was light outside and then Rose's voice came again. I thought maybe I was dreaming of the fire but in a second I could hear her again.

"Your bull is out. Get out here!"

I put clean clothes on and without tying my boot laces ran towards her voice. She was standing, hands on hips at a broken fence around the mink yard. She glared at me as I came up.

"The bull is out. He's broken down the fence and tipped over some pens. Some mink are out. Keep that damn dog outta here and help me catch these mink."

I heard West flapping down the driveway from the house on the hill. He grabbed King by the collar and tied him with a rope to a corner post. Then we took some scrap wood and temporarily repaired the bull-dozed fence, enough so mink wouldn't get out of it.

Rose had inventoried the smashed pens and determined six mink were out and God only knew what happened to the kits. Within five minutes we had captured four of them. We spent the next two hours rebuilding the nesting boxes and getting the females and their kits back together again. Mink don't take kindly to new surroundings. They like the smell and feel of familiarity of their old nests and they get cranky when they are made to live in something new. But we didn't have any choice so we did it.

"I've got to eat something or I'm gonna fall apart," Rose said. "And I can't sit around moping over the boys if this place is going to survive. If I'm going to survive." With that she strode to the Buick and drove away.

West came up to me, his eyes red, the lower lids sagging. His breathing was noisy. "Where's she goin', she say?"

"I don't know."

I hadn't had time to think about Paul and Ronny or decide how to start telling West and Rose how sad I was for them. What do you say when somebody has lost all of their children all their belongings and their house, and then still have a business to run with the day after day work that starts at dawn and goes to sunset and they're camped out in a shell of a house?

I looked at West and started. "I'm really sorry about the boys and your house. I've been thinking of it and can't think of anything different we could've done. Paul and his short wave radio and Ronny...."

He tilted his head down and cleared his throat before he spoke. "No." Then he shook his head. "It's too bad for the boys. But for the house—we didn't lose much." Tears collected in his eyes and ran down his cheeks. "Wished I'd died in there with 'em."

"No, West."

"I let 'em down.

"You did the best you could. You were right there."

"Didn't do any good."

"It was too far gone by then. Nothing you could have done."

He sniffed and took a sharp breath. "You know—I was surprised to find myself alive. The last thing I saw was black. I couldn't breathe." He shook his head. After a moment he said, "Ronny got his wish didn't he?" He turned to look at me—tears dripping off his chin. His face held the years and disappointments poorly this morning.

"I guess he did," I said.

"I don't blame him none either." He wiped his chin, lit a cigarette and we stood there close enough to touch but not touching. He sucked in on his smoke then coughed and pounded his fist against his chest until it stopped. "I wouldn't want to spend too much time living like that." He ran the sleeve of his shirt across his eyes and cheeks.

I nodded. "You got stuff in the big house so you can make it ok?"

"Oh—we'll need some things. Kinda like camping right now but it won't take much to make it livable. Smells like the Johnsons. I think they must have used one of the rooms for a toilet at night—too cold to go out to the outhouse."

I had that same sense when I had supper up there but I didn't comment. We sat silent hearing only the burbling of the swollen river rolling through the shore bushes' reminding me how sound travels uphill. I looked down the driveway across the road and the pasture and into the gray water. It was moving and I wasn't.

"What would happen if we built a raft and put it on that river and just took off?" I said.

"We'd end up at the coast." That was it for him. You got on something until you got off. It wasn't so much a destination as it was life that took you along on many different rides. You hung on and did what you could where you ended up.

I stretched my back. "We gotta find that bull."

West nodded. He mopped his eyes once more and finished his smoke.

We found the bull where West thought he would be, nosing the cows through the upper pasture fence.

"Just as well get this started," he said. "Open the gate, will ya, Jeff?"

He led the bull through the gate, removed the strand of rope that was left from the halter and slapped him on the rump. There were only three cows. It wouldn't take him long to get them with calves. Then they would freshen one at a time and each morning and evening give out with a couple gallons of fresh whole milk as white and clean as new snow.

I will never again question when someone tells or writes about the roar of a fire. It is a noise that cannot be compared to anything else. Some say it sounds like an airplane engine but having heard both I can tell you it does not. It has a sound all its own and it is a commanding sound. Brave King lay on the ground and whimpered. He will never look at fire the same way again and neither will I.

As I sit on my bed in the trailer it is hard to believe Paul and Ronny are gone. I think back to the Seven Devils road trip with a smile. Think back to the exploding window out of their room today and cry. They didn't have a prayer.

I sure miss Ladd. He would be such a comfort to me and West today and we need that something fierce. I'm already missing Ronny and Paul—finding it hard to believe that after the days work I won't be hearing Paul try to sell me some punches on his new punchboard and Ronny gurgling away on the couch, supporting his brother in the only way he knows how.

We found the bull and caught most of the mink that had gotten out. The day just went on without much time to think about the house and Ronny and Paul. It was too full of today's work.

My heavenly Father, I'm hoping for some time to think, to recoup my senses, to put this all in a container and be able to look at it without the distractions.

CHAPTER 36

Rose came back late in the afternoon with some hamburgers and French fries for us, as cold as the well water we had been drinking. She was followed up the driveway by a delivery truck that drove on up to the big house on the hill.

While West and I ate we could hear her telling the men where to put stuff. It looked like all kinds of household goods. We could see her packing in sacks of stuff but she didn't call us to help so we didn't go.

The men waved at us as they glided down the hill from the house, brakes squeaking, and turned down the driveway onto the river road. On the side of the truck were large letters: SALVATION ARMY. West and I looked at each other. He cracked a smile.

"Hope Ronny and Paul can see that truck," he said.

"They can." I thought about how we were grabbing food here and there and not sitting down with them in the house. "I miss them a lot," I managed to get out.

He nodded, looked down at his feet and spit between his boots. Then he looked at his legs and arms and raised his head. "These are the only clothes I own now."

"You'll need new underwear," I said.

He turned his head, smiled and nodded. "More'n likely."

Before dark, Rose came down to check on how we were doing with the feeding. She wore new Levi's and a flannel shirt and a jacket with a team emblem on it. Her new billed cap said 49'ers across the front.

"Did you find those other two mink?" she said.

"Haven't looked," West said.

"Well—my gawd! I can't do everything around here." She walked through the gate and looked in the upper corner of the yard.

"Probably up around the old pens," West yelled.

"I know it."

I bit my lip. Where was the respite? Where was the sense of tragedy and sense of loss and closing out the lives of Ronny and Paul and the memories of the melted house? Does this day continue with no let up after yesterday and all the tomorrows to come?

"Jeff—come here."

I stood up.

"Hurry up," she said. "Here's one of the mommas."

I put on thick leather gauntlet gloves and reached through the rusty wire and rotten wood of our abandoned pen pile and put my thumb and fore-finger around the mink's neck. She squirmed and tried to bite me but I held on. She buried her teeth in the heavy leather. The other momma mink was trying to get over the fence. She was easy to catch.

After West got through throwing hay to the cows and bull and we had finished the mink feeding, Rose and West walked side by side up the hill to the house. It looked as dark as a pile of rock. She had let us know there was no cooking tonight but by tomorrow she would have things set up. You can't starve to death with a hamburger and French fries in you so I did a quick sponge bath, (the kind my mother used to call a whore's bath) put on clean clothes and walked down the road in the twilight.

I knocked on the door. Her mother opened it. "Hi Jeff."

"Hello Mrs. Swensen. Is Rassel here?"

Rassel appeared with rollers in her hair.

"Can you take a walk?"

"Come on in while I take my hair down."

"Leave it. Let's take a walk."

She tied a scarf over her hair and closed the door behind her.

We held hands and walked down her driveway to a washed-up log by the river. We sat down and just stared at the river for a couple of minutes.

"That was terrible about Helner's boys. And the house. Everything gone."

"It was a lot of bad and some good," I said. "There is a clean start for them if they can take advantage of it. I can't tell how much they are grieving over Ronny and Paul but so far I haven't seen much regret about anything. The day to day work is just too much to stop and take measure. It shoves everything out of your head but what needs to be done next."

"Did she hire anyone to replace that red haired family?"

I shook my head. "So far we haven't missed them except for the cooking and since the fire the cooking has been haphazard. We're supposed to have stuff set up for tomorrow's cooking. Rose spent a few hundred dollars at the Salvation Army and got the essentials and last night West hooked up the range and refrigerator."

"That old house looks spooky at night."

"Well—it won't now. It'll have some lights in it."

Rassel took my hand. "Let's don't talk about them anymore. Let's talk about the future."

"Boy—I haven't thought about the future for a couple of days. How far in the future are you thinking?"

"A week—a month—a year. I don't know. Just somewhere ahead of today. I'm not going to sit on a dairy farm for the rest of my life and I'm not going to stay in this wet pit where the river floods every two months and leaves you on an island. This is an existence but it isn't living."

"What are you thinking?"

"Portland. Eugene. Somewhere where you can stretch yourself a little, where you don't work from dawn to dark and you know what a day off really is." She sat with her hands in her lap, my hand on top of hers. She took out one hand and patted her hair. The clean smell of her hair was like fresh clover on a hillside.

"You know anybody there?" she said.

I nodded. "Some."

"What do they do?"

"Well—couple of guys I know work in construction. One is a photographer. Another works in an outdoor sports store."

"Could they get us jobs?"

"I imagine. I'd have to ask but I think so. But we don't need them to find work. I've never had any trouble finding a job." It took me a minute to realize I had used 'we' when I said that. I swallowed and squeezed her hand.

"I'd like to work and go to school. They have colleges in both those towns. That's what I'd really like to do."

"And take what?"

"I've always thought I could teach school. I practically raised my brothers and sisters. I taught them to read before they went to first grade, their numbers too. I'd like that and teachers are scarce I hear."

"Don't know about that but it's a nice goal."

Here I was having a perfectly normal conversation with a lovely girl that wasn't dominated by mink or calves or bulls or hogs. She has a good head and clear understanding. I hadn't realized how much I had missed her.

"Oh Jeff—let's do it. You could get started on writing. I'll go to college and we can see each other often. Let's just get there and start living."

"I'll have to think about that. You could go a long way towards convincing me if you kissed me."

"That won't be hard."

CHAPTER 37

I didn't get back to the trailer until after midnight. Sometime during the night I heard a scratching on the door. I was instantly awake.

"Ladd?"

I had my feet on the floor before I knew it wasn't Ladd. I opened the door to nothing but night sounds and smells. I missed him and the more I thought about it I got a catch in my throat. I almost started talking to him. I had erased the shooting image for some time but now I let it swim back in and just held it for a few moments. I drifted back to sleep.

IT DIDN'T FEEL LIKE getting up time when I heard West getting the cows in for milking but I couldn't go back to sleep. I had just opened the door when I heard a wild commotion up by the barn. I couldn't make it out but there was a lot of snorting and stamping around.

When I got there West was spinning an old work jacket around and around the bull's head trying to drive off a swarm of bees. Every time the bull got stung he lunged one side or the other, dropped his head and snorted. West had his eyes on the bees. He missed seeing the bull's head drop and couldn't dodge the bulls face that jammed into his hip. The bull knocked him ten feet. I ran between the bull and West, grabbed the jacket out of West's hand and slapped the bull across the face with it. He turned and drove toward the other fence hitting it with all his weight. It popped the big nails we'd driven into it, and clear of us, the barn, and the fence, he ran up the hill full speed, the bees like a cloud over his back.

I turned to West. He was up on his hands and knees.

"How's it feel? Anything broken?" I said

"Don't know. Don't think so. Help me up will ya?"

He stood and ran his hands over his body. "Don't think I'm killed."

"No. I guess not unless it's a delayed reaction."

He smiled. "I don't want to join Ronny and Paul yet."

Rose walked through the barn door. "What the hell was that all about?"

We turned to look at her. She was looking at the missing fence where the bull had gone out.

"Bull had a bunch of bees on him," West said.

"When you gonna de-horn and castrate that bull?"

West looked at me then down at his feet. "Not gonna do that."

"He's already bred the cows. De-horn him and cut him or I'll shoot him." She turned and disappeared back into the barn.

West looked up. "He's just doing what an animal does. She thinks shooting everything is gonna cure it."

"Ladd didn't chase sheep after that."

"No. No, he didn't." He reached in his bib pocket for the tobacco. "I miss that dog."

"Yeah, I do too. Dreamed he scratched on the trailer door last night and I got up to let him in," I took a big breath.

West's eyes were red rimmed and watery. He nodded and bit off a chew. He revolved his jaw around it and ran his eyes over what needed to be done, surveying the hole and planning on how to fix it.

"Jeff—you put the corral back together and I'll get the bull. Those bees ought to be done with him by now."

"You gonna bring him back here?" I said.

"Yeah, she's not gonna shoot him. She might shoot me but she's not gonna shoot him."

"You feeling pretty sure of that, are you?"

"Thirty-five years of marriage I know the woman. Besides," he smiled, "the gun burned up in the house."

"Hope you're right." I went to the tool shed and got a hammer, some rope and a handful of big nails.

BY THE TIME WEST had calmed the bull down enough to bring him back to the corral I had the rails up in suitable fashion. I nailed them inside the corner posts and cross-wired them in. That left the rest of the corral with the railings nailed on the outside of the posts. The bull could go through those if he knew the difference.

I was standing in the far corner where West had buried Ladd when he led the bull into the corral. He glanced at me and at the dirt I was standing on. His scowl lasted but a second. I realized where I was standing—on Ladd's grave and moved off. I hadn't thought about him being touchy about Ladd's grave. The cows stood there all the time. It was their favorite place to stand and when it rained and the wind blew they churned the surface into mud soup. It looked like an old fashioned buffalo wallow.

"How far did he go?" I said.

He nodded his head up the hill. "Back near Iverson's east fence line."

"You gonna hive the bees?"

"No. I don't know that business."

I closed the gate and watched him move. "Did he hurt you much?"

"Pretty sore but I don't think anything's broken."

VIENNA SAUSAGES, CHEESE SLICES, apples and crackers made up the first supper in the empty house on the hill. Rose ate it like it was what she regularly served. She ate looking out the big window toward the lower pasture, the raw dirt edge of the road and the river. I looked around to see what she had bought at the Salvation Army warehouse.

There were odds and ends of furniture, six dining chairs of which only two matched, two easy chairs of different color and material and height and a brown radio on a small end table between them. A floor lamp stood beside each chair. Other than the range and refrigerator that was it.

"I'd call it contemporary sparse," I said.

Rose smiled. "We don't need much, Jeff. I like it simple."

West scanned the room. "Think I'll put the heater over there," he nodded toward the opposite wall. "Between that and the range—should keep it warm this winter."

"You need to get the septic tank hooked up and some running water in here," Rose said. "I can't get dishes and clothes washed without that."

"Lots of stuff to do," he said.

"First thing you do this afternoon while I can spare Jeff to help you is de-horn that bull and cut him. I'm not going to have him causing trouble all the time when we've got the mink to take care of. Pelting season is gonna start in another few weeks and we'll have our hands full without him busting up the place."

West turned his eyes and looked at me. I put my tongue between my lips but neither of us moved our head. He piled his silverware on top of his plate and stood up and started for the door.

"You can carry your plate to the tub," she said.

West stopped, turned around and limped back to the table. He picked up his plate and silverware and hobbled over to the galvanized tub sitting on a stool. He stopped above it for a second then threw the plate and silverware into the tub.

Rose didn't flinch. She stared out the window and sipped her coffee.

He took his hat off the nail, set it on his head and pulled it down tight making the long gray hairs spring out over his ears. That haircut hadn't lasted as long as he had hoped. He limped out the door leaving it open. I picked up my plate and silverware and put them into the tub.

"Thank you for lunch," I said.

"You're welcome, Jeff."

She was still sipping coffee when I closed the door behind me and walked down toward the barn.

The dehorning shears and West's pocket knife were on the work bench. West limped back with the sharpening stone from the slaughter house, spit on the stone and started the slow circular motion of sharpening the blade. His eyes were dead. He was going to do it. He was through arguing about it.

I hadn't dehorned an animal nor seen one castrated. I learned a lot that afternoon. I learned how much pain an animal can take and not pass out, how much blood he can lose and still stand up with blood spurting down his legs and how he didn't hold it against the man who did it or the woman who ordered it, or against me who helped tie him down so the old man could cut him. I watched but I don't remember much of it. Always before, when I had cut into an animal's genitals the animal had been dead.

When it was over and the bull was bawling in the corral and West and I had washed up we sat on the bench outside the barn while West opened his bib and took a chew. He handed it to me.

I shook my head. "No, thanks. Makes me woozy."

He smiled. "Did me too at first."

"When did you start chewing?"

"Logging. Can't smoke while you're logging. Chew works fine."

I took a deep breathe. "What a day. Who would have guessed when we got up this morning that all this would happen?"

He nodded, crossed his legs and settled his arms in his lap. "I cut him proud."

"You what?"

"Cut him proud. He won't ever know he can't make a calf."

"My gawd—is that gonna work?"

He nodded. "I've done it before. You have to cut the testicles off just right so there is still a vascular route. He'll get excited and mount the cows but he'll be more docile."

"What'll she say?"

"Don't think she'll know and I don't care."

"Isn't that something."

He spit between his feet. "I didn't want to do that. How'd you like to be cut in the prime of your life?"

"I am in the prime of my life."

"That's youth. That's what I saw in him. Strength, desire. All the stuff that leaves you when you get older. You know—I'm not the man I used to be."

"I know. You've said that before."

"Well—it's true."

I wondered how long it would be before I felt the same way. Would I ever? Could the strength and invulnerability leave me at some time later in life when I had been worn down by the events I passed through?

"How come you didn't ever take off?"

"Oh," he said. "The boys." He paused and looked at the ground. "And the devil you know might be better than the devil you don't know."

I nodded. "Suppose that could be right. She gonna be looking for somebody to help during pelting?"

"Probably. We'll need an extra hand."

"We could use someone like Jack now," I said in a mocking manner. "Someone who can do everything."

He had a stern look in his eye. "Jack's right here."

I turned. He stopped chewing and nodded.

"Here?"

"Yes. You can't never tell anybody."

"Maybe I don't want to know about it."

"Maybe not." His gaze was riveting.

My mind ran through the possibilities of what he was saying. Was whatever he was going to tell me worth my knowing and then locking it away in my memory forever? I already had Johnson's mink episode tucked away. Had I gone too far to stop now? I didn't want to know but then again—I did.

"What then?" I said.

He nodded his head toward the corral. "He's buried beneath Ladd."

"In the corral?"

He nodded.

"How in the hell did that happen?"

"He spent all one Saturday parading around here drinking and saying he was gonna kill me. Rose heard it. Kids heard it too. You remember that farmer that came in here with those two calves that he had rowed across the river?"

"Yeah."

"Well—he was here with some calves and Jack told him the same thing. Everybody put it off to the fact that he was drunk and getting drunker. He didn't come to supper that night so I walked up to the trailer and listened. There wasn't no sound so I knocked. There wasn't no reply so I opened the door. Jack was lying on the floor dead and as cold as one of those calves. I figured what was left of his liver give out on him. I put him in the wheelbarrow and buried him about six feet deep in the corner of the corral."

I shook my head. "For crying out loud, West, why didn't you call the sheriff?"

"Don't know. Just figured I'd get the last word."

"I guess you did."

"He didn't have much stuff so I buried it with him. Took couple of gunny sacks of bottles out of the trailer next day and told everybody he'd cleared out. That was that."

"That was that," I said.

He nodded.

I was stunned. Then it started to make sense to me and after pondering it while we sat there it seemed like an ok thing to have done and I began to nod my head. "How old are you?"

"Be fifty-two come November."

"Then I need to forget it for about forty years."

"Doubt I'll make ninety-two."

"Not the way you're going."

I guess we had said everything we were going to say about that and we sat with the sun setting behind us shining under the high clouds slanting its light across the river and illuminating the trees that were dropping yellow leaves in a neat circle around the drip line. It was a peaceful time.

Can't write what I want to write tonight. Learned something today that will die with me—untold. Never thought I'd be in this predicament. The last few days have been a swirling hell. Change coming so fast it is hard to adjust to it. I think when change comes this fast there is a psychological distraction to avoid going off the edge. I should talk to some of the soldiers returning from Korea about this. When I figure this out I'm going to write it down and use it somewhere.

When I think about the months I have been here and how different it is from the other places I've worked I wonder how many people ever in their lives get to see the raw day to day life of a real farm.

I took care of the hogs today. Part of my job now. The runt has grown almost as large as the others. I smile every time I think of Paul holding the runt thinking it was a full sized piglet we had brought him. I miss those guys.

CHAPTER 38

West finished splitting wood. I stacked it while he sat down and drew out a smoke. We sat there together, each knowing it would be our last evening together. How we knew I don't know. We worked together, we sweated together, we got sick inside together, we knew what each thought and we didn't speak.

"Where will you go?" he asked without looking at me.

"Somewhere." I picked a piece of bark off the ground and threw it for King. "Rassel's wanting to go to Eugene or Portland. We might head up that way."

He drew in on the cigarette and exhaled. He was pursuing a life-long practice of slowing down his life with a smoke and sitting still as a statue. "She's a nice girl."

"Seems to be." I threw the bark again for King. "I'm not thinking about getting married or living with anyone. Just didn't cross my mind yet."

"She wanting to do that?"

"Well—not in so many words but she has intimated it."

"Humm. Wouldn't think her folks would like that."

"No. Guess they wouldn't."

There wasn't much time but we sat still watching the evening leave us and finally we were in the dark with just the red glow of West's cigarette. He got up.

"See you in the morning?" he said.

"Yeah."

He walked to the house, a dark moving figure leaving shadows from the light filtering through the windows.

I walked down the frontage road. The river seemed very quiet tonight. I could see the lights on at Rassel's house. When I knocked she came out with a hair dryer in her hand.

"Hi, Jeff."

"Hi."

"Come in a second while I change."

"Okay. You want to take a walk?"

We held hands and walked down her driveway to the washed-up log by the river. "Just came to tell you I'm leaving," I said.

"I thought that was probably why you were here."

"You thought that?"

She nodded. "You just aren't their type."

"It's something more," I said.

"What?"

"It's trying to live right there and being part of something that isn't right. It's not my life style, not my way of thinking. Can't ever be. Being forced to say this is right...this isn't right with nothing in-between."

She nodded.

I pulled her to me and kissed her.

"I don't know what to say," I said.

"Don't say anything. Things like this just pass. Like the mink ranch: It's just a dream. All that killing and choosing...it's just a step in your life and I guess this is one, too, only...this is the love that always comes with life."

I put my finger on her lips. "What about us?"

"That's the way life is everywhere, the sweet and the sour."

She stepped close. "Now kiss me and walk away up that road. Let me remember it just this way."

As the sun climbed over the horizon, I took a deep breath and smelled the early morning in the air. The smell of blood and calves and dung-hay and mink came back anew and I realized that I had become unconscious of those odors in the months working among them. It was good to tell the difference. I reached for the new smell, the clear, sweet odor of green fields and seacoast smell, salt water and fish and moss.

I put my things in the pack and looked over the trailer house again. I left the rubber boots and some magazines. I took down the calendar and left it on the table. The blanket that Ladd slept on was rolled up in the closet. I took it out and smelled it. Just like him. I walked out and let the door slam shut behind me.

Rose was walking down from the house. "Good morning, Jeff."

I nodded.

She looked at my pack. "You're not leaving are you? We've got a lot of work to do here and I need your help."

"Rose..." I looked down at the clay soil I stood on then back to her stern face. "It is time for me to go. I've learned all I want to learn about the mink business."

"I need you to stay a couple more days until I find someone?"

I shook my head. "That might be too much."

"Too much?" She frowned at me.

West was standing beside the old Plymouth, a cigarette dangling between his lips, the smoke curling as always, up around his nose making his eyes squint, his old hat setting on his white hair, that half-quizzical smile on his face.

I handed him a piece of paper.

He unfolded it then pulled his glasses from his bib pocket and read it.

BILL OF SALE

Thirty mink and pens are sold this 11th day of August 1953 to West Helner for ten dollars and other valuable consideration.

Signed: Jeffrey Baker

We stood there, him pulling the white hairs at his throat and letting the cigarette burn, our eyes talking, saying the words that we knew would be left unsaid. He extended his lumberman's hand and I took it, firm.

"Goodbye, West," I said.

He nodded. "Goodbye."

"Reckon you'll be fine here now."

"Seems like it don't make much difference what I do, so I'll just do what I want. Won't be the same without you, though."

"We've been through some times."

I SHIFTED THE WEIGHT of the pack and started down the hill. King shuffled over and I patted his head. He was grown up now and a good barker. I missed Ladd. I looked back and West was still standing beside the Plymouth, the gray house looming up behind him. Rose crossed in front of the old man—paused to light a cigarette—shifted her weight to one leg and looked at me shaking her head. Then she turned and walked toward the mink yard.

West shrugged his shoulders. I waved from the end of the driveway.

The dust hung in the air from the last truck. It covered the smell of the ranch and when I walked over the bridge, only the bleating of some sheep and the warm sun drew my attention. It was easy to walk in the road and I made good time across the bridge up toward the service station where West and I usually stopped for gas and a candy bar. As I neared the station I could see someone standing outside in the sunshine leaning against the cinder block wall, a pack on their back. Every step took me closer and the figure began to look like someone I knew.

"Which way you going?" Rassel shouted.

I smiled and raised my voice. "I was thinking of Eugene or Corvallis."

"I know the way."

"Oh you do, do you?"

She nodded.

"Think you can keep up?"

"No problem."

"Well—since we're going the same way we just as well travel together."

"My thinking exactly."

I held out my hand. She walked over and took it.

WE WERE TIRED WHEN we stopped outside of North Bend. The quarter moon was well into the night sky. It was growing— a good sign of the moon.

Cover and interior book design by
Jonathan Friedman
Frame25 Productions
www.frame25productions.com

Comments from Readers:
For What He Could Become

"I was not expecting a full blown action and emotion packed, transporting reading experience. I could not put it down, and once the race started, did not. When I had finished...I reread it cover to cover. In forty years of fairly steady and broad based book devouring, I have seldom done that! You are in good company; Kipling, Faulkner, and Scott."
—Skip Lynar

"Great book!!!! Cathy got hold of it first and almost could not put it down until she finished it. She *never* reads a book. Then my turn. I didn't like it, I loved it. The story was so true to life and what I have seen so many times throughout Alaska. The race part was so perfect that I got cold, was elated, depressed, all the emotions one gets while actually running. It took me out on the trail again, especially the early years. Congratulations."
— Dick Mackey, Winner of the 1978 Iditarod,
and author of *One Second to Glory*

"I stayed up till about 12:30 this morning...can't tell you how enjoyable the book is and am looking forward to your next. Found myself laughing in some parts and sniffling in others. Exhausted at the finish line pushing the dogs and Bill along all the way."
—Joyce Delgado

"I can see that old church where the natives stayed, walking to an early death. The effort the Gospel Mission gave to those people was incredible. In your novel the struggle of the Alaska native who leaves the village and subsistence lifestyle is clearly depicted. I sweat and bled and cried with him as he struggled to come back through the running of the Iditarod. An outstanding story."
—Don Jack

Comments from Readers:
The Most Expensive Mistress in Jefferson County

"This is Great Stuff! I could not put this down in spite of
having a business associate in town for two days."
—Mary Ann Shaughnessy Krum

"I tried, but I couldn't put it down. I ate lunch reading it, then
scotch at 5:00, then dinner, alone at the dining room table
with the lights full on, and finished it in bed. What a ride.
Gimmie another one."
—Darry Gemmell

"Most entertaining, uplifting book I've read all year. Makes me
wish he would write a novel a month. Having spent a good deal
of my life in real estate, I can feel for the protagonist as he gets
caught up in trying to close that large of a transaction, knowing
he has every chip he owns in the deal. What a close one."
—Don Jack

"The characters were so real I could see, smell and feel each one
and see inside their heads. Their emotions were mine. The
humor had me laughing out loud while tears of tension and frustration welled in my eyes. The dialogue was faultless and kept
the pages crackling. You have captured the essence of Native
Americans with sensitivity and understanding. And you have
given heart to a big business deal. Thanks for a great read."
— Jeanne Tallman

"Jim Misko's novels celebrate the spirit of
adventure and the strength of perseverance."
—Irena Praitis, Author of *Branches* and *One Woman's
Life*. Professor of Literature and Creative Writing at
University of California State, Fullerton

To My Readers . . .

Thank you for buying my books. The publishing business is changing faster than most traditional publishers can change and many are consolidating, going on-line, and reinterpreting how they connect with the readers who buy books.

I have found that along with Barnes & Noble, Amazon, and Google Books, there are hundreds of other ways to reach book readers. One is through book clubs. Several book clubs have purchased my novels. At book signings, I get email addresses of buyers who want to know about future books I write. My books are all available as e-books on Kindle or Nook or Sony.

If you want to ask me any questions, have me speak to your book club, or order a bunch of books, just email me and we'll figure out a way to do that.

If you would like to be in my "readers club" and get advance notice of when I'll be in your area for a book signing or about to publish a new book, just send me your name and email.*

You can always reach me through my website: *www.JimMisko.com* or email me directly at *Jim@JimMisko.com*

*All names and email addresses are kept confidential. They are not shared with anyone.

Praise for:
The Cut of Pride

"In *The Cut of Pride,* Jim Misko's third novel, a group of interesting, cantankerous misfits attempt to run a mink farm in rural Oregon. The resulting black comedy lifts the characters off the page and into our hearts."
—Leonard Bird, author of *Folding Paper Cranes, an Atomic Memoir*

"A home run. Misko's taut tale explores a life few people will ever glimpse: relationships and life on a mink farm in the Oregon hills. I want to know more of the hardworking, straight-up protagonist, Jeff Baker. Is there a sequel in the works?"
—Sally Petersen, author of *Tea, Pie, Love and Reality,* memoir-essays

"Jim Misko's love of writing is evident in this richly detailed and closely observed account of the forces that hold a family replete with resentment, strength, weakness, and love in thrall to a life that leads inevitably to destruction."
—Lynn Schooler, author of *Walking Home, a traveler in the Alaska Wilderness*

"Jim Misko, in his new novel *The Cut of Pride*, does something that is really rare in modern literature; he writes about hard, brutal, unpleasant physical labor. And he does it with such vivid detail that the labor itself becomes one of the major entities in the story. His cast of complex, dysfunctional characters—owners and employees of a mink-raising farm in coastal Oregon—nearly destroys itself in its struggle with the endless, nasty toil. These are unforgettable characters, and their pride and distrust and bitterness make for grim drama. Like Hemingway, Steinbeck and Ruark, he writes close to the edge."
—James Alexander Thom, author of *Follow the River*

"'Nature is tough on the young,' observes Jeff Baker, the protagonist of Jim Misko's newest novel *The Cut of Pride*. In this gritty, evocative book, Misko looks unflinchingly at the harshest realities of running a mink farm on the Oregon coast. In doing so, he reveals the dirty underbelly that supports the glamour of mink coats and the violence that underlies so much of human existence. His characters sort through the work, the killing, and the fatigue to find the few factors of life that offer meaning. As they struggle with endless labor, each other, and their thoughts on living, they find friendship, pride, tragedy, and endurance. The characters, images, and emotions of this book will stay with a reader long after the novel ends."
— Irena Praitis, Professor of Literature and Creative Writing at California State University, Fullerton, author of *One Woman's Life*

"A sober and candid look at those still living off the land in the Pacific Northwest just a half century ago. A true slice of Americana."
— Dick Couch, author of *Sua Sponte: The Forging of a Modern American Ranger*

"Jim Misko is the sort of writer whose visual imagery takes you deeper into your own imagination and keeps you reading. Added to that is a dynamic and interesting protagonist whose impressions of the world he finds himself in adds even more to this journey and experience in a setting that will be most unusual and fascinating to the most demanding reader. "
—Andrew Neiderman, author of *The Devil's Advocate*